LORD EDGINGTON INVESTIGATES...

BOOK 6

THE
CURIOUS CASE
OF THE
TEMPLETON-
SWIFTS

A 1920s MYSTERY

BENEDICT BROWN

COPYRIGHT

For my father, Kevin,
I hope you would have liked this book an awful lot.

NOTE TO READERS

As with most of the titles in this series, this book is spoiler free and does not give away the solutions to any of the previous mysteries. Many people enjoy reading the books chronologically so as to see the main characters' relationships develop, but, for new readers, there is no reason not to jump in with this joyous romp of a summertime mystery. I hope you love every word!

Deer Eglglore—

Finding. Times changes exe-
edly. My wife was too babus
the women day to one.
day he tred retlist. But
day the t. Thise or then
I say it she's the one.
Shes trying. TO KILL ME!
If you're there!

Hugo Templeton.
Lucif t.

CHAPTER ONE

"Chrissy!" a voice at the window hissed. "Chrissy, come here."

I was trapped within an exceedingly dry passage on soil erosion that I needed to memorise in time for my geography exam the following week. The library was silent and the only other person in sight was the school librarian, Miss Radish, who appeared to have fallen asleep.

Assuming it was one of my fellow pupils, who wanted to distract me from my endless days of revision, I ignored the interruption.

"Chrissy, come out here. Quick smart!"

I finally recognised the voice, packed up my books and sprinted to freedom.

"No running, Christopher Prentiss!" Miss Radish managed to declare with her eyes still closed. I'd always known the woman had strange and unusual gifts, and this just proved it.

"What could possibly have taken you so long, my boy?" Dressed in his favourite dove-grey morning suit, my grandfather was standing in the school quad with his loyal golden retriever, Delilah, at his side and an incorrigible smile on his face.

"I've got ten different exams over the next month. If I don't pass at least six of them, I'll have to stay here for ever."

He raised one doubting eyebrow. "I do not believe that is how the British education system works, Christopher. But the proximity of your examinations is all the more reason for you to rest your mind for a period."

I was typically bowled over by the force and equanimity of his words, and my brain seemingly became locked. I was trying to make sense of his logic but, as I did not respond, and stood there with my tongue hanging out – much like dear Delilah – he tapped his cane on the gravel path and said, "Jolly good. I'll see you in the car."

"I... If... Why..." I'm awfully good at starting sentences. If they had an exam on that, I'd be top of the class. When the old fellow didn't look back, I shouted, "Oh! Fine. I'll meet you there in a few minutes."

By my final term at The Oakton Classical and Commercial Academy for Distinguished Young Gentlemen, I had come to realise that this supposedly worthy institution was nothing more than a cramming factory. The school had been built for the sole purpose of squishing as much information as possible into young boys' heads so that we could pass our final exams and never return. I had reached my eighteenth year on this planet without the foggiest idea of what I hoped to do with my life.

All I knew was that I would have to work terribly hard in order to put off that decision for a while longer. To achieve this – and, at the very least, stop my parents from looking so disappointed in me – it was essential that I obtained my Higher School Certificate. Which is why, instead of running after my illustrious grandfather, the Marquess of Edgington, to discover what he had planned for us that weekend, I returned to my dormitory to collect a few essential possessions.

"Take me with you, Chrissy," my friend Marmaduke begged. "Please, I'll go crazy if I have to stay here with all these awful, brain-corrupting books." He was lying on his bed with dusty tomes all around him. He clawed at them a little to illustrate his predicament. "In fact, it may already be too late."

"Sorry, old chap," I said, without a hint of smugness. "If Grandfather is here, it means he drove his new Bentley. I'm afraid it's only a two-seater. But I'll be sure to tell you about my adventure when I return."

"Adventure?" he practically drooled. "What adventure?"

I stuffed every last book I might need (along with a few I didn't) into a travelling chest, before realising I would require some assistance to move it.

"All right, Marmaduke, if you help me take this outside, I'll reveal all." I obviously didn't have a clue what my grandfather had in store for us, but I wasn't going to tell him that.

After much huffing and heaving, we made it to the car.

"Is that a Bentley 3 Litre Green Label?" Marmaduke asked in amazement as, apparently, I was the only person in Britain who was not infatuated with automobiles.

Grandfather was standing proudly beside his purring vehicle and his barking dog. "That's right. It comes with guaranteed one-hundred-mile-an-hour performance."

The shiny burgundy beast, with its four wheels, windows and

doors, was certainly an attractive vehicle. The old lord hadn't stopped talking about it since he'd bought it a month before. I believe it was his third new toy of the year and, at this rate, he would soon run out of space in his barn-like garage... or should that be his garage-like barn?

Marmaduke was struggling to express himself and eventually muttered something along the lines of, "One hundred miles an hour! The future has truly arrived."

Delilah woofed with excitement and ran around the vehicle, as, apparently, I was the only *creature* in Britain who was not infatuated with automobiles.

Grandfather eyed my baggage somewhat suspiciously as we loaded it into the back of the sporty car. "There'll be no time to study, Christopher." I think he might even have tutted at that moment. "We have a case to investigate. An actual case, rather than a body upon which we happen to stumble."

"Please take me with you," Marmaduke begged once more. "I'll sit on the bonnet if necessary, but please let me come."

Perhaps recalling his former role as a superintendent in the Metropolitan Police, Grandfather stood up straighter and spoke as though addressing a new recruit. "Not this time, my boy. This isn't the sort of mission upon which one can bring spectators. But it's a pleasure to see you. Do send my greetings to your father."

He opened the car door and stiffly climbed aboard. I felt terrible for my dejected friend and decided to offer him one small, vicarious thrill.

"What's the case, Grandfather?" I asked to fish for some more details.

"I've received... a *letter*." He pronounced this last word as though it was really quite electrifying.

"And what did it say?" Marmaduke's eyes grew wider as he hung off the side of the Bentley.

"There's going to be a murder!" I'd never heard anyone so excited about the possibility of a crime before.

"You mean it hasn't happened yet?" I had to ask.

"Evidently not." Grandfather's face displayed a look so withering I considered hiding behind a tree. "In fact, it is just such instances for which the future tense is reserved."

I tittered nervously in response. "Well... terrific. There's nothing quite like a good murder."

He motioned with his head for me to climb in next to him, and I duly obeyed.

"I'm not excited about the murder," he was quick to explain, whilst pulling on his driving gloves. "What I find so enticing is the chance to set off across England to investigate the wicked ways of man."

As though he hoped to stop us leaving without him, my tall ginger friend wouldn't let go of the car. "Where's this murder going to take place?"

Grandfather looked more mysterious than ever and drummed his fingers on the steering wheel. "Not far from Salisbury."

"Oh." Marmaduke clearly wasn't impressed. "That doesn't sound particularly exciting."

"It is if you wish to visit some exquisite countryside and one of the finest examples of English Gothic architecture still standing."

"I see… Well, I don't." Suddenly losing interest in the looming investigation, Marmaduke shrugged and wandered back towards school. His despondency had reached a new low.

"Salisbury Cathedral has the highest spire in the whole of Great Britain," my grandfather called after him with an indignant edge to his voice. It would do nothing to convince the boy.

Delilah hopped onto my lap, and Lord Edgington turned the car around on the circular drive in front of the school. With the intensity of my revision, (or rather my necessity to make up for the time I'd spent daydreaming, reading old novels and bird-watching) I hadn't been back to Cranley Hall for weeks. It felt wonderful to see the old chap.

"So, tell me what everyone has been doing in my absence? Has Cook invented any new dishes? Have any more of the maids got married?"

"Yes and no," he responded in short order. "I would ask you the same thing, but I've no doubt that your teachers have been working you like mules." I winced in reply, as a truer word had rarely been spoken. "Never mind all that now, boy. Just for one weekend, you can forget the world of academia and submerge yourself in the machinations of some malevolent soul's diabolical plan."

I was once more uncertain what to make of his cheery attitude on the matter. He seemed really rather gruntled – if such a word exists. "How can you be so sure that someone is going to be murdered?"

"The letter, boy. The letter." Sometimes even his simplest responses could seem like riddles. "I received it in the post this morning, and it has certainly whetted my appetite for–"

"Murder?"

"No, no. We may even prevent someone from getting killed. But think how long it's been since we had a mystery into which we could sink our hungry teeth. This is a rare opportunity, my dear boy. We would be fools not to seize it with our four collective hands." Delilah gave an indignant bark as, apparently, our dog could count. "And an identical number of paws."

As the sun broke through the trees on the lane that led off the school grounds, I thought I should pre-emptively warn him that, just because a car is capable of driving at over one hundred miles per hour, that doesn't mean it's necessary to go so fast.

"So who wrote the letter? The murderer or the murderee?" This sounded dreadfully clever, though I'd only said it because I couldn't remember the more obvious word *victim*.

Grandfather had a flair for the dramatic, and he was in a particularly effusive mood that day. "Hugo." He spaced out the words for effect. "Templeton." Like this. "Swift!" He positively bristled with excitement and took his eyes off the road to watch my reaction.

"Who?"

"Hugo Templeton-Swift!" he repeated. It still meant nothing to me. "The businessman who was implicated in the Marconi scandal all those years ago. You know, Lord Murray of Elibank's cousin."

He might as well have been listing mathematical equations for all I understood of this. "Grandfather, I believe I was only three years old at the time of that unfortunate event. And the only reason I can remember the date it occurred is because of my former history teacher's fanatical insistence on every boy knowing such tedious facts."

"Hugo Templeton-Swift?" he tried one final time, as though he suspected me of having a hearing deficiency. When it was clear I would not be convinced of my knowledge of the man, he deigned to explain. "He was a real titan of the City at the turn of the century. He made a fortune investing in Latin America, then used his wealth to buy a place on the board of Marconi just as–"

I must have yawned as he interrupted himself to ask, "My apologies. Am I boring you?"

I tried to think of an excuse but couldn't. "No, I just… well, I was hoping for something more interesting."

He shook his head and gripped the wheel a little tighter. "This is *interesting*, Christopher. Believe me. A man – a millionaire in fact – who has not been seen in public for more than a decade has written to explain that he believes someone is attempting to kill him in his own home."

Now this woke me up. "Well, that's more like it."

"There you go." He clapped his hands together, and I shot my arm out to steady the steering wheel before we could veer off the road. "What's more, I think this is the second letter he's written. The first was almost indecipherable. Whoever wrote it failed to put a return address, and I could make out little of what was written except for one clear phrase that repeated several times in amongst the scrawls. Unless I'm very much mistaken, I believe it says, 'She's the one. She's trying to kill me.'"

I admit, he'd trapped me in his web by now and I was caught up in the (admittedly slow-starting) story he'd woven. "To whom do you think he was referring?"

Much like a spider – if spiders could smile – his mouth curled up at that moment and he raised his chin with pride. "It would take an incredibly capable investigator to discover such a fact from the scant mentions there have been of Templeton-Swift in the papers over the last few years, but I happen to be an excellent delegator and nosed out the information we require."

"Sorry. Are you taking credit for someone else's discovery?" This seemed arrogant, even by his standards.

"Not at all. I'm taking credit for choosing the right person to search out the information we require. Delegation is not as simple a task as you might imagine."

"Undoubtedly," I replied, as I am no longer afraid of sounding sarcastic in front of the old boy.

"The point is that my acquaintance as Scotland Yard, has unearthed a small notice in The Western Gazette which revealed that Templeton-Swift got married a little over a year ago to a woman by the name of Christabel Quintin." He looked at me once more as though this was yet another figure by whom I should be impressed.

"I'm sorry, Grandfather. I haven't a clue who that might be."

"No, neither have I." His mood lightening a fraction, he had a brief laugh at his own expense. It made for a nice change.

"Christabel Quintin." I liked the way words formed in my mouth. "It sounds like a perfectly made-up name to me. Like a character from some foolish romance."

Grandfather cleared his throat and recited a poem.

"A sight to dream of, not to tell!

O shield her! Shield sweet Christabel!"

I didn't know what to make of it, so I continued clinging to the leather upholstery of the car as he navigated past a horse and cart, apparently without checking to see what was coming towards us. The man was a menace behind the wheel.

"Samuel Taylor Coleridge," he explained.

"Well now, I have heard of him!" I was overjoyed to be in the know on a topic he had broached. "He was a..." I'd begun to doubt myself again. "Well, he was a poet, wasn't he?"

"Yes, Christopher. He was a poet. And his ballad 'Christabel' concerned a supernatural temptress. But it's the real woman with whom I am most concerned – the new bride of a man in his eighties. Perhaps she married Templeton-Swift in the hope of inheriting his fortune and has decided not to wait until he dies of natural causes."

"Isn't that rather a leap to assume such a thing?"

We had already made it to the gates of my ancestral home by this point and he, at last, slowed down the Bentley to roll onto the long driveway. I caught my first glimpse of the impressive golden towers of Cranley Hall and couldn't suppress a sigh of admiration. He seemed to be enjoying the sight of the old place just as much as I was, and he breathed in the scent of the flowering borders that led up to the house. Spring had well and truly sprung, and summer was on its way.

"You're correct. And I wouldn't have indulged in such lazy detective work, but then a second letter arrived this morning and it only reinforced the idea."

"Why? What did it say?"

It's impressive that a man who was already so excited – so evidently beaming with enthusiasm – could attain another level of cheer at that moment. He smiled so much that the two ends of his perfectly white moustache almost touched. "It said that he fears he is being poisoned. The hand looked much the same, but the writing was a good deal more legible, and the message was far clearer this time. He wishes me to go to his house to prevent a great injustice from taking place."

"That's wonderful." I tried to sound positive for his sake. I hadn't mentioned my exams once since we'd left school.

Grandfather pulled the car to a stop at the front of the house and enjoyed another celebratory clap of his hands. "Yes, if this Christabel really is a dark spirit, sucking the lifeblood from her ailing husband, we'll soon exorcise her."

"Oh really?" a voice from the steps above us enquired. "What are the pair of you up to now?"

CHAPTER TWO.

"Mummy!" I pushed the dog from my lap and jumped from the car without opening the door (or falling flat on my face). Delilah thought this was wonderful and copied me.

My mother had descended the great stone staircase by the time I reached her, and she held her arms out for a hug. Is it terribly juvenile of me that, aged seventeen, there was still nothing quite so comforting as being wrapped up in the arms of a parent or two? Of course, my father's idea of affection was a pat on the back once a year on my birthday, but Mummy more than made up for it.

"Violet?" For all his skills of charm and deception, my grandfather couldn't disguise how surprised he was to find his daughter there. "What a pleasure it is to see you."

She wouldn't be duped by his performance and, once the embrace was over, looked between the pair of us disbelievingly. "Who's this wicked woman I've caught you discussing?"

"No one, my dear. No one at all." I think he even tried to whistle at this point in the hope of distracting her, but it wouldn't work.

"I really expected better from you, Father. Not only have you taken Christopher away from his books when he most needs to be studying, you're filling his head with lurid tales."

I might have pointed out that my head couldn't fit nearly so much in it as most people's and was already occupied with any number of useless topics, but I rather wanted to go away for the weekend and didn't want my mother refusing.

"So?" she asked when it was clear her father had no intention of providing an answer. "What are you hiding?"

"Hiding, my dear?" he said in a perfectly innocent tone and then, as the whistling hadn't worked, he tried to distract her with a song.

"The girl with the golden hair
In the ballet had little to wear,
For she went to rehearse with her clothes in her purse
Did the girl with the golden hair."

With a hesitant look on his face, he danced past her up the stairs. "I have to attend to a few matters before we leave, Christopher. Please be ready in–"

"I think I should accompany you to wherever you aren't going to meet this woman who doesn't exist," my mother interrupted, and the old lord stopped in his tracks.

"Oh…" From the twitching in his face as he looked down the stairs at us, I can only imagine that he carried out a series of complicated mental calculations before speaking again. "Ah…" I thought this was all he would produce in way of a response, but his computations eventually concluded. "That's wonderful. I will be so happy to have your company on our voyage, though I am afraid you'll have to drive in the Rolls with Todd. I will be taking the Aston Martin, and it's really only comfortable for two."

Delilah whimpered disappointedly, yet again proving her mathematical agility. Perhaps she could sit my algebra exam for me.

"Two and a dog." He hurried off before my mother could complain, and I believe that we were both left to wonder what new scheme he was hatching.

"I didn't know you would be here," I said, once he had disappeared through the immense double doors.

"Clearly, neither did your grandfather." She remained gazing after him, then seemed to come back to herself and turned to me with a smile. "But it's so nice to see you, Chrissy. Tell me everything. How has your work been going? Have you decided what you'd like to study next year? Do you know which university you will attend?"

These were probably the three questions I had the least interest in answering at that moment. The truthful replies would have been:

Terribly.

No, I haven't a clue.

Possibly none of them.

I wasn't about to tell my dear mater any of that, though, so I feigned a smile and prattled at her unconvincingly. "Jolly well, thank you. It's going whizzingly. Really, things couldn't be better. Now, why did you come to Cranley? I imagined you'd be in the City seeing father this weekend."

She had a distracted look in her eye at that moment. I thought she would realise that I'd changed the subject without answering her questions, but she was still so distracted by her father's eccentric exit that she accepted the shift in the conversation.

"Albert has a new sweetheart I was hoping to meet, but they've had to cancel the appointment."

"Another girlfriend?" My brother was forever falling in love with pretty young ladies who, of a kind, enjoyed nothing more than breaking his heart. "What happened to poor Miss Bowen? I rather liked her."

We began the walk up the stairs, and Mother looped her arm through mine and whispered conspiratorially. "My spies inform me that this new girl – Cassandra Fairfax is her name – swooped in to steal dear Albert for herself. I knew the Fairfaxes growing up, and they are certainly a mercenary lot. It doesn't surprise me that the next generation has followed suit."

There was one particular detail in her story which alarmed me. "Spies, mother? I hope you don't have anyone surveilling me at school."

Her eyes sparkled with mischief, and I knew I'd have to be careful about what I said around my Oaktonian friends for ever more.

"Oh, wouldn't you like to know!" She giggled and I could see so much of the girl of sixteen who had been so fond of tricks and jokes, but whose acquaintance I had only made through photographs.

"I should prepare for our trip," I said, studying her cheeky grin and wondering just how much she knew about my life away from the family. I set off on the long journey through Cranley Hall to my bedroom in the east wing. There were maids getting ready for a weekend of tidying in the lord's absence, and I spotted a new arrival in the house. An Electrolux Model V vacuum cleaner! As Marmaduke had so astutely observed, the future had most definitely arrived.

Not wanting to upset my alternately cheerful and cantankerous forebear, I packed some clothes for the weekend into a knapsack and went back outside to await our departure. To my surprise, the old detective was already out there. Lord Edgington was issuing a series of complex instructions to his usual team of staff. Cook was standing with our footman, Halfpenny, who was in a real fluster as he listened to whatever instructions my grandfather had for him.

Our cooler-headed chauffeur, Todd, had removed my chest of books in order to carry it in the ferry-like Silver Ghost in which he would drive my mother. My grandfather liked to bring a reserve team of staff wherever we went, and so I was most surprised when he dismissed everyone but the driver.

"So you're not bringing fifty servants with you this time?" I must have sounded rather astounded.

"No, of course I'm not." He looked even more devious than before. "You know, I am capable of travelling light and carefree. During my days in the police, there was no one to cook me meals or wash my clothes. You and your mother seem to be under the impression that I can't survive without being waited on hand and foot."

I felt a bit guilty for thinking exactly this. "Well, I look forward to our time together as a family, then."

"That's the stuff, Christopher. There's nothing like a bit of enthusiasm!" He rubbed his hands together before another thought occurred to him. "And punctuality. Enthusiasm and punctuality will surely set us on the right foot. I see a great adventure ahead of us. A great adventure indeed." He was perhaps becoming a little wordier in his old age.

"And what, pray tell, will this adventure entail?" My mother had surprised us again. She appeared once more at the top of the staircases in a really very elegant cornflower blue hat. Thanks to the matching dress, which trailed behind her as she descended, she looked as though she had stepped out of an elegant painting of a picnic beside the Seine.

"Violet, how marvellous that you've joined us." Grandfather immediately sounded circumspect and, as she arrived at the foot of the stairs, he led her to the waiting Rolls Royce. "There's no need to go into all that just yet. Though I can see now just how fortuitous it was that you should come here when you did. You will be essential in winning the trust of the lady in question. I have heard reports that she is what the French would call *une femme fatale*, and I will need someone of your subtlety to pass her defences."

"Would this be the same lady who didn't exist before?" My mother was the only person I knew who had the intellect and experience to see through her father's stratagems. She took her place in the rear of the large tourer and barely spared the old chap a glance as he helped her aboard.

"The very same, my dear. And though, at first, I was uncertain how you would fit into my plans. I have no such reservations now."

"So you'll tell me where we're heading?"

Grandfather gave a florid bow. "Of course, my dear. Of course."

She looked back at him dubiously. "And so?"

I was amazed he didn't tell her to speak in full sentences, but that wouldn't have fitted with the charming demeanour he had adopted. "I will definitely tell you every last detail… when we stop for lunch." He closed the door and winked at the driver. "Have a safe and leisurely drive. I will see you there."

We waved them off, and our chauffeur, Todd, gave the old man a wink as they passed. I could only assume he was a co-conspirator in Grandfather's plot, or at the very least a lackey.

I have to say, I was grateful that we would be travelling in our usual grey Aston Martin Cloverleaf, as opposed to the new Bentley. The top speed couldn't have been more than eighty, which meant I had a twenty per cent higher chance of surviving the journey. Bearing in mind that I'm no statistician – and that my maths teacher had recently told me that, if I succeeded in passing my exam, he would run three laps of the school completely naked – this is only a very rough estimation.

"Where are we off to first?" I asked and, just as I was getting into the car, I heard a furious growl from one of the windows. Delilah was looking out at us from the entrance hall and did not appear happy that we'd forgotten her.

"Silly girl, we're not leaving without you," Grandfather shouted up. "Come down this moment and you can sit in the dickey seat."

She barked twice more and disappeared from view.

"Of course we'll wait for you." Her master shook his head and tutted. I was yet to understand whether he really believed her capable of speech. Perhaps the conversations in which the pair engaged were solely for my entertainment.

We boarded the elegant motorcar, and Delilah bounded down to us. She did not accept the offer of the small drafty seat at the back of the car. Almost inevitably, she dumped herself on top of me so that my legs had fallen asleep by the time we left the grounds.

Grandfather put his arm out of the window to bang on the side of the vehicle with great agitation and declared, "Next stop: Winchester!"

CHAPTER THREE

The first part of Lord Edgington's deception was soon made apparent. While Todd took my mother on a scenic tour of the Surrey and Hampshire countryside, we would be visiting an old acquaintance of my grandfather's.

We drove for over an hour across the South Downs and through picturesque villages with duck ponds and cricket greens. The sun was bright, the air was warm on my skin, and I was quite intoxicated by thoughts of the season to come. It was almost enough to erase the bad memories of my teachers screaming at me to read faster, remember facts more accurately and be cleverer. I knew that, as soon as we reached our final destination for the day, I would have to split my time between my revision and resolving the mystery of Hugo Templeton-Swift, but just for a while, I felt perfectly free.

We made it to Easton in the Itchen Valley and parked in front of a house that, somewhat perversely, looked a lot like my school. At some point in the past, someone had stuck a few Doric columns onto the south façade, but otherwise it was a squat, boxy building of red brick, just like Oakton Academy.

And yet this place had something unique about it. The creeping plants which covered one wall were wild and overgrown, as though Easton Manor had grown out of the ground with them. There were ponds, sunken gardens and the odd trickling fountain here and there, and I got the sense that the estate we had entered belonged to someone who understood the countryside that surrounded us.

"It's awfully quaint, don't you think?" Grandfather asked, and I could see that he held a similar opinion to the one then forming in my head.

Delilah barked her agreement and went skittering off to the woods to look for rabbits. I'd yet to see her catch one, but she certainly loved trying.

"Awfully," I agreed with her agreement. "Who lives here?"

He sat in the driver's seat for a few moments longer, then, without another word, hopped from the vehicle. "It's hard to explain." He looked back at me and stroked his long white beard, as though puzzling over the riddle I'd presented. "It's best if you see for yourself."

By the time we reached the front door, a servant had come out to greet us. He wore no livery and was not like any footman I'd met before but, from his bow and obsequious good manners, I was certain of his position in the house.

"Lord Edgington?" he asked with his eyes dipped low. "Lady Highley-Summers is expecting you in the music room." He held one arm out to indicate the way and we passed through the glossy red doorway before he pulled ahead of us to navigate the corridors of the comfortably appointed dwelling.

"I'm so glad that Lady Highley-Summers knew we were coming," I whispered to my grandfather as we tried to keep pace with the sprightly employee. "Though I wish you could have informed *me* what you had planned."

Undeterred by my barb, his face became quite cheerful. I was trying to make sense of why he had brought us here when a man's life was at risk, but my mind was blank.

"Vivian!" His voice announced our arrival in the room. It travelled ahead of us, like a calling card dispatched by one's servant, all the way to an elegantly attired woman who was sitting at an ancient harpsichord, playing most sweetly. The notes she produced filled the room, and I felt I could have listened to that music for the rest of my life (if I hadn't had so many exams for which to prepare).

"Oh, Lord Edgington, my beloved friend." She rose to greet us. "What a pleasure it is to have you at Easton Manor. I thought I would never have the chance to entertain you, and here you are."

Grandfather found a new sense of vim with which to speed across the room to our host. Standing in a beam of sunlight, she was dressed all in white and wore her hair in almost architecturally perfect ringlets. As we moved closer, I could see that she was some years younger than my grandfather, not more than fifty, perhaps, but she spoke as though they had once been intimate acquaintances.

"You are simply too kind to receive us, my dear. May I introduce my grandson, Christopher?"

She stepped forward to offer me her hand, and I took it before bowing. There was a touch of magic and mystery in her smile. With our formal greeting concluded, she examined the boy in front of her.

"The famous Christopher," she said approvingly. "Whatever this old character might say to your face, let me tell you that he thinks you are wonderful. He went into great detail on the phone this morning about all you've done for him over the last year."

Grandfather suddenly looked shy and even stuttered as he denied this interpretation. "I... I said he is a well-meaning boy, though he still has some way to go." He risked a glance at me then and, as I was smiling at this hint of his grumpier side, he qualified the statement. "But it's true that men of such character as my grandson are few and far between."

Obviously not wishing to deal in such flattery for any longer than was necessary, he changed the subject. "What a house this is, Vivian. I remember it from my youth, of course, but you have very much made it your own."

She glanced around the spacious room, as though unfamiliar with her surroundings. It had incredibly tall windows to let in great swathes of light, and the walls were lined with framed sketches and musical instruments. "Since Archibald died, I've tried to make the place my own, but you've no idea how I've missed him. The life of a widow is a lonely one."

I'm not going to claim to be the quickest-witted boy in the world, but even I could see that there was a hidden meaning to her words. Something suspicious was occurring; I simply couldn't be sure what it was.

"Yes, it was a great tragedy when the old codger popped his clogs, but I hope you can console yourself with the fortune he left you." Grandfather even let out a hearty guffaw at this, and my mind boggled with thoughts of what had passed between them. It almost sounded as if former Superintendent Edgington – that merciless bulldog of Scotland Yard – had plotted to murder this woman's husband. Surely, that couldn't be right.

Lady Highley-Summers pointed us to a chaise longue and two armchairs which were positioned in another patch of light in one of the window bays. The servant had already disappeared and returned with a silver trolley that was laden with refreshments. I spotted a variety of cream cakes, tartlets, fruit flans and gateaux and decided that I no longer particularly minded whether I was in the presence of two lascivious criminals, as long as I could have my pick of those delights.

There was even homemade lemonade to accompany the delectable treats. The Itchen Valley was clearly some kind of heavenly plane I had not visited before.

"I must confess, I was surprised to receive your call," Vivian revealed, perching prettily on the chaise longue.

She certainly was an attractive woman. I probably say that about most fine ladies I meet, but, in a white dress, with a few well-placed flowers in her long grey hair, there was something ever so natural and perhaps even pagan about her. I wondered whether she was a wood spirit who had come into the house one day and enchanted its former owner.

"I hate to intrude," Grandfather said as the footman poured Assam tea for the adults and orange juice for the almost-adult. "But the situation is quite out of the ordinary. You will know at least one of the players involved, I believe. Hugo Templeton-Swift has written to me. He claims that his life is in danger."

She gasped at the mere mention of the man's name and Grandfather looked at me as though to say, *you see, he is famous after all.*

"I have brought the letter with me. Would you care for me to read it aloud?"

Lady Highley-Summers took some time to compose herself before motioning in the affirmative. I realised then that it was more than the man's status that had caused her to gasp. It was quite evident that she had known him personally.

Grandfather cleared his throat and began.

> **"'Dear Lord Edgington, etc… I write on a matter of sensitivity. I assume you are acquainted with my name and know, therefore, that I am a man of some wealth. Perhaps you will think me foolish for the fact that, at the age of eighty, I took a wife some forty years younger than myself.**

> **"'I have suffered from various ailments over the last decade, but meeting my Christabel seemed to restore me to good health. As such, the pair of us were married on the fourth of March 1925.**

> **"'Our life together started happily enough, but as my health deteriorated, so did the relations between**

us. I wished to believe in my new bride and not think
her capable of such evil but, based on my condition
these last few months, and the fact that my doctor has
only the vaguest notion of what could have caused my
malady, I can only conclude that I am being poisoned.'"

Grandfather paused at this moment to explain a minor point. "I am having to read between the lines, at times, as certain words are difficult to decipher and there are a number of spelling mistakes."

Vivian did not respond. In fact, she had not moved one eighth of an inch since the old man commenced his reading.

"'Perhaps it is cruel for a man to think so poorly of the woman he has wed before the eyes of God, but I am unable to come to any other conclusion than that the person I first knew as Christabel Quintin married me with the sole aim of inheriting my estate at Riverside Keep. I'm at a loss to know how to escape from the dreadful situation in which I find myself.

"'I have managed to get word to my three children over the last month and the last has just arrived from America, but I request your presence here to observe the machinations of my heirs. I am no longer certain whom I should trust, but I know that the great Lord Edgington will not fail in his duty to uncover the truth.

"'I will be indebted to you for any service you may render, but please make haste in coming to the above address. Yours sincerely, Hugo Templeton-Swift.'"

Vivian released a strangled gasp before the teacup she was holding fell from her hand to smash into a hundred pieces on the wooden floor.

CHAPTER FOUR

The clatter seemed to pull our hostess out of her malaise. A passing servant must have heard, as a maid came rushing into the room to clean up the mess. In the meantime, Vivian rose to standing. Her hands rubbed nervously against one another, like two carding panels working at wool, and she took a short turn about the room.

"Are you perfectly all right, my dear?" Grandfather's voice was full of concern. I would have stood to make sure the poor woman wasn't in shock, but I'd just taken a bite of a rather delicious vanilla slice, and I had cream all over my fingers.

"I'm fine," she replied after a few seconds' contemplation.

I caught another glimpse of the disquiet within her then. There was so much sorrow peeking out at the seams that I had to wonder at the life she'd led. "I'm just a little shaken by Hugo's letter. Perhaps Christabel will turn out to be entirely blameless, but I pray that you will get there in time to save him."

Grandfather waited for her to return to our sunny spot. "You know the woman, don't you? I was hoping that was the case. I discovered that, like you, she was born in the Old Nichol and moved to Dalston when they cleared the slum."

It occurred to me then that grandfather knew more about Hugo Templeton-Swift's new bride than he had revealed.

Vivian nodded slowly, the implications of that letter still troubling her. "Christabel's parents were my neighbours when I was a child. I tried to keep an eye on her, even after I left London."

"And what sort of person is she? Do Templeton-Swift's suspicions match your own impression?"

"No. Quite the opposite." Walking past my chair, she stood in front of the window and the light of the sun seemed to enhance the beauty in her face, just as a match transforms a candle. "I thought she was an angel – a truly kind-hearted person – and yet…"

"And yet there is some flickering doubt in your mind," Grandfather continued, so that Vivian didn't have to speak ill of the woman. "You cannot say whether she really is as innocent as she appears?"

"That's just it." Her head snapped towards the old detective at this point, and it was clear that she was impressed. "I adore her. I always have. As a child, she was whiter than Snow White. And yet I heard something recently which made me question whether any person could be so pure as she presented herself. How did you know what I was thinking?"

Lord Edgington is no clairvoyant, though he does a terrifically good impression of one. "I read it in your face, my dear. In the tone of your voice and the near-imperceptible flicker of your eyelids as you spoke."

I was perplexed by all that I'd heard since entering that handsome room. Grandfather must have noticed this too as he paused his questioning to ask a favour from his old… friend? I wasn't sure how else one could describe her.

"Vivian, would you be so kind as to describe all you know of Christabel and her husband from the beginning?"

Still not as animated as when she'd received us, she nodded absentmindedly and came to perch on the spare armchair of the suite. "I did what I could for Christabel, and…" She hesitated once more. "…I don't want to think badly of a woman who has lived a life in parallel to my own. But, you see, Hugo is not Christabel's first husband."

I could see that Grandfather was anticipating this very revelation. "Yes, a former colleague of mine in the Met discovered that she had been married twice before."

She looked up at him then, as though shocked that the police were already involved. "I heard that she…"

As she appeared unable to finish this thought, Lord Edgington took pity on her. "Perhaps you tell us about Hugo instead. Would that be a little less painful?"

This suggestion seemed to soothe her nerves. She nodded, took a quiet breath and started again. "In truth, it was all very odd. I had been widowed some ten years when I saw a notice in the newspaper about him. It was the queerest thing. Once I knew him better, I came to understand that it was actually very much in keeping with his character, but I can't honestly–"

"What did it say in the newspaper?" I asked, a touch precipitously.

She jumped just a fraction, as though an electric current had passed through her. "Well, I suppose a proposition is the best word

30

for it. It was only a few lines in The Western Gazette. It said, 'Hugo Templeton-Swift is in need of a wife. A woman of good breeding, rank and manners. Apply to Riverside Keep, Hanging Langford. References may be required.'"

"How fascinating," my grandfather chimed, much like his horological namesake in the corner who, upright and steadfast, informed us that it was a quarter to twelve.

"As you know, I was rather lonely after Archibald died, and I considered Hugo's companionship to be the perfect solution. You see, I had met him once, years earlier. It was at the Guildhall in London. There was a grand function for a visiting diplomat, to which I was lucky enough to be invited. Hugo gave a speech and, as I was quite fascinated by it, I introduced myself. We spent the evening talking, and he was a true gentleman throughout."

"What happened after you responded to his notice?" It was Grandfather's turn to hurry her along. I might have said something similar, but I'd helped myself to a strawberry tart.

Her smile then was partly shy, partly amused. "I was summoned. That's just the word for it. I was told when my presence would be required at Riverside Keep, and Hugo sent a car for me. It was an unfathomably strange experience. The driver took me there in silence and, when I arrived at the house, there was no one to welcome me. The doors were open and so I walked inside unaccompanied. Hugo was in his wheelchair in the sitting room and, when he saw me, he seemed to grow decades younger in just a few seconds.

"He remembered me; that was what I found most surprising. I didn't have to remind him. He told me exactly where we had met and what we had discussed. By the end of the day, we were the best of friends."

"And then?" Grandfather asked in a downcast voice.

"Well, we saw one another several times, and it was just as convivial on each occasion. Most of all, though, he really did seem to be in good health. I would push him around his garden and tell him about all the plants we were growing here. The last time I spoke to him, he suggested that he might pay a visit to my home, but he never called again. It was most unusual and, when I rang the house, I was told that Hugo no longer wished to see me. Six months later, I discovered he had married someone else."

I felt rotten for the poor lady. It was clear that the old devil had been toying with her affections. "And you suspect that Christabel had beaten you to the prize?"

She hesitated before answering me. "No, not that exactly. Though I am curious as to the sequence of events that led to their engagement. I can only think he was interviewing various candidates at the same time."

"So then, what was it?" I placed my empty glass on the marble-topped table in front of us, and the percussive clink punctuated my questions. "Why did you have such suspicions of her?"

Vivian looked at me as though she wanted to apologise for what she was about to say. "You must understand that Christabel and I grew up in true poverty. In fact, if it hadn't been for your grandfather, I would most likely have remained in such a state." Her old friend adjusted his tie as she spoke of him, but she held my concentration completely. "I did much the same for Christabel but, after she married, I began to wonder whether she was quite as sweet as she seemed."

"What exactly happened to her previous husbands?" Lord Edgington leaned forward, clearly eager to discover the answer.

"The first was really very young. The pair seemed happy together and Christabel mourned for a long time after, so I really thought nothing of it. The doctors put it down to overwork, stress, poor diet, those sorts of everyday explanations that no one questions."

"But you were less sure?"

She shook her head. "No, not at first. It was when her second husband died that I became suspicious."

"She killed him, too?" I let out an unintended screech, and Grandfather turned to glare.

Vivian didn't look at me this time. She could only stare at the space where the broken pieces of china had previously lain. "I do not know all the details but... it was only a short time after they were married. He'd been to war but was relatively healthy and so, when he died, people began to talk. They called her the spider – one of those insects who eats their mates for sustenance. I thought it rather cruel and I'm sure there's an innocent explanation, but it still made me question what I really knew of her."

Her explanation came to an abrupt halt, and Grandfather sat with his back perfectly straight, his chin high and proud, and his gaze cast off through the window. He said nothing, but I could tell that he was considering the various paths down which this new case would take us and the possibility that Christabel Templeton-Swift was a killer.

CHAPTER FIVE

I finished my cake, took a few chocolate eclairs for the journey and said goodbye to that gentle lady who seemed perfectly happy there in a world of her own design. This did beg the question why she would have wanted to marry the invalid Hugo Templeton-Swift in the first place, but that was only one entry on a very long list of things I did not understand.

"I'm sorry, Grandfather, but I have a few questions," I revealed once we'd driven off the Easton Manor estate and were gliding along a dappled country lane. I could tell this came as no surprise to my companion, and so I started on my first. "Who exactly was that lady?"

"Vivian," he pronounced with some pleasure, clearly enjoying the way the letters sounded in his mouth. "She's unlike any other person I know."

This was typically opaque, and so I prodded him for more. "Which leads to my next question. How exactly did you meet her?" Exactitude was always important when talking to that singularly evasive fellow.

"I arrested her." He started laughing before the words had passed his lips and was evidently keen to scandalise me. I can tell you this: it worked!

"You mean she's a criminal?"

"Yes, but only a sneak thief." He clearly felt the need to underline her insalubrious connections and offered a few synonyms to add emphasis. "A pickpocket, a cutpurse, a fingersmith. Quite the loveliest criminal I've ever met, I must say, but a criminal nonetheless."

"Then how did she become Lady Highley-Summers?" Her words came back to me, and I added another question. "And what part did you play in such a transformation?"

He was luxuriating in my discomfort and didn't even feel the need to break the speed limit as we spoke. "The truth is, Christopher, I met young Vivian when she was at the lowest point in her life. She was a thief and an exceedingly good one, but she was neither cruel, greedy nor selfish. She stole because that is what her father had brought her up to do. She stole so that her little brothers and sisters did not starve. She stole to survive, and I showed her a modicum of human kindness out of fear of what might otherwise have befallen her."

"That doesn't explain how she ended up marrying a lord."

I could see the pleasure he took in knowing that he had the whole story preserved in his mind, like a book in a library, while I had mere scraps of torn pages. "Fine, I'll tell you what happened from the beginning, but you must promise you won't be shocked."

In response, I could do nothing but stare at him… in shock.

"There was a man I knew named Honest Bill. He helped disreputable people become acceptable in the eyes of society. Your friend Marmaduke's father would have used the services of just such a person to go from gang master to baron. Well, Vivian was seventeen and a diamond of a beauty, which meant that she was vulnerable.

"She was living in a slum, surrounded by poverty such as you've never seen. I knew that, if I did nothing, those nefarious characters in the Old Nichol would exploit her. I was afraid that I might never see her again if such a tragedy were to occur, and so I introduced her to Bill. With my financial support, he gave her a new life. We created a whole identity for her, and I presented her at court as the daughter of a deceased friend."

"You presented a criminal before the King! Of Great Britain!?"

"Well, as it happens, Christopher, we had a queen at the time, but you promised you would not be shocked."

"I did no such thing. Now finish your story."

He had to wait at a crossroads for a rickety cart covered in straw to roll past. "Vivian was the belle of the season and any number of men wished to marry her. But I did not want her to feel that she had been sold off to the highest bidder. Trading her to a man against her wishes, whether it be a duke or a dockworker, was against my principles. I counselled her carefully and arranged a marriage with an elderly blowhard by the name of Lord Archibald Highley-Summers."

"And how was that any better for poor Vivian? Couldn't you at least have found her a young man she might have loved?"

"That wasn't my concern. I chose good old Archie because he had been paralysed in the Second Opium War and required nothing more from his wife than light conversation and her company at grand functions. I knew that he would die when Vivian was still a relatively young woman and that she could enjoy a long and happy existence in the comfort of one of the prettiest estates in Hampshire."

I tossed the tale over in my head, trying to understand exactly what I felt about his morally dubious plotting. "I suppose that was a kind thing to do."

"Yes…" He didn't sound so sure. "But perhaps you were right. Perhaps I should have thought more about her heart than her purse. When I heard from a mutual friend some time ago that she had been connected with Hugo Templeton-Swift, I realised that she must have been lonely to entertain the idea of marrying such a man."

His face had grown stony, and I knew that Vivian's life had touched him more than anyone could say.

"There's something else, isn't there, Grandfather?"

His eyes were fixed on the road ahead of us, which is never a good sign. For a man who liked to boast about his own skill at reading those around him, he sometimes had the most fantastically expressive visage, and his bad moods were never in doubt.

"She came to see me." His voice had dropped lower, and I could barely make out his reply over the sound of the roaring engine. "A year to the day after your grandmother died, Vivian came to Cranley. I'm sure you can imagine what happened."

My grandfather had seen no one outside the family during the decade he had mourned his wife, and I knew exactly what he meant. It took me a while longer to realise why Vivian would have been visiting him, though.

"She must be fifteen years younger than you!" This was an extremely diplomatic estimate, but I didn't tell him that. My grandfather had recently turned seventy-six and, though he was still an active chap, Vivian was a spring lamb in comparison.

"And why should age be an obstacle to anything?" His eyebrows shot up his forehead, and I was relieved that he was looking at me again (though I'd have preferred him to watch the road).

"I merely meant that…" I had no idea what I meant; I was still reeling from the idea that a vivacious woman like Vivian Highley-Summers could have entertained thoughts of a romantic relationship with my grandfather and, far worse, Hugo Templeton-Swift.

He broke into my frantic puzzling with a neat summary of the facts. "None of that is relevant now, of course, but you asked for the details. The only thing you need to know is that I trust Vivian and believe everything she told us this morning."

"So you really think this Christabel woman is plotting to murder her husband?"

"I can't be certain." He bit his lip as he considered the point. It entered my mind that, much like a chess player who is familiar with the different sequences of moves with which to win the game, he had already calculated any number of hypothetical solutions to the case. "We won't know anything until we reach Riverside Keep this afternoon."

His speech had become more forceful as the conversation progressed, and I found myself falling silent. It would be an hour before we reached our next stop, and I spent that time deep in thought. It wasn't just the case itself that danced about in my head. It was tangled up with thoughts of my family, my exams and my future.

From what my brother had told me, university sounded like an awful lot of fun, but I hadn't a clue which institution would want a silly goose like me or what I might like to study if I got there. Of course, I hadn't mentioned this minor issue to my parents, who still expected me to follow in Albert's footsteps.

One thing I could say for certain was that I now understood why my grandfather hadn't wanted his daughter to come with us to visit Vivian. Though he had revealed some minor details of their relationship, I felt there was more still to be unearthed about this attractive figure from his past. Lord Edgington was a bag of secrets shut away in a safe that was safely ensconced in a locked room some three hundred yards beneath the surface of the Earth. He always expected me to work for the information I required, and I was lucky to have learnt as much as I had.

The hour soon passed, and we parked the car at the end of a track in the middle of a grassy plain. Todd's Silver Ghost was already there and, except for a few bleating sheep, the only sign of life was a man in a wooden pay box who was cheerfully awaiting our custom.

"Afternoon, gentlemen," he called over, as we got out of the car. "Quiet here today. You're only my second visitors. Tomorrow's Saturday, though. We normally have more folk stop by at the weekend."

"I believe that my daughter and our chauffeur have arrived ahead of us," Grandfather replied.

"That'll be them, guvnor. They've gone off to start the picnic.

They only arrived a quarter hour ago. I should think there'll still be some pork pie left if you hurry." For some reason, he looked at me when he said this.

"Wonderful." Grandfather handed over the coins for our admittance.

"Enjoy your lunch now," the chap said, and we nodded our thanks and walked away.

I should probably have worked out where we were going from the general direction in which we'd driven, but it was only when I saw the ring of monoliths on the horizon that I realised.

"Oh my goodness," I began. "This is Salisbury Plain, isn't it? I've always wanted to see Stonehenge."

The ancient circle of standing stones was bigger than I had imagined. My only disappointment was that there were no hooded druids about the place to complete the scene. The sun shone down upon the mythical site, just as it would have when it was first built. If it hadn't been for a few houses in the distance, I could have pretended we'd travelled back to pagan times.

"Inspiring stuff," my companion cheered as we cut a line towards the centre of the circle, where Mother and Todd were presumably hidden. "Can you believe that a few years ago this was all private? I know the chap who bought the land and donated it to the public. Such antiquities should be preserved for the good of all people, not just the rich."

This gave me pause for thought. "If that's how you feel, why don't you donate Cranley Hall to the National Trust?"

He stopped walking and grinned at me. I knew I would regret the question even before he'd answered it. "How do you know I won't leave it to them when I die?"

He thundered off ahead, and we soon found the others sitting on a blanket in the shade of one of the great trilithon structures. Well, Mother was sitting, Todd was busy preparing our plates. That clever chap must have heard the car arriving and decided to make a start on his duties. Delilah instantly ran up to him and demanded her lunch.

"Where have you been?" Mother was less than impressed by our tardiness and, I can only imagine, suspicious of what we had been doing.

"It's such a lovely day, we decided to take a scenic route," Grandfather told her, his tone light and jolly.

"Yes," she replied, her forehead creased with doubt. "Todd said the very same thing. It was quite the least direct road we could have followed. I had to ask him where we were going at one point, when I noticed a sign for Oxford."

Todd winced at this. Though he was always a willing accomplice to his employer's schemes, they tended to backfire. "My apologies again, madam. But, as I said at the time, the North Wessex Downs are a sight we simply couldn't miss."

Mother said nothing in response but bit the head off a stick of celery with some aggression. Cranley Hall's cook, Henrietta, had clearly been charged with preparing the repast. In addition to the usual picnic food one might expect like scotch eggs, cucumber sandwiches and thinly cut fried potatoes, she had included flasks of a Ukrainian soup known as borscht. Instead of the traditional beef stock with which the dish is associated, she'd used trout broth. I took a few painful sips to be polite, whereas my grandfather had second helpings.

As we ate our lunch, a pair of biplanes circled lazily around one another in the sky.

"What marvels of the modern world." Grandfather craned his neck to look up at the aerial acrobatics on display. "Such a contrast to this phenomenal place, don't you think?"

His gaze travelled back down to Earth and, now that I had stuffed my belly, I took the time to look around us. There were only a few of the three-part stone structures still standing, but it was fascinating to imagine how the site would have looked in its heyday. It was such a warm and dozy afternoon, I would have happily lain down to go to sleep, but my grandfather decided to give me a lesson instead.

"There's a chap called Lieutenant-Colonel William Hawley who has spent the last six years restoring and investigating this place. He found a number of skeletons buried beneath the stones and believes that it must have been sacred to generations of different people, centuries apart. He's even postulated the theory that the main function of Stonehenge was to host funereal rituals. Personally, I don't mind why they built it all those millennia ago. I'm just thankful we can still visit today."

He sighed again and fell to reflecting on the beauty of nature and the ingenuity of humankind. I suppose that some of my dreamier qualities must have come from him.

My mother, meanwhile, was a pragmatist. "Are you ever going to tell me where we're going this weekend?"

This certainly pulled him from his stupor. "Of course, my dear. Once we finish here, we will be driving directly to the country pile of a man named Hugo Templeton-Swift. He's—"

"A wealthy investor, yes, I know." Why was I always the ignorant one? Even my dear mother knew more than me. "I've been married to a stockbroker for a quarter of a century. I've probably heard Templeton-Swift's name more often than that of the prime minister."

"Excellent." Grandfather really was excited about our investigation and rubbed his hands together with glee. "Well, we're going to his house, as he's written to me claiming that his wife is trying to kill him. So it will be your job to—"

"To win the trust of his potential murderer." She rolled her eyes then and looked just like her father. "What could be easier?"

CHAPTER SIX

"Not a chance."

"You have to do it one day." Grandfather could barely look at me.

"And what makes you think that day has arrived?"

Todd had pulled away in the Silver Ghost and the old man and I were shouting across the bonnet of Grandfather's car. He'd just handed me the key to the Aston Martin, and I was considering running off across Salisbury Plain to escape.

"I've never driven so much as a horse before," I told him, throwing the key back in his direction. He was an incredibly good catch for a man of his age.

"You ride a horse and drive a car. Surely you know that much?" He threw it straight back to me, but I dropped it.

"If you think that, you have far too much faith in me."

The old dictator climbed into the passenger seat, and I had no choice but to sit down next to him.

"Just see how it feels sitting there. I won't force you to do anything."

Even as he said this, he leaned across me to poke the key into the hole. He started the motor and the fearsome machine shuddered into life. I had never before noticed what treacherous beasts cars can be. Placing my hands on the steering wheel felt like I was gripping the horns of a charging bull.

"That's the ticket. Easy does it." Grandfather was full of charming platitudes, but I'd yet to hear him offer any useful advice.

"I have no idea what I'm doing," I assured him.

"You've seen me drive plenty of times. You must have some idea how it works."

"Stuff and nonsense. I've never seen you drive because, as soon as you start the car, I close my eyes and say a prayer."

He waited a few seconds in the hope I'd calm down. The chap who'd sold us our tickets to Stonehenge had come out of his box and was enjoying the spectacle.

Grandfather hadn't given up hope. "Come along now, Christopher. It really is the simplest thing in the world. All you have to do is press your left foot down on the clutch, and–"

"Which one is the clutch?" I had warned him just how ignorant I was.

"The one on the left." He waited for me to remember my left from right. "That's good, now move the gearstick into position and gently raise the pedal again until you feel the car pulling forward."

I tried exactly this, and the engine cut out.

"That was excellent, my boy." I didn't believe him. "Now, we'll try it again and, this time, press your right foot gently on the accelerator as you ease off the clutch."

I tried again, and the engine cut out.

"That was the brake, not the accelerator. We'll have one more go and, this time, do everything a little more slowly. We're in no hurry whatsoever."

The engine cut out for a third time, and I must say, he did well to not to lose his patience. It took me another fifteen minutes, but I managed to navigate off the field and onto a public road – it helped that it was downhill all the way.

"You're a natural, Christopher. An absolute natural!"

Obviously, it was not the smoothest drive. I suspect I reached a top speed of seven miles an hour, and much of that movement was backwards. For some reason, every time I accelerated, the car seemed to jerk to and fro as though someone had grasped hold of it. I did manage to get into second gear at one point, but that was an accident; I had taken a wrong turn and was trying to reverse.

"How far do we have to go?" I asked when I'd been at it for a good half an hour.

"Nine… miles." Grandfather finally showed a first hint of irritation.

"And how far is our destination from Stonehenge?"

"Nine and a half!"

I don't know what came over me, but I suddenly found some confidence. I can't say whether it was my newfound familiarity with the vehicle, a desire to please my wise forebear or because we'd both got used to the fact that I was a truly terrible driver, but Grandfather's beloved Aston Martin suddenly started doing as it was told. Delilah had taken the wise step of travelling in the front seat of the Rolls with Todd and was spared the torture of my early attempts, but I think she would have barked with approval at this moment.

"Well now," Grandfather said, looking about with surprise. "That's better, lad. Yes, you're really getting the hang of it. I knew you would."

He pulled out his Bartholomew map of Wiltshire to check the route, but I spotted a sign for Hanging Langford and headed in that direction. Speaking of signs, I noticed the hilariously named towns of Little Wishford, Fisherton de la Mere and Nether Wallop! I pointed them out to my passenger, but he didn't find them funny.

I must say that the subsequent part of the journey went quite perfectly. I still crunched the gears occasionally, but at least we rolled along at a good pelt. We reached an exceedingly straight road at one point, and so I decided to go even faster.

"Don't get carried away now, boy," my instructor told me, perhaps enduring a taste of his own poison. "The turn for the house will be coming up shortly."

We were blazing down a hilly road with high hedges on either side. I was greatly enjoying myself. Experimentally at first, and then with more belief, I pushed the gear stick up to the third position.

"Nicely done, Christopher, but slow down a little. We'll be taking the next left."

I did just as he said. I changed gear, slowed into the turn and drove straight into a meadow.

"What are you doing!" he boomed, as we shot through the long grass.

"You said, 'next left,' so I took the next left."

"This isn't a left turn, Christopher. It's a field."

If he'd found my driving bumpy before, this was a whole new experience. It rather reminded me of the rollercoaster we'd enjoyed at the Great Yarmouth Pleasure Beach. Well, I'd enjoyed it. He'd turned quite green as we hurtled down the wooden mountain. In fact, that wasn't so different from how he looked at this very moment.

"That must be the house," I pointed to our right as we sped forwards, narrowly avoiding a sheep. "It looks very nice."

He had abandoned his map by this point and was gripping his seat, the whites of his eyes consuming much of his face. I tried to slow the car down, but I was still in a higher gear and momentum pulled us onward down the slope.

"I suppose we might as well keep going now that we've got this far," I suggested with a nervous laugh as we reached the middle of the field; the idea of reversing back the way we'd come was not an enticing one.

He did not reply, but I spotted another open gate some distance away and charted a course towards it. I really didn't come too close to any of the trees there, and yet he yelped and squirmed in his seat as though we were rushing headlong towards the abyss. I'd never known him to be such a fusspot.

"Here we are," I said as I steered us back onto the road with some skill. I'd managed to shift down through the gears by now, and we were once more jerking along at a snail's pace. It turned out that it was really only driving in first gear that caused me any problems. Everything else seemed relatively simple.

For some reason, he was clutching his heart.

"Yes, here we are." He needed a moment to catch his breath. "If you could take the next left to pull into Riverside Keep, we'll–" He felt the need to interrupt himself then. "The left with the large stone gate, not the small ditch just before it that would almost certainly destroy the car."

"I'm not an idiot," I said as, though I'm no genius, idiot is surely too strong a word for me.

"No, boy. Of course you're not. You're only seventeen and you've almost mastered the art of driving. I have no doubt that you'll be competing in the Grand Prix of Endurance in Le Mans next year."

"Grandfather, I think I detected a touch of sarcasm in that comment."

"Thus proving once again that you are no idiot." He had recovered his nerves and slapped his thigh like Dick Whittington in a pantomime. "Come along, Christopher, it's time to meet our suspects."

CHAPTER SEVEN

Just inside the drive, we discovered the Rolls parked behind a row of bushes.

"What in heaven's name are you hiding there for?" Grandfather asked his usual chauffeur after I'd managed to stall our car in approximately the right place.

I'd never seen our heroic servant look so nervous before. "Well, M'Lord, you said there might be a murderer in the house."

Grandfather pulled his neck in like a startled turkey. "But you've met any number of murderers. I fail to see the problem."

"That was different, M'Lord. They'd already done the killing when I dealt with them. This chap hasn't yet begun."

It was hard to follow his logic, but I think I understood what had unnerved him. "So you mean there's more chance of you becoming his target?"

"Exactly, Master Christopher. That's just it. I don't want to be murdered. I'm my mother's only son. She'd be heartbroken." He was a good-natured chap, and even Grandfather couldn't be upset by such selfless reasoning.

"You've nothing to worry about, man. I'm here now." He sounded like a mother himself then, comforting a nipper who'd had a bad dream.

My mother had observed this exchange from the back seat of the Rolls and looked just as bewildered as she had all day. No doubt she thought we men were being very silly. She climbed out of the car and, without waiting for us, walked across the wide, oval drive towards the house with Delilah close at heel.

It was a unique place. Neither so old nor grand as most of the houses in my family, there was something very different about it from most estates I'd visited. It had a checkerboard exterior and five gabled roofs set back behind protruding bays. After staring at it for some seconds, I finally realised what marked it out so greatly. Unlike many of the other lavish abodes I'd seen, the exterior didn't try to wow visitors with just how grand or opulent it was. Its design was for the sake of art, beauty and originality, which I thought rather special. The only thing that disappointed me was the fact that, despite its name, the house was nothing like a keep. I suppose there were crenellations on the roof, but that was hardly enough to earn such a moniker.

Before my mother could ring on the doorbell to be admitted, two figures burst from the house.

"I won't remain under this roof for another minute," a young woman wailed. She had shoulder-length blonde hair and wore a loose-fitting white suit with black spats over patent leather shoes. She marched straight past my mother without noticing her.

"Come on, Lettice. Don't be so wet." The man who was pursuing her couldn't have been more than forty and had a precise, yet jolly manner. He seemed to place his feet in the woman's footprints, as though afraid of upsetting the paving stones.

"That joke wasn't funny the first time you said it when I was seven years old, and it isn't funny now." She turned to face him, and I tried to make sense of what was happening. Were they friends, lovers or relatives? I detected no immediate family likeness, but then people tell me that I'm a rounder version of Albert, and I can't see that either.

"I'm sorry, Letty, but our father needs us." There we go. One mystery solved. "We can't abandon him now."

"I won't watch him die." She was crying by this stage and, though she remained oblivious to her audience, her brother looked from one to another of us. "I won't watch that woman slowly kill him."

The man wore a golfing jumper and slacks, as if he'd just stepped off the fairway at St Andrews. Walking a little faster now to catch up with his emotional sister, he seized her by the shoulder to turn her round. "We won't let that happen, but we can't just abandon him."

"I'm terribly sorry to interrupt," my grandfather... interrupted. "Clearly, this is a trying time for you both, but Hugo Templeton-Swift wrote to me to request my presence here. I imagine you must be his children."

The pair froze for a moment longer, as though the intimacy of that scene simply wouldn't permit such an intrusion. It was, perhaps inevitably, the sporty-looking chap who would respond. "That's right. And who the devil are you?"

I was interested to see how the great detective would react to this question. His usual tactic was to wave the flag of his brilliance for all to see. In this case, I thought perhaps a more subtle approach was in order.

"I am the Most Honourable Marquess of Edgington, former superintendent in the Metropolitan Police. I imagine you've heard of me."

But then, what do I know?

Drying her eyes, the woman nodded. "Of course we have, but how did Daddy come to write to you without anyone knowing?"

Grandfather bowed a fraction to acknowledge the effort she had made in responding. "That, I cannot say, but I must reveal that he wrote to me because he fears for his life. I am here to prevent a murder."

"We don't need anyone's help." A third man had walked out of the house and was striding towards us. He was not dressed for the season but wore a long leather coat, much like a soldier in the trenches. "We'll deal with our problems as a family. We don't need outsiders sticking their noses into Dad's business."

It was hard to imagine he came from the same family as his two siblings. Not because of any great physical difference, in fact he had similarly dark hair and eyes to his brother's, but because of the brutish manner in which he addressed us. He was as rough as a hedgehog's back.

"That's all very well," Grandfather replied, as politely as ever. "But Mr Templeton-Swift has requested my presence, and I feel it is my duty to fulfil his wishes."

My poor mother was still standing near the entrance to the house, looking quite bemused by the drama we had witnessed.

"Come along, Devyn," the sister began. She spoke with real hesitation, and I wondered if it was this gruff ruffian whom we should investigate, rather than their stepmother (wherever she might be). "It will do no harm to have another person here to help."

The savage Devyn glared about at us, as though he wished to square the discrepancy between the one person his sister had mentioned and the four of us standing about gawking.

"That's right, Dev," his brother tried. "Let's give Lord Edgington a chance… for Papa's sake."

The beast's nostrils flared, and he scratched his mutton-chop sideburns before throwing a dismissive hand through the air and stomping away from the house. The sheen of fear that had been visible on his brother's face now disappeared, and he tiptoed across the stones to offer my grandfather his hand.

"I'm Tiffin. Hugo's eldest boy. You've just had the pleasure of meeting Devyn, and over there is my sister, Lettice." He was one of those carefree, lively chaps who seem to go through life without the slightest thing worrying them. Or at least, that was the mask he wore. After what I'd just seen, it was somewhat hard to believe.

"I'm very pleased to meet you." Grandfather nodded efficiently and took this opportunity to size up the larger-than-life character in front of him. "I must also introduce you to my family. This is my grandson and assistant, Christopher and, standing by the front door, is my daughter and occasional assistant, Violet."

He sometimes took his meticulousness to unnecessary lengths. I was surprised he didn't introduce his chauffeur (and frequent assistant), Todd.

"Perhaps you'd like to see Daddy?" Lettice suggested, and we walked across the driveway together. I noticed that Todd stayed behind to lock himself in the Rolls.

When we drew level with my mother, her natural generosity meant that only a few seconds would pass before she looped her arm through the bleary-eyed woman's. I could tell that they were on their way to becoming firm friends. Delilah looked just as cheery and wagged her tail incessantly as we walked into the old manor.

The entrance hall, and much of the house beyond, was replete with works of art wherever the eye landed. Every room we passed had deep red wallpaper and countless frames on display. Once again, rather than sticking with tradition to present an assortment of hunting scenes, landscapes and family portraits, Riverside Keep's artistic selection was far more varied. Each wall held twenty to thirty pictures of differing sizes. I spotted everything from colourful, modern daubings to religious art by ancient hands. The more experimental pieces reminded me of the work of my favourite artist, Augustus Harred.

But what made Riverside Keep so different was the fact that it felt as though real people lived there. It was nothing like the theatre sets I'd so often visited in the houses of family friends. Whoever had overseen its decoration had no interest in screaming, *this is how much money I possess,* so much as, *this is where I live.*

I think my grandfather must have been a little impressed, too. He frowned appreciatively as we passed dining rooms, salons and sitting rooms, on our way to the see the master of the house.

"You don't live in the area?" he asked the two siblings, as we paused to open a final door. "Is that correct?"

"Indeed," Tiffin replied, before turning the handle. "The three of us flew the coop some time ago. In fact, Devyn only arrived yesterday from New York. I have an estate of my own up near Edinburgh, and Lettice is on the other coast from here."

She winced a little, apparently feeling the need to expand upon this phenomenally vague description. "My husband is from Sutton-on-Sea. We live there with our two children."

With this information divulged, Tiffin pushed the door open, and we entered a large room that was all dark wood and bookshelves. To my horror, there was not a single book upon any of them, and I almost changed my mind about the place after all.

Instead, the space was filled with interesting artefacts from across the world. There were statues of Indian gods, great wooden masks, skulls of animals that I couldn't identify and countless unusual ceramics in every colour. There was even a small sculpture of a monkey made from the husks of two coconuts.

In place of the paintings that had marked out the other rooms we had seen, one wall was covered in photographs. I should probably have been paying more attention to the occupants of that cosy space, but I was travelling around the world in eighty seconds. The images that I first noticed were of Latin America, where Hugo Templeton-Swift had made his fortune. But the photos on display were not dry images of building projects or mining concerns. They showed temples, jungles, rivers and waterfalls.

From there, I hopped across to Africa, on to Asia and back up through Russia and Europe once more. The only major oversight was Australasia, though I'm far from certain I'd be able to identify that region based on a photograph – assuming there were no kangaroos, koalas or kiwis present.

Whilst I was peering about the place, my subconscious mind must have been doing its job as I vaguely recall the conversation that took place. There was quite a lot of shouting, so it's hardly a surprise.

"Who are these people?" a woman enquired.

"Oh, so you knew nothing about it, did you?" Lettice's voice had turned quite cold.

The other woman became more anxious. "What are they doing in my house?"

"This is not your house, my dear," Tiffin said with some force. "This is our father's estate, which, if there's any justice in the world, will be left to us when he dies."

"How can you be so cruel? What have I done for you to treat me in such a way?" The woman groaned, and I finally turned to look at her.

Lettice did not need long to find an answer. "You wish to steal what's ours. You're trying to take away my children's birthright."

"Thank you, everyone." Grandfather physically placed himself between the warring parties and held up both hands to keep the peace. "There is no need to argue. I am not here to serve as an umpire. I am a detective, and I have come to–"

"A detective?" the woman I took to be Christabel Templeton-Swift exclaimed, her mouth hanging open in quiet disbelief.

In the silence that followed, I could finally examine the antagonist who had brought about so much upheaval in that house. Dressed in stunning pleats of green silk, she was quite the beauty and there was a remarkable innocence to her, just as Vivian Highley-Summers had attested. She had truly golden hair, much of which was tied in a single plait at the back of her head, with the rest tumbling about her shoulders and halfway to her waist. Her skin was as fine as the white Chinese porcelain that sat on the shelves behind her, and her lips were full and pert.

She was a great deal younger than Vivian and was quite the most handsome woman I'd seen since the last case we'd investigated. That really isn't saying much, though, as a beauty contest at Oakton Academy would be a toss-up between our ageing matron and a boy in the third form with thick blonde hair.

Sitting beside her in a wheelchair was what I can only describe as her exact opposite. A man with more wrinkles than hairs on his head was propped up at an uncomfortable angle and appeared to be asleep. There was a slate in his lap with a piece of chalk resting upon it. In his letter, Hugo Templeton-Swift had implied that he was in his eighty-second year on Earth and yet, to look at him, I would have guessed he had already celebrated his centenary.

My grandfather allowed the intense atmosphere to simmer down before responding. "Yes, my dear. My name is Lord Edgington. Your husband wrote to request my assistance on a matter of some sensitivity."

Her face fell as her stepchildren grinned. "But… I've read about you. You were in the paper when that newspaper baron died in London a few months ago. You investigate murders and all sorts of unpleasantness. What could you possibly think would require your attention at Riverside Keep?"

He glanced away then, and I was surprised by just how coy he looked. Before he could answer, Lettice had stepped forward to reveal the harsh truth.

"Daddy summoned these people here to prevent his murder. He evidently believes that someone wishes to do away with him, or he wouldn't have written to Superintendent Edgington of Scotland Yard."

"Now, now." Grandfather attempted to play peacemaker once more. "We mustn't get ahead of ourselves. As far as I know, no crime has been committed and there's absolutely no reason to think that anyone is going to die."

I'm one hundred per cent certain that he didn't believe what he was saying. Even if I hadn't known what was written in Hugo's letter, as soon as I walked into that house, I would have thought, *Well, blow me tight! Someone's going to get murdered here!*

Another argument erupted, as both siblings snapped at their stepmother, and even Delilah had a bit of a growl. The outburst woke the sleeping patriarch, and Hugo drowsily managed to open his eyes and cough out a few words.

"Not myself. She's the one," he grumbled, then fell asleep once more.

In the excitement, I hadn't noticed the maid tending to a fire, just behind the spot where Christabel and her husband were sitting. With this task complete and the flames eating up the logs and kindling she'd arranged, she rose. She wiped a sooty hand across her face and, without a hint of good manners or the necessary training to work in such a house, she announced, "Tea'll be ready in a minute. There's only just enough for everyone, so come and get it soon or you'll miss out."

Grasping her back with a groan of discomfort, she left the room without even curtseying. I'd never seen such behaviour from a domestic. While I'm all for equality and the avoidance of unnecessary stuffiness, her disregard for the usual rules of polite society bordered on the scandalous.

"Oh, and don't expect nothing fancy," she put her head back around the door to warn my grandfather. "You may be a Lord or what have ya, but we're simple folk around here. Mum's cooking ain't up to much at the best of times. So you'll get what you're given."

CHAPTER EIGHT

"Did you hear that, Hugo?" Christabel asked in a tender voice, as she bent down to her husband's level. "We'll go into the dining room for afternoon tea now."

He opened his eyes a little wider this time but could do nothing more than nod and grasp hold of his wife's hand. She placed it on his shoulder affectionately and walked around him to push the chair.

To my genuine surprise, her elder stepson, who had previously been shouting at her, stood aside with a smile to let her through. Tiffin even bowed a little as they passed and kept smiling as he ushered us forward. Lettice maintained her sullen demeanour, but her brother was very light and frivolous as he chatted away about several breezy topics before we reached the dining room, which was, in a fashion at least, laid out for tea. Plates were stacked in piles. Cutlery was thrown about willy-nilly and the teacups and saucers were still on a trolley at the side of the room. Lettice apparently didn't find anything strange in this and began to finish the job that the maid had presumably abandoned halfway through.

Hugo was wheeled into place at one end of the table and Grandfather took his seat opposite, while the rest of us sat wherever we could. Evidently no order or thought went into the rules of the house and, to my surprise, I longed for our matron from school to pop up and shout at everyone to observe a little decorum. I swear I am no snob, but seeing a man seated next to another man at a dining table seemed quite unnatural. What next? Women next to women?

Grandfather acted as though he hadn't even noticed – that wily fox – and, once we were all seated, and the table was laid, a cook appeared to toss food at us like sea lions in the zoo.

"Ham, cheese, ham and cheese, cucumber and cheese, cucumber." It took me a few giddy seconds to realise that she was listing the different types of sandwiches which she had assembled on a tray. There was a big pile of the things and, for all the information she had provided, there was no way of telling one from another. "Fish paste, radish and garlic, tomato and anchovy, and cucumber."

"You already said cucumber," the maid informed her as she rolled in another trolley with a samovar on top. She looked the spit and image of the older domestic, and I remembered that she had previously mentioned her mother's cooking. "You forgot about the egg and cress."

"Oh, egg and cress too. Basically, you've got all the usual sandwiches, plus garlic and radish, which is one of me own creations." The older of the two had a bright red face, and I had to wonder whether she'd stuck her head in a boiling pan before delivering her victuals. She had a thick moustache on her lip – which made me a little jealous, as mine was taking its time to appear – and her fists were like two loaves of bread that had been left in the oven too long. The woman was terrifying.

"Very kind of you, Betty," Tiffin muttered, as she smashed the enormous tray down in front of him.

"Well, go on then." The cook stood next to the table to make sure that we ate with those great hands of hers on her hips. I know I said that I wished my school matron had been present to whip us into shape, but this wasn't what I'd had in mind. "Dig in!"

My mother was the first to take the initiative and stood up from the table to provide each person with a selection of small white triangles with the crusts removed. As she went about this task, the young maid set to work, lighting another fire. I had to assume that this was for the invalid's benefit, as the room was as hot as a bakehouse. Once the sandwiches were distributed, we all took a nervous bite and Christabel helped her husband with his. I crossed my fingers that mine would not be radish and garlic.

"Lovely stuff," Betty beamed and, wiping her hands on her sides, she marched from the room with a final promise, or perhaps I should say threat. "There's plenty more where those came from."

I was still trying to identify which flavour I was eating. There was definitely something fishy about it, and yet the predominant taste was cheese. Unlike our chef at Cranley, who never rested on her laurels and put experimentation before all else, Betty had somehow succeeded in taking a few simple ingredients and doing the unthinkable; she'd managed to make a sandwich taste bad.

Almost everyone nibbled at the bready snacks, with each of us doing our best to pretend that the afternoon meal was really quite edible. Grandfather was the only one who refused to make such a pretence, but then, at his age, he could get away with anything and frequently did. He glared across the table at me as if to say, *now do you understand why I always insist on bringing my own staff when we travel?* I made a mental note to never complain about the delicious offerings that Henrietta provided back at Cranley for as long as I lived.

The final sibling reappeared at this moment. Devyn's eyes were as big as cartwheels as he spotted the refreshments. I was only surprised that he sat down at the table – next to his brother! – instead of filling his pockets with sandwiches and charging off again.

Grandfather took this opportunity to address the family whose home we had invaded. I think it was mainly to hide the fact that he had no interest in that dreadful food.

"Though some of you may wish to pretend otherwise, you all know why I've come to Riverside Keep. Hugo here wrote to me because he suspects that one of you is plotting to kill him." He must have been right in his assertion, as no one seemed particularly alarmed by this. Even the maid continued with her task as though she hadn't heard.

I watched Hugo himself at this moment and he seemed surprisingly alert. He kept his eyes fixed on Lord Edgington and raised his hand to point down the table at him and nod. It was hard to tell exactly what was wrong with him. I'm obviously no doctor, but he seemed more sleepy than sick, and he kept fading in and out of consciousness.

"While I am in this house," Grandfather continued. "Things are going to be a little different. For a start, I or my daughter will be in charge of overseeing Hugo's medicine. No one is to give him anything unless one of us is present."

"Steady on now," Tiffin began. "We can't all be under suspicion. If Papa wrote to you, it was because he suspected the hussy currently sitting next to him. What exactly did he say in the letter?"

"Letters, plural," Grandfather corrected him. I watched the suspects' reactions for some sign of surprise but detected nothing. "The first reached me over a week ago but was almost illegible. The second arrived just this morning."

Lettice's expression hardened. Though I'd taken her to be a sweet, soft-hearted woman when we'd seen her in tears outside, there was a fierceness to her that I hadn't previously anticipated. I tried to give one of my sandwiches to Delilah under the table whilst no one was looking, but even she didn't want them.

"My husband goes through phases of mental cognisance." This was Christabel speaking, not our dog. "One day he can be most jolly and the next quite at sea. That should explain the difference between the two missives." I thought that this sounded like a good excuse for something, though I couldn't imagine exactly what that would be.

"So what did *they* say?" Tiffin asked again.

"You were correct." Grandfather paused to let his audience absorb these words. "Hugo claimed his wife is poisoning him. May I ask if he ever speaks sense?"

"Not often, I'm afraid," Lettice replied, and it seemed that Christabel took particular exception to her presence there. This apparently innocent comment ignited a brief firefight across the table.

"What right have you got to comment on such a matter?" Perhaps it was the casual mention of her intention to kill her husband, but she looked as though she might explode at any second. "You aren't the one who has been here for the last year. You didn't even respond when we invited you to our wedding."

"And you wonder why?"

Grandfather was quick to bring the discussion under control. "Thank you, both." He nodded to them in turn before addressing the widow-to-be. "Would you disagree with your stepdaughter's appraisal, madam?"

She took a deep breath and looked at her husband. "No, the substance of her response was accurate enough. My dear Hugo rarely speaks more than a few words. It is often difficult to understand to whom they are addressed or exactly what he wishes to communicate. He is more lucid when writing and sometimes uses a slate and chalk to facilitate the process."

Grandfather wiggled his moustache for a moment, as if to say, *oh, how convenient,* but showed no other sign of doubting the woman's words. "Devyn, I've heard your brother and sister's thoughts on the matter. Do you have anything to add?"

The scruffy chap had inserted any number of sandwiches into his mouth but replied all the same. "I reckon they're right. I might not have been around for the last few years, and I've never lived up to Dad's expectations, but I know what he used to be like, and this isn't it." There was a constant aggressive edge to his voice, and I wondered how he could have grown into such a very different beast from his brother and sister.

Christabel could take no more and released a lupine growl. "Of course he isn't. Your father is sick. He's an old man who suffers from any number of physical maladies. I am not to blame for his poor health."

"That is enough." Lord Edgington brought his fist down on the table like a lightning bolt. The sandwiches shook in fear. "I have already explained that I am not here to adjudicate between you. I am a detective and I intend to root out the potential murderer before any evil can befall this house." He rose and, addressing the sooty maid, exclaimed, "My family and I will be staying the night. Please show me to my room."

The cook returned at this moment carrying a silver platter with a large carrot cake upon it. "Where are you off to? You 'aven't had the sweet yet."

He gave another courtly bow, complete with bended knee and twisted hand, before delivering a veiled insult. "I thank you kindly, madam. But I have eaten quite enough of your food."

She clearly didn't know how to read his words but dropped the dish on the table with yet more belligerence. Afraid that I would be forced to eat the grey monstrosity that had been set before us. I pushed back my chair, nodded politely to the lady of the house, then ran after my grandfather before my mother could object.

Just imagine! Christopher Prentiss running away at the sight of dessert? The very idea is preposterous.

CHAPTER NINE

"Young lady, what is your name?" Grandfather asked, as the maid led us upstairs.

"I'm Billie Crower," she replied without looking back.

"Isn't your mother's name Billie?" All these B names were confusing me. I already had three Billies to deal with back at school.

She stopped on the landing and let out a pained huff. "No, she's Betty, short for Elizabeth. I'm Billie, short for Wilhelmina."

Grandfather looked as though he could make no sense of this equation. "Very well, I will call you Wilhelmina."

I thought that "Billie" suited the girl a great deal better than that singularly regal name, but I said nothing more. Delilah walked with us as we navigated the upper hallway of the comfortable house. Despite the servants' lax manners, the place was clean, tidy and generally well maintained. Perhaps the girl was a harder worker than her mother was a capable chef.

"I will need your help this weekend, Wilhelmina," Grandfather announced in that confidential manner of his, which was often useful for drawing our suspects into his confidences. "I have no doubt that you know what goes on in this house better than most people."

"Are you talking about the poison, or what?" She was a very matter of fact young woman and clearly wasn't afraid to address the macabre reason we had come to Riverside Keep.

"Among other things. Tell me, when did Lettice and Tiffin arrive?"

She did not reply at first but punched open one of the doors off the corridor we were descending and pointed a stubby finger at me. "You're in that one." She crossed to the door opposite and did the same for my grandfather. "And you're in there. As for being your spy, I'm not sure I like the idea."

Grandfather peered into the room and found the large bed and the view much to his liking. Through the window, I could see a pretty garden and a river beyond. He was less enthused by Wilhelmina's response but was willing to negotiate.

"I will give you a shilling a day."

She smiled. "On second thoughts, I love the idea. And as for those two stuffy heirs, Lettice showed up on Monday and her brother came down from Scotland two days later. What else do you want to know?"

Grandfather had entered the room by this point and was testing the springiness of his bed.

"Excellent, and what about the letters that your employer sent?"

She rolled her fingers up into a fist and said in a menacing voice, "What about 'em?"

"Well, how did he send them? I doubt he could pop to the post office in his state."

She immediately brightened, and, when she answered, her voice was as sunny as the sky outside. "Oh, that was me. He asked me to go, and I popped 'em in the box for the postie."

Something had caught his eye through the window, and he raced over to look out. "Who's that man outside?"

"That's my pa. He makes sure the garden is neat and tidy." The upkeep of Riverside Keep was clearly a Crower family business. "He does a good job."

"And how many other members of your family are there?"

"I've got four brothers, as it happens, but they don't work here." Wilhelmina sat down in an armchair to get more comfortable. "Except for a girl who comes in on Tuesdays to do some cleaning, it's just the three of us." She looked up at the ceiling and had a brief yawn. "He's been good to us, old Hugo. Kept us around when most lordly types wouldn't."

"I don't suppose he has much say in the matter, these days," I said and immediately regretted it. The impetuous maid glared at me, and I suspect she would have clipped me round the ear if my grandfather hadn't been there to protect me.

He had another question for her. "So you've been working here for some time?"

"A couple of years now, I'd say. That's when we saw the advert for the job in the paper and Ma and Pa came for an interview. We was with an old maid in Wimbledon before this. But she was an ancient thing and went into an old people's home in the end. Ma always says we're helpers, not carers."

Grandfather looked as though he would ask another question. It caught in his throat, though, and he ended up dismissing her instead.

"That will be all for the moment. Thank you, Wilhelmina."

She rose but would not leave. Instead, she stood there with her cheeks inflated and her chin sticking out. Like her gnarled mother, she was no beauty, but this was a particularly unflattering pose.

"Well?" she finally said when Grandfather stared back in abject confusion.

Coming to understand her meaning, he reached inside his long grey coat in search of his purse. "This is for the weekend," he said, handing over a few coins. "But if you discover anything very useful, I will consider a further reward."

The coins seemed to sparkle in her eyes before she curtsied and hurried out. Grandfather remained at the window, watching the gardener go about his work, but I had a point to make.

"This is all rather strange, don't you think?"

He seemed excited by the observation and turned to look at me. "The fact that all three siblings could be so different? Yes, very unusual. Though not unheard of. My own three were quite dissimilar from a young age. Just consider the gulf between your mother and her dearly departed sister. I sometimes struggled to believe they were related, and I was there at the births."

"No, not that. I was thinking of how difficult it will be to investigate a murder without a body."

"Hmmm..." he replied, which wasn't particularly helpful. After a few seconds, he explained his thinking. "I'm not so sure that we are here to investigate a murder. Or at least, not yet."

"So why did we come?"

"We came, dear boy, to resolve the question of Christabel Templeton-Swift's guilt." He was evidently in a pedantic mood.

"Isn't that exactly the same thing?"

He needed no time to consider the possibility and replied with a resolute, "No! It is quite different. Have you wondered exactly why we are here? Why I, a former superintendent, would not simply call the local police to investigate?"

I hadn't a clue but felt certain he would be only too thrilled to explain. "No, I can't say I have."

"Tut, tut, Christopher. You really must be more inquisitive." He paced about in front of the window and said nothing for a minute or two as he formulated the answers to his own questions. "We are here to investigate the suspicions of a dying man. Whether his illness will kill him this weekend or ten years from now, it is clear that he is in no great health. And yet, his letters intrigued me."

"So you're suggesting… Wait…no. what are you suggesting?"

He stopped for a moment to shake his head in despair and then continued his pensive ambulation. "I'm saying that the local police would have no interest in this case. No crime has been committed. There is no suggestion that Hugo Templeton-Swift was tricked into marrying his much younger bride and, for the moment there is no clear evidence that his life is in danger."

"Then why did we come?"

"That's a very good question." He crossed his arms, and I didn't think he'd tell me anything more. Even for him, this was perplexing behaviour. "Something about those letters and the behaviour of his three children that we've seen so far tells me that we have a case to investigate. Though, I admit, it still is not apparent what such a process might entail. And so I return to the first question that the letters presented: is 'The lovely lady Christabel' as innocent as she appears? Or are her husband's suspicions warranted?"

"Which is all very well," I countered. "But how do we go about proving it one way or another?"

Grandfather smiled at this and nodded as though he were very pleased with his own forethought. "That game has already begun. Your mother is downstairs, earning the woman's trust as we speak. It's a jolly good thing she sniffed out my little enterprise this weekend or our task would be so much greater. What no one in this house realises is that your seemingly demure, well-spoken mother is as good a bloodhound as any detective I've known."

He glanced down appreciatively at his neatly clipped nails. He didn't need to say, *I taught her everything she knows,* but I know that's what he was thinking.

"I don't see that Mother is in any great position to uncover the truth? She's probably still nibbling on that terrible food."

He rushed forward to address me in a whisper. "Violet accompanied me on countless cases when she was a little older than you. Women couldn't attend university or join the police in those unenlightened times, but no one objected to the celebrated Lord Edgington taking his daughter along on his cases. She is the investigator you could one day be if you try your hardest."

I was quite taken aback by his words, though whether this was due to the picture he had painted of my mother, or his own vanity in describing himself as "celebrated", was unclear.

"So, what should we do first?" I was eager to become just as good a detective as my mother reportedly was and hungry to start the search for evidence.

"You can settle in your room while I have a nap. There's no sense in depleting our energy reserves before we begin. We'll let your mother do her part and drop in to see her a little later."

I was hoping for a different answer. Grandfather had often told me that he did his best thinking when he was asleep, and who was I to disagree with him? I walked back across the corridor to my room and found that good old Todd had already delivered my chest and bag. This was wonderful as it meant I could get straight on with my revision, but it was also rather terrible as it meant I had no excuse not to get on with my revision.

I opened the great wooden box and stared at the different textbooks for geography, history, maths and chemistry. Buried in amongst them was my copy of H.G. Wells's 'War of the Worlds' which I must have read three times. I was tempted to make it four, when I heard a voice through the cracked open window.

Out on the drive once more, Lettice and Tiffin were enjoying some cigarettes.

"I can't help feeling nervous," Lettice told her brother. There was a hint of desperation in her voice and, peering over the windowsill, I could see her feverishly pulling on the paper tube in her hand.

"But there really is no need, my dear. I thought you did a wonderful job."

She shook her head and let out the smoke. "How can you say that? I was pathetic. Totally unbelievable from the first word I uttered. I fooled no one. Edgington will know it's an act. I bet that even the slightly dim-looking, pudgy boy was unconvinced."

"You're forgetting that I was there, and I thought you did just perfectly. The important thing is not to become overwrought. Stay calm and everything will be fine."

She took another quick drag, and this seemed to tranquillise her somewhat. "Yes, stay calm. You always know just what to say."

"Of course I do." He put one arm around her in fraternal support. "If we keep it up for the rest of the weekend, we'll be laughing all the way to the bank."

CHAPTER TEN

I was stunned by the revelations I'd overheard, and my first thought was to speed back to my grandfather's room to tell him all. Ultimately, though, I was more afraid of getting shouted at for waking him from his slumber than what the potential murderers would do, and so I stayed in my room instead.

I resisted the temptation to relive the Martian invasion and opened my history book. To my surprise, there was a rather interesting chapter on Stonehenge, and I learnt all about the modern theories of its original use and construction. Marvellous stuff! I was almost disappointed when Grandfather woke up and came to get his lapdog. Delilah had fallen asleep at my feet, and I had to wonder whether their daily rhythms had become harmonised over the years they'd spent together.

"With me, boy," Grandfather called, and I duly ran after him with Delilah trundling along less willingly. "We must see what we can get out of the man himself. He may be too far gone, but Templeton-Swift had a fine brain once. I believe that some part of it might still be accessible."

After listening to see whether anyone was in earshot, I stopped him on the landing and repeated the conversation I had heard outside my window.

"How very interesting," he replied, then sped downstairs without further comment.

He had a real spring in his step as we bustled off to discover that the owners of Riverside Keep had retreated to the garden to enjoy the afternoon sunshine and perhaps digest the questionable sandwiches they had consumed. I'd only had a few bites myself, which meant that I still had control of my internal organs. Sadly, however, I was now close to starvation. Skipping afternoon tea is surely not good for the health. I like a nice round six meals a day and could just about manage on the four they provided at school.

"Hello, all," Grandfather sang after we emerged into the fresh air and crossed the garden to find them. "What a glorious afternoon."

Mr and Mrs Templeton-Swift were sitting with my mother on a large terrace with a bubbling fountain and white wooden garden furniture. I watched the exquisite Christabel. She couldn't have been much younger than my mother but had an astonishingly youthful manner. I suppose that, in order to marry so many men who had apparently died off in unusual circumstances, she needed to take good care of her looks. It's a sad fact but, even in the twentieth century, a woman's strongest asset is often the speed at which she can make a man's heart flutter. There are women scientists, racing drivers and pilots these days, but some things never change.

She said nothing and so Grandfather continued. "I was hoping to have a talk with Hugo here." He was studying the woman just then. I watched as his eyes carved into her, so it was no wonder she looked so anxious. "If you have no objections, of course."

She hesitated, further unsettled by his prodding words. "I have no objections."

Mother cast a sidelong look at me as I sat down beside her. She knew the part she was to play and, though still not happy that I'd abandoned my studies before my exams, she was ever the professional. "Christabel, why don't we go for a walk in the garden and get to know one another a little better? I feel dreadful invading your home like this, but at least we can try to make it a pleasant experience."

"Very well. But Hugo needs a drop of tincture in a glass of water every two hours on the hour." She pointed to a small bottle with a pipette stopper on the table. "It is just a natural remedy, but it does appear to ease his suffering."

"Oh, if it's only a natural remedy, we could try without it for one day, don't you think?" Grandfather looked like a man who had backed the winning horse in the Grand National.

Christabel showed no fear as she nodded. "If you think that's best for him, very well."

My mother stood up and held a hand out to her new friend. The woman hesitated but, without a trace of a smile, finally acquiesced. The pair moved off along a path towards the river and we were left alone with Hugo.

Once they were out of sight beyond a bank of lavender, Grandfather took his pocket watch from his waistcoat to consult the time. He picked up the bottle of medicine and gave it a sniff before turning to the patient. "I think this may be a rare case where a little less medication might do the trick."

He placed it back on the table and moved closer to look into the man's eyes. I wasn't certain what he was trying to do. For a moment, I wondered if he planned to hypnotise the poor chap. Whatever he had intended, it didn't work, and he let out a frustrated grunt.

"Hugo, I believe you know who I am. My name is Edgington, and I used to be a police officer. Perhaps you could make some response if you remember writing to me."

Until this moment, the old gentleman had been gazing up at the sky, but he finally moved to acknowledge our presence there.

I believe he said the word, "Arm," though I can't be certain. Either way, he tapped on the slate on his lap, and it was clear that he was replying in the affirmative.

"Wonderful." Grandfather was happy with the result of this first phase of the interview.

"Can you tell me anything more about your suspicions?"

The old fellow… well, perhaps I should say the older of the two fellows, but after spending a few minutes with Hugo Templeton-Swift, I thought of my grandfather as quite the young buck. In any case, Hugo picked up the chalk that was resting in the folds of his burgundy dressing gown. He was purposeful in his movements, but when he pressed the utensil to the smooth black surface, he could make nothing more than a long, sinuous line. The effort apparently took a great deal of energy too, as he put his head back against the wicker wheelchair and had to close his eyes.

"I know this must be immensely difficult, but I'm certain you can do it." I really did feel terrible for the poor chap. "If someone here is trying to hurt you, my grandfather will stop them. We just need your help to understand exactly what is happening."

With his eyes still closed, he took a deep breath and tried again. The letters that slowly formed were spidery and wandered about the slate. One was small, the next big, but little by little, some words formed.

CaN't sAay

"You don't know who has been poisoning you?"

He looked across the room but did not answer. This definitely raised the question of why he had written the letter in the first place if he couldn't name his assailant.

"How do you know you're being poisoned?" Grandfather asked, though he seemed to be speaking to himself as much as Hugo. "Could it not simply be the medicine you're taking?"

A slow shake of the head followed and, this time, it was too much for him. He closed his eyes and would not open them again for several minutes.

"How very odd," Grandfather exclaimed. "Perhaps we've been sent upon a fool's errand after all. I came here believing that, no matter his affliction, the word of Hugo Templeton-Swift was worth trusting. He is clearly a shadow of his former self."

He rose then, and I thought he would give up on our task entirely. "You over there," he called across the garden to where the man we'd seen from the upstairs window was trimming back a bush of summer lilac. "If you'd be so kind as to send for coffee from the kitchen, I'd be awfully appreciative."

The grubby chap wandered over, taking his own merry time about it. "I believe that a shilling is the price of assistance around here." He had a wicked grin and a devious sparkle in his eye. Grandfather kept coins about his person for this very purpose and already had the desired scrap of silver at hand.

"Then be quick about it."

The man lumbered over to the side of the house and bellowed through a window. "Betty? Betty, make some damn coffee for his lordship. Make it strong and all; the fellow looks like he could do with a good jounce." Clearly unashamed that we would have heard his comment, he reappeared a short while later with that smile still bold on his face.

"What is your Christian name, Mr Crower?" Grandfather enquired of his new assistant.

I assumed it would be Bernie or perhaps Bobby, but it turned out that he was a "Ned. My name's Ned Crower. And what of it?"

"I was only wishing to thank you, Ned. I can see you do some wonderful work here in the gardens. Did you lay them out yourself, or were they always like this?"

He became a little more guarded then, as Lord Edgington inveigled him into an interview of his own. "I've done my bit. No one's ever complained. Specially not old Hugo there." There was a note of impish glee to his words, and I decided that Ned Crower was quite the rogue.

He had a gimlet eye, nails that were black with mud and bruises, and a perpetually shifting posture, as though he couldn't bear to stand still.

"Have you noticed anything unusual about Mrs Templeton-Swift?" Grandfather persisted.

"Ooh, I've noticed her." The gardener emitted a truly saucy laugh, which triggered a cough that he beat his chest to halt. "I may be married, but I'm still a red-blooded man."

Grandfather had no patience for such innuendo, and his stare hardened. "I'm more interested in her behaviour. Have you observed Christabel doing anything that might suggest duplicity or underhandedness?"

He at least took a moment to consider the question. "You know what? I can't say I have noticed any duplicity nor underhandedness. But I have noticed she's got a pretty pair of eyes. And that may well be the politest of my observations. I wouldn't want to scandalise the boy here now, would I?" He erupted in filthy laughter once more. "But what would I know? I'm just the gardener. It's my Billie you should talk to. Wilhelmina is the clever one in the family. Not like Betty or our boys, you know–"

His wife plodded over from the house then, and he cut the sentence short. She was carrying the requested cup of thick black liquid and I was faintly horrified to see that she hadn't brought a tray but held it in her own hand.

"What the heck are you bothering His Lordship for, Ned?" she shouted over, and her husband peery down at the ground like a naughty cur who'd been caught stealing sausages. It was clear who held the whip hand in the Crower family.

"Ain't doing nothing, my love. Just answering a few questions."

She addressed the detective in an apologetic tone. "You don't want to be bothering yourself with this grimy mucker, M'Lord. My Ned knows less than the earthworms he spends his days hunting. If you've got any questions, it's our Wilhelmina you wants to talk to. Girl's got a brain she has, not like her parents."

"That's what I already told 'im," Ned grumbled beneath his breath

Grandfather seemed quite amused by the exchange. "Thank you for the tip, Betty. I agree that your daughter appears to be a smart young woman. It seems she has told you about the task I have asked her to perform this weekend, but should either of you discover anything, I'd be equally generous in my compensation."

"Awful kind of you, sir. Such a gent you are." She pushed her husband back to his duties with a firm hand.

Grandfather bowed his head and waited until we were alone. As soon as his wife had retreated, Ned Crower rushed back over to add a caveat to the previous discussion. "Of course, as much as I like shillings, whisky's even better."

With his piece said, he gave one last wicked giggle and cantered off across the garden. With the help of the coffee, Hugo had opened his eyes and, with great determination on his face, took up the chalk once more.

"Have some more coffee first, man." Grandfather leaned forward with the cup. "It seems to have helped."

Hugo gave a short nod and allowed Lord Edgington to assist him. With this done, he peered into my wise ancestor's eyes and said his favoured phrase once more, "She's the one." He tried to expand on the sentence but no other words would come and so he attempted to write instead.

Beefor she CaMe, I wAs DiffeernT

Grandfather was buoyed by this development and spoke with a sudden rush of enthusiasm. "That's a sterling effort, Hugo. But what exactly do you mean? What was different? Are you suggesting that you're sick now and you weren't before you married? Is that it?"

He managed a brief nod, but then the energy drained out of the tragic character. It was hard to imagine he had once been a celebrated mogul of the London Stock Exchange. He wouldn't give up so easily, though. After another break with his eyes closed, and another noisy gulp of coffee, he tried one last time.

I waS HuMan.

CHAPTER ELEVEN

Grandfather couldn't hide his disappointment that our interview with Hugo had revealed so little. What I understood for certain was that he really did believe someone had impeded his well-being, and that things had been different before his wife appeared. This was enough for me. I'd been dubious at first but could now see that we really did have a mystery, if not an actual murder that needed solving.

Dinner that night was a strange affair, not least because my grandfather ducked out of it at the last moment.

"I'm sorry, my boy, but there is something I need to confirm in Salisbury tonight," he told me as he combed his moustaches up in his bedroom. "I can't imagine I will return at too late an hour."

"But you'll miss dinner," I told him and struggled to make this sound as though it were a bad thing.

"It can't be helped. I'll just have to eat something when I'm in town." He couldn't hide his joy at this statement. "I'm sure I'll be able to find a cheerful pub somewhere, or perhaps even an adequate restaurant."

"Take me with you!" I begged, falling to the floor in the middle of his room to make sure he knew how serious I was. It was a foolish gesture, and I hurt my knees.

"Don't overreact, Christopher. I have no doubt that the food here will be perfectly delicious. If I didn't have important business in town, I'd be joining you." He had allowed a note of amusement to creep into his voice and tried to hide it by issuing me with my orders for the evening. "However, I have a task for you."

He paused and glanced out of the window, in case one of our suspects happened to have grown wings and was listening from outside. "A meal is a wonderful opportunity to observe the various players with their guards lowered. If your interpretation of the conversation you overheard between Lettice and Tiffin is accurate, then this is the moment to find out what they're hiding. Try not only to watch them but to steer the conversation towards pertinent topics." He seemed to have second thoughts about this advice and quickly issued a correction. "Subtly, of course. You mustn't be too obvious about it. As you'll know by now, subtlety is a key tool in a detective's arsenal."

"Didn't you say the same thing about using one's imagination?"

He looked impressed that I'd remembered. "Well, quite. Imagination, subtlety and intuition are all key tools in a detective's arsenal."

I wondered what else he had stashed away in there, but he was out of the door before I could ask. "I've already informed Violet what she needs to do, but she's busy with Christabel. I'm expecting you to keep an eye on the three siblings."

I noticed him slipping a vial of something into his pocket then and, because I'm a better detective than I sometimes claim, I thought I knew what it was. He'd surely snatched a sample of Hugo's medicine which would, almost without doubt, be winging its way to some bright spark at Scotland Yard to uncover exactly what the old chap had been taking.

"Yes, Grandfather, of course I will." Though pleased with my mental dexterity in identifying the hidden object, I was a little disheartened that I was so thoroughly eager to please him. "I promise I won't miss a thing."

Wilhelmina was in the room next to mine, presumably cleaning it for my mother to have somewhere to stay, and Grandfather stopped in the doorway to peek inside. It was certainly in a terrible state. The maid was removing a thick blanket from the bed as we arrived. A cloud of dust whipped up into the air, and I had to stand back to avoid breathing in a lungful of the stuff.

"I'm heading out for the evening," Grandfather announced, perhaps aware that we had no other reason to look in on her.

"Lucky you." I very much doubt the woman had uttered a *M'Lord* in her life and curtseying clearly wasn't one of her skills. "Why my ma ever became a cook is beyond me. If anyone dies in this house, it's her food you should investigate."

Grandfather was flustered by her honesty and could muster little more than an "Indubitably," and a nod of the head in farewell.

We walked to the front door, where Delilah and I stood wagging our tails as our master abandoned us. Todd must have known exactly what was happening, as he had the Rolls ready on the drive and a big smile on his face. He opened the rear door and Grandfather disappeared inside.

"So…" I said once the car had passed through the stone archway.

"Now what do we do?"

Delilah looked uncertain how to respond.

"Are you talking to a dog?" that thug Devyn had crept up behind me without making a sound.

"I… Well…" I was uncertain how to answer his question but, instead of showing just how frightening I found him, I attempted to do what my grandfather would have. "Yes, I was." I put on my most Lord Edgington-esque voice. "In fact, they're far better conversationalists than most humans." And with that, I marched away.

If there was one lesson that Grandfather had taught me, it was never to confess to a suspect when you've done something stupid. Confidence is surely another key tool in a detective's arsenal, and former Superintendent Edgington had it by the boxful. Perhaps I would master the skill in real life one day and not just in our cases.

It's odd that things came easier to me when I was playing a part. Had the same situation arisen in my family or at school, I would have melted with embarrassment, but in front of that rotter Devyn Templeton-Swift, I had nerves of titanium… or do I mean thorium? I think I might have mentioned that chemistry is not my strongest subject.

Delilah must have been struck dumb by my performance. She stayed right where she was on the door mat, her eyes wide, her tongue hanging out and her tail wagging. Well, it was either that or she was waiting to be told what to do, but I prefer to imagine the former. "Here girl," I shouted from further inside the house, and she came running after me.

We explored the gardens before dinner. I thought that a good long walk would help me build an even greater appetite. There is surely a level of hunger that one can pass at which any food will taste delicious, and I was determined to reach it. I'd barely eaten anything (except the cream cakes I'd taken from our meeting with Lady Highley-Summers's) since our picnic at Stonehenge. A quick lap around the garden would do the trick. No doubt, I'd have eaten a brick slathered in mustard by the time I got back to the house.

I was once more impressed by my surroundings. They weren't as ornate or luxurious as some of the grounds of the grand houses I'd visited, but Riverside Keep had a charm all of its own. Neat intertwining paths cut across the garden in a crisscrossing mesh to divide flowerbeds from small patches of pleasingly wild growth. This ordered chaos dropped away as we approached the river, where we found a dock with a little boat next to it and an elegant wooden house on stilts on the water.

Beyond it, the river widened, and a flock of Canada Geese took to the air as Delilah splashed after them. Well, I assume they were Canada Geese. Perhaps they were the smaller Barnacle Geese, and they were closer than I had realised. It's difficult to say for certain, but one thing I am absolutely sure of (beyond any doubt) is that they were geese... or very muddy swans.

I spotted a kingfisher too. It was perched on a branch overhanging the water and would go diving beneath the surface whenever it saw movement. I adored the regular flash of orange and luminous blue and could have stood watching it forever. I once read that kingfishers have an extra pair of translucent eyelids which protect them when they dart into the water. It is just such ingenuity that makes me marvel at the perfection of this phenomenal world we inhabit. It is hard to imagine a universe more harmoniously balanced – though it is a good thing no one has to investigate fish murders. My feathered companion got through three minnows in the five minutes I was watching him.

Feeling confident that I was close to my limit of hunger-tolerance, I whistled for Delilah, and we charted a new path back through the garden. To the right of Riverside Keep, there was another house that I hadn't noticed before. It was smaller but appeared just as comfortable. Looking in from outside, I saw plushly upholstered furnishings in a neat sitting room. It was the kind of place in which I often thought I would be content to live. I'd never understood the need for such gigantic dwellings of the kind which my family and all their associates occupied.

Ned Crower must have finished his work for the day as he was sitting beside a large radio set, listening to a local broadcast with a glass of something in his hand. I could only assume his wife and daughter were still tending to their duties, but the garden was in a wonderful state, and he surely deserved his rest.

The pork pie into which he was tucking looked more appealing than anything I'd be eating that night, and I can't begin to tell you how jealous I was. After one last look around the tranquil garden, with its prettily bubbling fountains and the incredible collage of colours wherever my eyes landed, I sighed and trudged back into the house.

CHAPTER TWELVE

By the time I'd gone back to my room and changed, Wilhelmina and Betty had the meal prepared and we were called down to dinner. My poor mother looked quite tired from her work as a lady's companion-cum-bodyguard, but Hugo was still alive, so she was clearly up to the task. Lettice and Tiffin seemed jollier than they had that afternoon and were dressed in summery outfits, which befitted a dinner with new friends. Lettice had even forsaken the modern attire she'd previously worn for a more traditional dress. It was long, frilly and perhaps a touch Victorian. In fact, she looked a different person altogether.

I tried to put the conversation I'd overheard from my mind and treat them as I would any other suspect in a murder inquiry – with total suspicion at all times.

I started the conversation with a nice, easygoing question. "What do you do up in Edinburgh, Tiffin?"

"I've a house in the Highlands and a house in the city." He had a youthful, effervescent manner that was really most appealing. I didn't trust him for a second. "Scotland's an awfully nice place, when it's not too cold or rainy. I split my time between hunting and fishing."

I made a note in my head to inform Grandfather that Hugo's elder son had admitted to being a murderer – of animals, at least.

"What about you, Lettice?" I continued. "Do you work at all?"

She laughed, and I made a note in my head to inform Grandfather that Hugo's daughter had made light of our investigation.

"Work?" She laughed again. "Oh, no, no. I couldn't possibly find the time. I have two children of my own, remember. And their nanny has Sunday afternoons free, so it's never ending."

My mother and Christabel turned their eyebrows up at me disapprovingly, apparently unable to make sense of my inquisition. I had bigger problems to deal with than those two, however, as, at this moment, Devyn barged into the room. I suppose I should have been beyond feeling any outrage by this point, but the man hadn't even dressed for dinner. He wore a shirt with no jacket and was completely tie-less!

Up until this moment, Hugo had been silent. But, as his wife tied a napkin around his throat, he became quite agitated and banged his hand down on the slate in his lap.

"I know, Dad," Devyn immediately responded, his hands up in protest. "You don't want me here. You never wanted me here. But you wrote to me. It's too late to take it back now. And do you know what? I wasn't too desperate to come home neither." I suppose it was from the time he'd spent abroad but, just occasionally, his speech would become a little mangled, his English not quite so standard.

Hugo became agitated once again but could do little more than bang his hand in his lap and mumble. It made me wonder what had passed between the father and son to create this gulf. I couldn't get away with such hostile questions at the dinner table, though, so I returned to my previous topic as our host drifted out of consciousness once more.

"We were discussing our occupations, Devyn," I began, sounding just as breezy as a spring meadow. "What was it that took you to New York?"

He crashed down in a free seat opposite his father. His hair was unkempt, and he sat rolling his sleeves up before answering. "I moved there to get away from here. They say it's the land of opportunity, but I reckon that means it's just as easy to get in trouble in the States as it is back home in Blighty."

I was unsure whether it was wise to continue the conversation, or whether I should hide beneath the table until he'd gone away, but I pressed on all the same. "Did you take up a trade over in the colonies?"

"That's correct," he replied a little more cordially, before repeating my words back to me. "I *took up a trade*. Didn't have any other option after my old dad cut the purse strings. I ended up doing a bit of everything. I worked as a ratcatcher for a while, but I kept getting bitten. So then I deboned animals in an abattoir before I met a chap who trained me to be a butcher."

I made a note in my head to inform Grandfather that Hugo's younger son had admitted to being a mass-murderer!

"And what about you, kid?" the thug asked.

"Yes, Christopher," his stepmother encouraged me. "Why don't you tell us what lies ahead of you?

Her other stepson seemed most excited by the idea and smiled down the table. "Hear hear!" I hadn't considered it before, but Tiffin and Christabel were surely around the same age. That must have been strange to have so few years between himself and his stepmother.

"Me?" I had to ask, as I wasn't expecting the attention to ricochet back in my direction.

"Yes, of course." Christabel seemed amused by my shyness. "What would you like to do with your life? You're only young. You could be anything you choose."

I looked at my mother in case she had an answer to this question. The supportive smile with which she responded was no use whatsoever. "I... Well, I suppose I'm like most boys, really." I hoped this was vague, yet specific enough to suffice.

I was about to change the subject when Devyn placed his fists on the table and, with a truly ferocious scowl, spoke again. "What does that mean?"

I wasn't the only one to jump at his words. Tiffin tried awfully hard to keep the blithe expression glued to his face, but even he looked worried that his brother might explode. It was clear that I would have to answer the question, but there was a minor problem: I hadn't a clue what to say.

I'd been hiding my indecision from my family for some time and didn't feel this was the moment to tell my mother that I was unlikely to follow my father into a job in the City or my brother on his path through academia.

"Oh, me!" I finally sputtered. "I assumed you were asking about someone else." I cringed at my ridiculous response, but at least I had succeeded in killing another few seconds before I either made my mother cry or received a black eye from the Bill Sikes made flesh who was awaiting my answer.

Every eye in that room was pointed at me, and I suddenly felt very hot. What *did* I want to do with my life? My main skills consisted of misidentifying garden birds, eating breaded delicacies and following my grandfather about like a lonely puppy. Were there any jobs which could utilise such abilities?

"Christopher will go to university like his brother," my mother said, in an attempt to stop my bright red face from getting so hot it evaporated and the room filled with steam. "Isn't that right, Chrissy?"

I felt like a man facing his sentence at the Old Bailey. There was no doubt about it; I would swing on the morrow. The hangman was tying a fresh noose just for me, and my minutes were numbered. Betty arrived at this moment with a hot tureen filled with brown stew. It was not the sort of dish one might request as a final meal.

"Why yas all sitting in silence?" the robust cook asked.

I was possibly more scared of her than I was of Devyn, and so I blurted out something at last. "There are so many things I wish to do. I'd like to explore the world and visit every country on God's green Earth. I want to discover things that people have never seen before – plants, birds, insects and animals. I'd like to climb mountains and swim in every sea.

"And then I'll come back home and write books about all of it. Great long treatises on our understanding of the natural world, which will make Charles Darwin's ideas seem positively old fashioned. Then, when I've done all that, I'll fall in love with a beautiful girl, and we'll have six children." I paused and realised that even our chef was stunned by the answer. "So, all in all a fairly standard list of ambitions."

When the silence still wouldn't break, I coughed and straightened the cutlery in front of me. It was Devyn who finally made a sound. A great laugh burst out of him, which set off those around him like a fire spreading through the room. He clearly thought I was a fool, but his brother and sister seemed quite entertained by my story. Christabel's laugh was much like a child's; it was high and delicate and made me like her more than at any moment that day. I felt rather proud to have given her such joy, but there was one person who did not seem happy.

"So you don't wish to go to university?" Mother asked, with a stern aspect about the eyes.

I didn't know how to reply, so I emitted a nervous titter of my own, which made everyone else instantly stop. I must have looked quite mad, snickering away to myself as my beloved mother scowled.

"I… Well, I haven't ruled out the possibility. I simply…"

"Ooh, someone's in trouble." Devyn lacked subtlety, to say the least. "Don't go keeping secrets from your mummy, boy."

Even the cook had a giggle at my expense, but my mother's mood had not lightened. "Christopher, I'm surprised that you'd keep this from me. I really am. It's not so much your decision that upsets me as the fact that you chose to hide it."

"But I haven't made any decision. In fact, I think I might be physically incapable of making decisions, and that's the problem." I sounded like a whining piglet.

To my surprise, one person there was on my side. Lettice, who was normally the most taciturn of the Templeton-Swift clan, spoke in my defence. "How old are you, Christopher? Seventeen? Eighteen? You're still just a child, and it really is madness that society expects young men and women to know what they want to do with their lives so early." Her eyes scanned the room to rest on her elderly father. "If I had been given time and support at your age, I might have done something more with my life instead of marrying the first pleasant man who came along and settling down to have children."

Her words cut through the mirth and misery, and we all strained to listen.

"I'm not criticising you, Daddy. I just wish that my path had been a little different."

Tiffin held her hand across the table and, perhaps feeling he should show such solidarity, Devyn nodded his agreement. It was a great deal more sympathy than he'd shown anyone else that day and his first sign of fraternal loyalty. Yet, far from endearing him to me, this limited act only made me wonder whether the threat to Hugo came from his three children. They clearly held a grudge against their father and, even if they had only recently arrived in person, it didn't mean they were free from suspicion.

After this emotional climax, the dinner unfolded in a sedate fashion. I was awfully glad that the focus had shifted away from me. This was supposed to be my big moment to uncover the truth about the odd family but, somehow, I was the one who had been thrust into the spotlight. I had no intention of saying another word for the rest of the evening. I can tell you that for nothing.

Even Betty's terrible cuisine didn't break my silence, though it was ever so tempting to declare that I would never let any such vile nutriment enter my mouth for as long as I should live. It was more of a swamp than a soup and contained any number of lethal hazards. The undercooked chunks of potato were crocodiles, the gristly specks of pork were piranhas and the nebulous carrots – so mushy that they disintegrated on contact with the tongue – were some form of deadly creature that man has yet to name. Lamentably, that was only the starter.

I'd never eaten a main course before that was quite so black. Betty was clearly no expert when it came to cooking quail, and I could only assume that she had followed the instructions for cooking turkey. The tiny birds must have been crisping away in the oven for several hours. The gravy-like sauce, which at the very least disguised the charcoaled remains, tasted of milled pepper and nothing else. She must have dumped the stuff in by the cupful. This did have one positive consequence, however, as the intensity of the seasoning served to numb my mouth.

By the time the un-flambéed Cherries Jubilee was served, I could no longer taste a thing. I could smell that there was any amount of deadly strong maraschino cherry liqueur mixed into the dessert, but it might just as well have been apple juice.

Though she still looked really very cross with me, my mother occasionally attempted to spark some conversation around the table, but it soon petered out. The three siblings were strangely subdued, and Christabel clearly didn't want to speak in front of them for fear of how they would react. In fact, it was the intermittently awake Hugo who contributed most. He delivered a slow, laboured "She's the one," approximately once per course.

"Father," Tiffin whispered at the end of the meal. The old man's eyes shot open, and he banged his slate a little. "I think Cook's culinary efforts are likely to kill you before one of us does."

Devyn clearly didn't like the aspersion and clicked his fingers in his brother's direction. "Steady on, Tiffin. Betty's served this family well. They practically nursed Dad when he was first ill. You should show some courtesy."

Tiffin wore his strained expression and his hands pulled tight on the tablecloth in front of him as he attempted an apologetic grimace and a short, "Of course she has. A real battler is our Betty. She deserves all the thanks we can give her."

Lettice had no interest in watching her brothers arguing and glanced out of the window with disdain. Our maid Wilhelmina, meanwhile, found the whole thing hilarious and had to shoot from the room to hide her glee. I somewhat envied her. Christabel, my mother and I were forced to sit quietly and pretend we hadn't noticed the uncomfortable atmosphere that had seized the room. For perhaps the first time in my life, I found myself praying there would be no cheese course so that we could leave the dining room just as soon as good etiquette allowed.

I hid up in my bedroom for the rest of the evening. The only company I wanted was Delilah, who was terribly good at keeping me warm once the sun had set. She sat on my feet as I returned to my studies. I tried to stay awake to tell Grandfather what little I had been able to garner from that evening's spectacle. Unfortunately, though, reading my algebra notes for the fifteenth time that week was not the best way to remain alert and I soon drifted off.

"I think I was wrong to bring us here," came the voice that would wake me up some time later. It was hard to say the hour with any accuracy, as there was no clock in my bedroom. The moon was high in the sky and the stars were out, so it had gone nine o'clock at the very least. As I'd fallen asleep at around ten, this knowledge was of no great help.

I sat up in bed and rubbed my eyes to see better through the darkness. I could just make out the upstanding Marquess of Edgington's outline in the doorway.

"What's the matter, Grandfather?" I imagine my words came out as one long moan, as I was still half asleep.

"Nothing, my boy. Nothing is wrong. I just feel we have been misled somehow." It was hard to tell whether he had been drinking or he was at that point of the investigation where he momentarily doubted his abilities – only to be proved correct after all. It seemed a bit early for such an occurrence, and so I had to assume he'd partaken of some brandy on his trip into town. "If our inquiries prove fruitless tomorrow morning, we will drive home to Cranley in the afternoon."

I could just about see the straight line of his moustache in the moonlight. He sucked in his cheeks for a moment, which he often did when he had a serious thought to consider. Then, letting out a whistle, he said, "Goodnight, Christopher," and padded from the room for Delilah to follow.

"Thank you for waking me up in the middle of the night for no particular reason," I shouted (or perhaps silently thought) in his direction. Thirty seconds later, I was fast asleep once more.

CHAPTER THIRTEEN

I'd known some eccentric families in my life.

One good example is my father's cousin Aldrich, who dressed up as an admiral and raised his five sons to speak in naval jargon. The dining room was known as the mess deck, the kitchen was the galley, and the sons were all referred to by an arbitrary rank. I was twelve before I realised that my cousin Midshipman's real name was Peter. Perhaps strangest of all was the fact that Aldrich had never been in the navy and didn't know anything about ships. He was simply mad, but at least his eccentricity made sense at the end of a long line of similarly maladjusted ancestors. The Templeton-Swifts, on the other hand, were an altogether different prospect.

I lay in bed on our first morning in Riverside Keep and tried to make sense of the previous day. I had gone there expecting to find a man-eating monster in Christabel, and yet she was nothing of the sort. In fact, Hugo's three children who had been summoned to protect him seemed to have more against the old chap than the once and future widow.

I felt as though I was piecing together a jigsaw with the pieces from five different puzzles. The patch of sunflowers refused to go with the Spanish galleon. The sky was blue, though the stars were clearly shining, and what was that elephant doing there?

The sun rose over the fields at the front of the house, and I lay enjoying the first rays of morning light. I was in no hurry to get down to breakfast, though it is generally my favourite meal of the day – and the only one at which I can eat nothing but cakes without someone looking at me reproachfully. It was so warm and comfortable in that neat little room that I would happily have stayed there all day had I been able to reach my book on the nightstand. Its distance, just a few inches out of reach, told me that I would have to get up eventually. This happened far sooner than I was hoping as, just a few minutes after waking, I heard a scream.

I was not the first to react. Indeed, footsteps seemed to emanate from all parts of the house at once. My grandfather's door flew open before I could get my slippers on and, by the time I'd left my room, he had disappeared. The upstairs of the house was laid out much like a horseshoe with the central staircase in the middle and two wings leading off it. It wasn't just my superior hearing that told me the scream had come from the wing of the house opposite our own. Grandfather had shot off in that direction.

I passed the open staircase, which gave onto to the entrance below, and moved quickly to a parallel corridor. I slowed my pace and, in a reverent hush, crept towards the door where the others stood clustered together. Wilhelmina, my mother, and the three Templeton-Swift children were already there, but they were riveted to the spot.

Grandfather showed no such hesitance and pushed through them to enter the room. I would not have had the courage to do the same but, as I arrived, the crowd parted like the Red Sea. I found myself in the main suite, which must have belonged to the master of the house himself. And there he was in the grand four-poster, with his wife, Christabel, standing just a few feet from him, a pillow in her hand.

My grandfather didn't have to say the words for once, as it was apparent to everyone there; Hugo was dead. Sitting up in bed with his eyes closed, he looked no less active than he had at any time since we'd arrived, but dead he was. His head was tipped at an awkward angle, his hands palm up as though at prayer. Whatever he had asked for had not been granted, and the colour of his skin was unnaturally pale.

Lord Edgington, with his detective's cap firmly (though metaphorically) on his head, had stopped a few feet into the room. He was painting a picture in his mind, freezing that moment forever in time. All at once, my senses caught fire, and I tried to copy him.

I could hear Christabel panting softly, as though she had run around the house three times before entering. This did not appear to be her problem, though. It was the shock of her discovery that had robbed her of breath.

The scent of sweet perfume or flowers filled the air, but I couldn't say precisely which. Christabel herself was as pretty as a posy and every element of her spoke of grace and femininity, so I assumed the heady scent was coming from her direction.

Admittedly, my sense of taste was not much help at this moment, but I stuck my tongue out, just in case.

I wanted to talk to my grandfather and learn what he had spotted that I had surely failed to observe, but I knew there was one thing that had to happen before we could investigate further.

The recriminations were yet to begin.

Tiffin was the first to get things started. "She did this." He strode into the room until he was framed by a full-length mirror that was leaning against the wall beside the enormous bed. "That harlot killed our father."

Lettice followed her brother and put her hand out as if to stop him. As soon as she set eyes on Hugo, though, it was simply too much to bear, and she fell to her knees. She resisted the tears for a few seconds, batting her eyelids in the hope of fighting the emotion, but it would do no good and she soon transformed into a tiny fountain.

"You wretched wench," Tiffin continued in his theatrical tenor, taking a few steps back to put his hand on his sister's shoulder. "Look what you have done to our father. Look what you have done to this family."

My head flicked about as I attempted to keep everyone in my line of sight. Still standing at a distance in the doorway, it was Devyn whose reaction most surprised me. He didn't cry out or launch fresh accusations. He simply folded his arms and watched his siblings in their misery. It was as though they had summoned enough sentiment for the three of them, and there was nothing more he could add.

Tiffin had one last line to deliver before he went to comfort his poor sister. "You will hang for this, Christabel. I'll see to that."

"That's enough," I eventually responded. Grandfather was still somewhere far away, processing every last scrap of evidence he'd detected. But I didn't feel that Christabel should have to endure any more cruelty until we'd confirmed her guilt.

Mother walked across the room to see that her new friend was not too distressed. Before she could do anything to help her, though, Christabel found her voice. "This wasn't me." I wonder how many times she'd had to repeat this expression in her head before she managed to say it out loud. "I came in here and the pillow was over his face. I didn't kill him. I loved Hugo; I would never do this."

I performed a rapid calculation and could see that, from her words and the fact that the bedding was well tucked in on the other side of his bed, she hadn't slept with her husband that night. Although she was a sweet, pretty woman with some charisma and a true tenderness that I found ever so attractive, it was hard not to conclude that she had murdered her husband in cold blood. If that was the case, it surely wasn't her first crime.

Tiffin was down on his knees with his arms around his sister, and Devyn had finally come forward to pat Lettice's shoulder with one of his impressive paws. I suppose this was what passed for empathy from a former ratcatcher, turned animal deboner, turned butcher.

Grandfather now returned to us and lunged forward to inspect the dead man. I might well have done something similar if he hadn't. Not that I would have known how to go about such a task.

"Are we even sure he was suffocated?" I like to ask really simple questions such as this one to make sure that my grandfather has the opportunity to shine.

He didn't look at me but pressed the back of one hand to the man's forehead before opening the right eyelid with his other. "He has a blue tinge to the lips, red spots in his eyes, and there was a pillow found over his face. So I believe that suffocation is the likely cause of death. Bruising about the nose suggests that considerable force was used, but in the state in which I saw the man yesterday, it is unlikely he would have suffered for long.

"Tiffin is right," Lettice said, finding her voice. "Our *stepmother* is to blame. I found her like that with the pillow in her hand."

Before Christabel could deny the charge once more, Grandfather raised an interesting point. "Which of you screamed?"

He paused his investigation to look at the grieving daughter, who was still on her knees at the foot of the bed. "I can't say. I..."

"It was me." Christabel injected a touch more confidence into her voice. "And why would I have screamed if I had just killed him?"

Lettice had no answer and looked from brother to brother for assistance as the (at last!) widow continued.

"Why would I have killed a man for whom I've spent the last year of my life caring?" This was one question to which there was an obvious answer, but no one provided it. "Why would I have left the door open for someone to catch me in the act?"

As her words faded away, it was clear that she had undermined their argument, and the room was plunged into silence once more.

CHAPTER FOURTEEN

Tiffin was charged with calling the police, and his brother and sister accompanied him to the phone for... well... moral support, I suppose. I felt a little sorry for my mother. While Grandfather and I got to enjoy the thrills of poking around a dead body, she was once more tasked with looking after the weeping Christabel. Grandfather had told me just what a capable detective she was, and yet she'd been demoted to the position of hand-holder and shoulder-offerer.

"What do you think happened?" I asked the old man once we were alone.

He stopped rifling through the bedclothes to peer down his nose at me. "I think he was murdered, Christopher."

I huffed as only he could be so literal. "You know that's not what I meant. I want to know what you really think has occurred here."

He shook his head and got back to work. "Well, if you ask a ridiculous question, you should expect an equally nonsensical answer."

"Really, Grandfather, I only wished to know who you believe could be responsible for the murder."

"So why didn't you ask that very question?" He paused again, and I realised he'd managed to outdo himself. I genuinely thought that I was beyond being surprised by his pedantry, but it was clear he would go no further until I'd spoken the words he required.

"Fine. Who do you believe could be responsible for the murder?"

He looked inordinately pleased with himself and pulled his shoulders halfway to his cheeks in delight. "An excellent question. The most truthful answer I have for you would be that I suspect a member or perhaps multiple members of this household."

"So you haven't a clue?"

"I did not say or suggest such a thing, Christopher. But the man has only been dead for..." He pulled out his pocket watch and then glanced at Hugo's face. "Approximately five hours. Were I to kill someone in a house such as this one – not that I would of course–" He winked at me at this moment, and I wondered if he had something to confess. "If I were to murder someone, I would go about it at the time when most people are likely to be asleep. Between the hours of two and five would be the best option. After any late drinkers or card players have retired, but before the servants normally rise."

"It has just gone nine," I said, glancing at the clock on the mantelpiece. "And so, if you're right, there's no sense interviewing the suspects to work out who was where and when because they were all supposed to be asleep." I let out an exasperated moan. "I like this case less with every moment that passes. First, we had a murder investigation with no body, and now we have a body with no chance of finding the killer."

I don't know if Grandfather was waiting for the inevitable moment when I would suggest our task was impossible, but it was just then that his hand came to a rest at the side of the corpse, and he discovered something under the covers. I didn't like to think what it could be, but when he pulled it out, he was glowing like an angel in a Renaissance painting.

"Et voila!" I hated it when he spoke Latin. "Our first step on the path to solving the murder!"

He unclasped his fingers to reveal a small, brown medicine bottle. It was quite different from the medicine which we'd seen Christabel administering the afternoon before. For a start, this one had a label attached, and a word stamped upon it in large capital letters.

MORPHINE

I know so little about chemistry that my teacher once had to apologise to the rest of the class when he had to stop a demonstration to explain to me that carbon dioxide wasn't simply two lots of carbon monoxide put together. He once told me I was the only boy he'd taught who thought the chemical symbol Ca in the periodic table referred to carrots. And, despite all of that, even I knew what morphine was.

"Christabel said she only gave him a natural remedy," I began. She said it was some sort of tincture. Was this what he was really taking?"

Grandfather didn't answer but shook the clear bottle and the transparent liquid splashed about inside. It looked so innocent that it was hard to imagine such a substance could kill a man or leave him so dependent on the stuff he'd rather be dead.

"It makes certain things more likely now, don't you think?"

I wasn't sure whether to nod or shake my head and so I went for a gesture somewhere between the two – a sort of diagonal, shaking nod – and hoped he wouldn't notice.

"In fact, I genuinely doubt there was much wrong with Hugo's health. Since we arrived yesterday, I considered that his symptoms were more in line with drug dependency than a specific illness, and this surely proves it."

I remembered the words he'd written. "He said that he was fine before she came. Doesn't it seem likely, just as he suspected, that his wife was slowly poisoning him over a long period of time?"

Grandfather straightened his back and released a breath ever so slowly. He looked about the room, perhaps in the hope that some significant truth would slap us both about the cheeks.

"The problem with your assertion, Christopher, is that you are reliant on the word of the man who was taking this drug. He even admitted that he couldn't be sure who was poisoning him. So what makes you think we should believe his version of events?" He slipped the bottle into his pocket and moved away from the rapidly hardening cadaver. He closed his eyes then and took a few steps forward into the large space at the end of the bed.

"She didn't sleep here last night." I thought this was a truly revelatory piece of evidence. "Doesn't that suggest she was busy plotting her crime or that the relationship between them was not as harmonious as Christabel would have us believe?"

Somewhat predictably, Grandfather was unimpressed. "It does nothing of the sort. It merely implies she has a separate bedroom. It is not unusual for married couples, especially when one of them is an invalid. I don't think that your great aunt Clementine ever shared the same floor as my brother, let alone a bedroom."

Not knowing what else I could offer, I glanced around the room in which our victim had breathed his last. It was much like many others in the house, with frames all over the walls. The one significant difference was that, in the photographs of far-flung destinations, two people featured repeatedly. One was undoubtedly a much younger Hugo and so I took the other to be his first wife. Her name had not been mentioned since we'd laid siege to Riverside Keep. I knew nothing about her, but her demise, or dismissal from the house, would surely be worth investigating.

"Think a little on this, my boy." Grandfather held one finger in the air and spun around to face me before opening his eyes. "We don't know to whom Hugo was referring in his repeated refrain, 'She's the one.'" He slid sideways most balletically, and I thought he was about to begin a dance. "We cannot say whether he had been manipulated in some manner into saying it. We don't even know how this bottle of morphine came to be hidden here. The picture we have before us could be the simple truth, or it could be a trap of the most sophisticated design."

I considered the possibility that Hugo was a mere pawn in someone else's game. I wondered if they'd said the same phrases to him time and time again until he'd begun to repeat them – much like a parrot will learn to say rude words if it hears them often enough. "She's the one," was the most important, of course, but there might have been others too. Short, memorable expressions that certain questions would have triggered.

"But what about the letter, Grandfather. You read it out to me, and Hugo laid the blame for what had happened at the feet of his wife. He said you would think him foolish for marrying a woman several decades younger than him. There can be no doubt that it was Christabel whom he suspected."

He rushed forward to me, no longer a dancer, but a Shakespearean actor. His tone was rich, his movement bold and precise. "Come, come, my boy. Surely you must realise now what that letter really tells us."

I tried. I promise I did. I thought really hard for a good ten seconds before coming up with what I believed to be a rather clever answer. "It shows he didn't feel safe revealing every last detail in writing, as he was afraid who might read it."

He clapped then. His elegantly lined hands crashed together, and he despatched his applause across the comfortable boudoir. "Very good, Christopher. That is a fine piece of analysis and ingenuity."

He'd made me smile, but then reality dawned. "And yet it's not the correct answer, is it?"

"Sadly not." Off he went, searching the perimeter of the room and occasionally stopping to glance at the photographs. "What that letter should now tell you is that there is no possible way that Hugo Templeton-Swift was the man who composed it."

Oh! What a fool I'd been. "Of course he didn't. It was far too coherent for that. But then why would anyone have wanted to bring us here?"

92

He sat down on a padded box in the protruding bay window. "As I see it, there are two possible reasons. I will give you thirty seconds to determine them." He removed his watch once more. "Starting now."

A ticking started in my brain. A similar noise struck up whenever I was put on the spot in my maths class. I can't say it had ever helped me work out any equation, but that didn't stop me trying now.

I considered the various factors that were at play in the case. The warring sides of the Templeton-Swift family and the dead man's wife. I thought about parrots, strong medicines and terrible sandwiches. I threw all these pieces together and, to my astonishment, when the thirty seconds had passed, I had an answer for him. "Either the person who sent that letter really was worried about Hugo and wrote it on his behalf…"

"Correct!" He clapped again, but a little more earnestly this time. "Or?"

"Or… The second letter was only written in order to obfuscate the revelations of the first."

"Bravo, Christopher." Like a spectator at Covent Garden after the finale of an opera, he stood up to applaud. I'm sure if he had possessed a bouquet of roses, he would have thrown them at me one by one in appreciation. "You have outdone yourself."

I was suddenly afraid that this was yet another ruse, and he was about to tell me that it was a good guess but still not quite right. Happily, such a disclosure never came.

In a merry pin, he reached inside his grey cashmere overcoat – though why he was dressed already at such an hour, I never discovered – and extracted not one, but two letters. I had not seen the first before and felt a frisson of excitement.

"Regard the two envelopes," he began. "The first was addressed in the same untidy hand as the letter itself."

I did as instructed and observed the single line of scrawled text. It merely said 'Lord Edgington' but bore a franked 2d stamp. "How did it reach you if no one included your address?"

He suddenly became terribly patriotic. "Thanks to the Royal Mail, of course. The British postal service is one of the finest institutions on the whole bally planet. We'd be lost without them."

I'd never heard him use so much as a euphemism for a swear word before. He was clearly most passionate on the topic of postage.

"So, what does it mean?"

He held up the second envelope. Though the address upon it was not neatly written, it was complete and legible. "Whoever wrote this had the facilities to set about discovering where I live. I don't think for a second that poor Hugo would have been capable of such an act and, if his killer was watching him, he would not have been allowed to do so in the first place."

"Then what about Wilhelmina? She must have–" I cut my words short as Grandfather put one finger to his lips.

"Wilhelmina?" he asked, his voice rising as he held the last vowel like the final note of a song. "Perhaps you should join us."

That mischievous hoyden had been loitering outside the room, listening to every word we said. "Morning, Lord Edgington."

Grandfather's face was quite expressionless. "When I asked you to stay alert for anything I might consider useful, I did not mean for you to spy on Christopher and me."

She looked quite shy then and even managed an apologetic tone. "I'm sorry. It's just… Well, I didn't want to get into any trouble. I knew I should never have sent them letters for Mr Templeton-Swift."

"So you still say that you sent them both?" Grandfather raised his left eyebrow.

Wilhelmina looked from one to the other of us, perhaps afraid that she'd incriminated herself further. "That's right."

"Very well. Can you tell me the circumstances in which you obtained them?"

She thought about her answer before replying. "Well, the first one I took straight from Hugo's hand. It was while his missus was having an afternoon nap. She never left him alone for long, except when she went for a nap each afternoon, and so he had an hour to himself. I suppose that was when he wrote it. I was tidying the library where he normally liked to sit, and he pressed it into my hand. He didn't say nothing, but then that was generally his way. He just gave me the letter, and I told him I'd get it to where it needed to go."

"You didn't think it strange that he had only included a name and no address?"

She turned a touch redder. "Not really. I thought that, if even I'd heard of ya, the postie surely would 'ave. I reckoned he'd know where it needed to go."

It was Grandfather's turn to blush. "You did very well, my girl. Now, tell me about the second letter."

"That was in a pile of them at the front door. I walk to the post office every Thursday in Wylye. It's only a couple of miles and I like the exercise. I didn't think nothing of it until I handed the letters over to the post mistress and noticed your name."

"And it didn't strike you as strange that Hugo had found the address in the meantime?" I hope I didn't sound too harsh on her. She'd obviously tried to help the old duffer when no one else would.

"Not really." She frowned for a few seconds, presumably recalling what had passed through her mind two days prior. "I figured he must've remembered it. You see, he had his good spells, did Hugo. He never said much, but there were days where he seemed a lot more alert and alive. We'd smile at one another, and he'd give me one of his little waves as I tidied."

"I see. Well, thank you for your candour." Grandfather turned away, presumably distracted by something she had said. With a flick of the head that signalled his renewed vigour, he soon returned to the conversation. "Now you must earn your wage. What suspicions do you have of the three Templeton-Swift children? They present something of a puzzle to me."

"I can't say for certain. What I do know is that there was some sort of falling out between them and their dad, but I never found out exactly what happened. Tiffin is always very jolly. His sister is as much fun as a sleepy badger, and I don't reckon that Devyn is quite as beastly as he wants everyone to believe."

Grandfather clearly would have preferred detailed evidence over vague impressions. "So you haven't noticed anything specific you'd like to share with me?"

Her face turned blank. "Not really. I spend most of my time working, to be honest. It's true that no one here pays me much attention, but that doesn't mean they natter away when I'm nearby."

The old detective paused again, and he held the young maid's gaze. "Thank you, Wilhelmina. A less honest person would have made up a story for me, and I appreciate your sticking to the truth. I have one last question and then you can go." His burst of energy had dissipated, and he became quite pensive. "Tell me, what was Hugo like when you first came here?"

She was quick with her answer. "He was never a well man, if that's what you mean. He soon needed a wheelchair and had various problems with his health that the local doctor always came to inspect."

"But it was only after he married Christabel that his condition worsened to such an extent?"

She hesitated once more, opened her mouth to reply, then changed her mind and simply nodded.

"Thank you, my girl. That will be all for now."

She was evidently a terribly loyal servant. The only thing I couldn't be certain of was to whom her loyalty belonged.

CHAPTER FIFTEEN

"Christopher, tell me this…" We had gone to the front of the house to wait for the police, and he was pacing back and forth, over and over, on the hexagonal paving stones. "…who are our suspects?"

I knew it was a trick question but answered it without thinking all the same. "That's an easy one, and we're lucky this time because there are really only four people who might have wanted to kill the old chap."

"I see. So you're sure it was a member of the family?"

I smiled in affirmation and began to list them. "Christabel, Devyn, Tiffin and Lettice." This sparked a thought. "Why does no one use good dependable names these days like John or Terrence?"

He stopped walking. "Is that relevant to the investigation?"

"No, but–"

"Four suspects, you say… Excluding you, your mother, and your esteemed grandfather, there are seven people currently residing in Riverside Keep. Can we really say that the servants weren't involved in the murder?"

"I believe so," I responded with some conviction. "What could they possibly gain from it? There's a chance Hugo would have left them some small bequest, but it would surely be worth less to them than the jobs they now have. Based on Betty's cooking, it's unlikely that whoever ends up inheriting the house will keep them. They could find themselves out on their ears."

He winked then, and I knew he'd been testing me. "And what did you make of Wilhelmina? Are we to believe her version of events?"

I considered what she'd told us about the two letters. "I think so. I didn't notice any contradictions in her story. In fact, it made perfect sense to me. The question we must ask ourselves now, though, is who wrote the second letter?"

"Indeed."

"I haven't finished." I'd indulged in a little pacing of my own by this point and found my mind full of ideas. "Furthermore, we must surely conclude that, despite any other evidence we have amassed, Christabel is unlikely to be our killer."

He evidently enjoyed this comment and had a good laugh at my expense. "Weren't you just saying the exact opposite? What made you change your mind?"

"Because someone wrote to you to implicate her in Hugo's murder that hadn't yet occurred. She wouldn't have written the letter herself, would she? Someone here has set out to inculpate the poor woman. As the letter was only sent from Wylye post office two days ago, it could be any one of them."

I heard a car chugging along the lane then, and Grandfather had just enough time for another question before it arrived. "Who do you think is our likely culprit if Christabel is innocent?"

"I would think that goes without saying." Some part of me must have realised that what I was about to say would be dismissed as balderdash. "Devyn is the obvious choice. The man is a monster."

"Despite the fact you overheard his brother and sister discussing their fears that a ruse they had been perpetuating would be discovered?"

"Ummm… yes."

A quaintly old-fashioned, pre-war Vauxhall cabriolet rolled onto the property and two identically dressed men in black suits, hobnailed boots and bowler hats stepped out on either side of the vehicle.

"Edgington?" the one on the left enquired, but he didn't wait for an answer. "I'm D.I. Simpson, and this is D.I. Simpson – no relation. We've been informed that there has been a murder?"

Grandfather adopted the same brusque tone as the inspector. "That's right, I'm Edgington. This is my grandson, Prentiss." It was hard to tell if he was imitating them or had fallen into a particular style of policing with which he was familiar from his days on the force. "I'll show you up to the body, and then we can all have a cup of tea."

"Grand," D.I. Simpson responded.

"Grand," the other Simpson echoed, and they strode after my grandfather into the house.

I was a little surprised to see that every last one of our suspects, from heir apparent Tiffin Templeton-Swift to the gardener Ned Crower, was standing in a crescent in the entrance hall. They were presumably hoping to work out what suspicions the police already held and whose head would end up on the chopping block.

The three police officers (including former Superintendent Edgington) stopped in the doorway and there was an odd moment as we waited for someone to say something. When no one did, the silence overwhelmed me and I muttered, "The dead body's this way, inspectors."

I was about to lead them upstairs when Grandfather put his hand on my shoulder and motioned for me to take the suspects away and ensure that everyone got a drink. He was a very capable mime.

I did as I'd been instructed and, rather than going to the same room where the deceased chap had spent so much of his time, I found a bright, airy lounge that looked on to the garden.

"Betty, would you be so kind as to prepare some refreshments?" I asked, only half expecting the cook to agree.

"No trouble, my lad."

I didn't hold out much hope for what she would deliver, but beggars can't be choosers.

"Ned, you lazy good for nothin'." She started hitting her husband around the back of the head and wouldn't stop. "You'll help me carry the tray. What were you thinkin' traipsing those muddy boots through the house? Just because the master is dead, it don't mean he can't see what a mess you're making."

It was not the first time that I'd noticed a member of the household staff entirely ignore the presence of their mistress. As we trailed into the lounge, Christabel's eyes were full to the brim with tears. I didn't think she would stop crying all day and, if it hadn't been for my mother, there would have been no one to comfort her.

The room I'd found had an upright piano in the corner and various modern styles of painting filled each frame on the wall. Bright colours and abstract shapes, along with a few pastoral scenes, gave the room a more cheerful appearance than many of the others I'd visited. If it wasn't for the fact a man had just been murdered, I might even have said it was a jolly little spot.

My mother, the siblings and Hugo's widow spaced themselves out around the room, while I stood in space, wondering what to say. It felt wrong to allow the silence to control us, but I didn't have the faintest idea where to start with our investigation. I was sure I'd say something silly if I tried, and so I just stood there, watching the various suspects and wondering what they were thinking.

In her favour, Lettice looked quite distraught after the events of that morning. At the slightest sound of Wilhelmina cleaning outside, her eyes flicked to the door, and she took a sharp breath. Tiffin really was a markedly different kettle of fish to his sister and kept smiling as though everything was dandy. He let out an occasional, unbelieving, *hfffff,* as if to imply that he was confident someone would be along at any moment to solve the little problem. Every time I glanced at him, he gave me a wink and a smile. It was hard to know what sort of person we were dealing with as, though he was clearly an insouciant chap, I would have expected a little more discretion from him so soon after his father's death.

"Allow me," he jumped up to say when Betty reappeared with Ned in tow to bring the tea things. Why they hadn't simply brought everything on a trolley, I couldn't say.

"Nothing like a good cup of tea to set the world to rights, what?" Tiffin beamed.

His sister glared at him then, and he finally appeared to realise that even a hot drink couldn't bring their father back. Perhaps feeling guilty for his previous frivolity, he slumped into a chair and bowed his head in sadness. It was a most dramatic transformation.

Much as she did everything else, poor, sweet, potentially murderous Christabel sobbed in a soft, understated manner. It was almost as if she were a supernumerary actress in a play who had been told not to make too much noise whilst the other characters talked. I was torn between wanting to rush over and comfort her and screaming to the rooftops of her guilt. It made for an interesting elevenses.

And yet, my key suspect, Devyn – the man whose rough hands and savage visage would have been enough to convince any jury he was a born killer – sat looking aloof. It was hard to tell what was going on behind his eerily dark eyes and thick brow. He was a slab of granite that a sculptor had never finished shaping.

I rather wished I could have consulted my mother at this point. For one thing, she would have come to a conclusion by now on exactly what sort of person Christabel Templeton-Swift was. Mother was far more perceptive than me and an excellent judge of character. I'm certain that, when I'm fifty years old, I'll still be calling her on the telephone to confirm whether I really should trust my neighbours, the local milkman or, indeed, any woman who even attempts to speak to me. A young man can always rely upon his mother, that's what I say!

100

By the time the inspectors returned, and tea was served, I'd compiled quite the list of burning questions. Disappointingly, it was too late to ask a single one of them. Simpson and Simpson had a look of sheer incredulity on their faces, which told me that my grandfather had veritably roasted their brains with his interpretation of the case.

"Nothing like a cup of tea," Tiffin tried once again, though in a far more morose tone this time. He said this before he'd taken a sip, of course, and having raised the cup to his lips, the twitching muscles in his neck told me that what he had just drunk was *nothing like a cup of tea*.

"I'm sure you know why we're here," the first Simpson said. It seemed he was the talker of the pair. "The owner of Riverside Keep, Mr Hugo Templeton-Swift, has been murdered. We can only assume that the assailant was known to him and is still present in the house."

He appeared quite flustered and spoke with his head at an angle, as though he couldn't quite believe what he was saying. "There is no evidence of a stranger entering the property overnight. The exterior gates were kept locked and, had someone found a way to break in, it seems likely that we would have found some evidence of it. We cannot rule out the possibility entirely, but, for my money, this was no burglary."

"And nothing appears to have been stolen," Simpson number two added.

"That's right. To our knowledge, nothing was stolen."

As the pair spoke, Grandfather leaned on the mantlepiece and was clearly enjoying every moment. I'd told him a number of times that he really must make more effort to hide his glee when investigating a murder, but would he listen?

"It is our belief that the people who would benefit most from the victim's death are all here at this moment. His three children, his wife and..." The primary Simpson looked at my mother with some confusion. "...I'm sorry, madam. I don't know who you are."

Grandfather whispered an explanation into his ear, and the man shrugged and returned to his summary of the facts.

"Mr Templeton-Swift was murdered sometime in the middle of the night. As I believe you are all aware, he was suffocated. His doctor has just arrived and is upstairs, attempting to determine a more precise time of death."

He allowed these last words to hang in the air, and I expected him to make some threat or perhaps a promise. You know the sort of thing, *I'm warning you now, if anyone in this room was responsible for the old man's death, there'll be trouble.* Or, *I'll get to the bottom of what occurred here even if it takes me the rest of my days.*

When nothing came, Lettice raised her skinny hand to push a lock of her hair behind her ear. "So what do you plan to do about it?"

"Do about it?" the first Simpson replied in one quick breath. "What am I going to do about it? I'll tell you exactly what I'm going to do about it. I'm going to request the assistance of an expert in the field. A man so respected that they still haven't found anyone like him some fifteen years after he left the police."

Around the room, our suspects shifted in their seats as they tried to work out to whom the inspector was referring. I thought it was perfectly obvious.

"I'm talking about former Superintendent Edgington of the Metropolitan Police." He gave a humble nod and withdrew for his would-be superior to take over the investigation.

I doubt I was the only one who felt a little baffled by the announcement. Simpson and Simpson had seemed so efficient, so professional and yet the sum total of their conclusions was that they should step aside and let someone else do the work. I knew better than anyone just how good a brain my grandfather had. He was a superlative detective, and yet I'd still expected the actual police officers to have a go at solving the crime.

"Detective Inspectors Simpson and Simpson will, of course, be assisting me when necessary," the celebrity in our midst revealed. "And I believe that, together, we have the resources, nous and wherewithal to bring a good man's killer to justice in record time." He sounded as though he was giving a speech to a group of browbeaten officers rather than the potential suspects. "I will be interviewing each of you in turn, and I appreciate your assistance with this inquiry."

He bowed and, much to his chagrin, no one clapped.

"Come along, Christopher," he said, just as I was about to bite into a biscuit. "There's no time for that." He swept from the room, leaving me to follow behind most reluctantly.

CHAPTER SIXTEEN

Grandfather was treating this new mystery with a touch more formality than he often managed. Instead of allowing the wind to take us where it wanted, he set up a centre of operations in the dead man's study. It was another chance for me to find out something about Hugo himself and another space to enjoy a gallery's worth of photos depicting his exciting life. It looked as though some of them had been removed over the years as there were spaces about the place, but the original Mrs Templeton-Swift featured heavily and so did their young children.

There were blurry photographs of the family of five, fishing on the river beside the boathouse, a picture of Lettice's birthday when she was perhaps seven years old, and one of the three children sitting in a park as the sun went down.

Hugo had clearly been a modern man, whereas my father was the opposite. I don't think there was a single photograph of my brother and me in our house, and yet the Templeton-Swifts appeared to have captured half of their lives on film. I looked at the mother of the family and wondered where she had gone. Which of Henry VIII's preferred methods of ending a marriage had befallen her? Divorced, beheaded (in a manner of speaking at least) or died?

I looked at an open ledger on the desk, but the only details of interest were the three addresses of Hugo's children in Scotland, England and New York. Grandfather made himself comfortable behind the wide desk with its inlaid leather surface, and we awaited our first witness.

"Ah, Dr Merrick," he cooed, as a man with white hair cut very close to the skin entered the room. He had an attractive style to his dress, which belied his provincial calling. He wore a well-cut jacket, matching black trousers over patent leather brogues and walked in a confident fashion. He took a few steps into the room before replying.

"Hello again, Lord Edgington." He spoke in a strong Welsh accent and held onto every vowel as though it were precious. "I believe you were right in your assertion. It appears as though my old friend Hugo died at approximately four o'clock this morning."

"May I ask how you came to that conclusion?" Grandfather motioned to a chair in front of the desk and the man sat down.

"Of course. When a person dies, their body slowly cools to acclimatise to the room. From his current temperature and the signs of rigor mortis now visible, I think it is fair to state that he died approximately seven hours ago." He consulted his wristwatch, as though to confirm the theory he would already have recorded in his notes.

"That's excellent." Grandfather certainly looked as though he was impressed by the man's work, but something suggested that his praise was not sincere. It's hard to say whether it was the gleam in his eye or the tiniest pulsation in the muscles around his temple, but I knew he was about to qualify this statement. "In that case, it seems as though you know more about the dead than you do about the living."

"I beg your pardon. Are you suggesting I somehow failed my patient?" Dr Merrick pulled his shoulders back and puffed up his chest. He'd clearly never been so insulted in his life. "I have never been so insulted in my life." See!

"Oh, I think I can do better than that." Grandfather smiled benignly. I hadn't realised until this moment that my dear old mentor had lost his mind. I'd never seen such a rude display from him. "What was your diagnosis of Templeton-Swift's symptoms when he was still with us?"

The good doctor looked at me then, but there was nothing I could do to help him. I was still chewing on Betty's biscuit – more as a challenge to myself than out of any hope it would possess some nutritional value.

"The man had suffered a stroke. It was quite evident from his behaviour."

"When was that?"

The doctor had a pompous voice and spoke as though he believed that every word he said should be revered. So he had that much in common with my grandfather, at least. "I'd have to consult my files of course, but I would say that the most debilitating attack occurred almost a year ago."

"That would have been shortly after he married his second wife, then?"

Dr Merrick weighed up the words as though checking them for some amphibolic second meaning. "It may well have been, but I cannot say with any great certainty. Would you like to tell me exactly what you are implying?"

Grandfather rose up on his forearms like a gorilla attempting to intimidate... well... another gorilla, perhaps. "I am suggesting that Hugo Templeton-Swift suffered no stroke. In fact, I am inclined to believe that he was quite well."

Merrick sneered and wafted one hand across the table in dismissal. "You're talking nonsense. Do you have even a modicum of medical training?" He waited a few seconds before continuing. "I have been a doctor for over forty years, and you think you know better than I do? Very well, tell me why my patient acted in such a fashion if there was nothing wrong with him."

Grandfather was only too happy to comply. "The man had been drugged. Any fool could have seen it. His condition wasn't constant, as it would have been in the case of a stroke. He had good days and bad. His speech would come and go, and he could write quite legibly depending on the amount of morphine he had ingested."

"Morphine?" The doctor sounded shocked by Lord Edgington's diagnosis but did not rule out the possibility.

"That's right. I found a bottle of the substance at his side when he was murdered. I can only conclude that whoever killed him had seen to it that he was kept immobile and near senseless. I came here to prevent a murder, though I fear that, if anything, my arrival only precipitated Hugo's demise."

Far from raging as he previously had, Dr Merrick now fell quiet. He was appalled at the idea that he had made a mistake. "But... his symptoms... his symptoms were surely in keeping with the effects–"

"Give it up, man. I've no intention of reporting your blunder, but it was your misdiagnosis that led to the situation in which the deceased found himself. If you'd spotted what was happening, he would never have had to write to me in the first place."

The doctor conceived of the glimmer of an argument at this point and launched himself into it. "You're finding excuses for your own failings now. That's it, isn't it? You know that you could have saved the chap from whichever savage snuffed out his candle, so you're looking for someone else to blame."

Grandfather was an old hand at resisting such obvious bait. He sat back in his chair and waited for the next allegation to come.

"If you thought he was in danger, you should have removed Hugo from this house as soon as you arrived. But, no, you let him die. It was your oversight that led to his murder, not mine. Why didn't you do more to protect him?"

"On whose authority do you suggest I could have removed the man?" he asked, a lighter tone in his voice to show just how little he thought of the desperate ploy. "An Englishman's home is his castle; I couldn't come strolling in here to cart the fellow away without a scrap of evidence. His children would have called the police to have me locked up. And, the truth is, I wouldn't have blamed them."

The mutual grenade throwing appeared to be over, and calm descended. The two experts in their field would no longer look at one another but peered down at the desk. It was the perfect moment for me to say something significant, but the only thing I could think of was, "Grandfather, if someone has been drugging Hugo all this time, doesn't that mean that his children can be eliminated from the investigation? Devyn was in America. Tiffin was up in Scotland, and Lettice lives somewhere near the sea." To be perfectly honest, I couldn't remember where.

He at least considered the possibility before disproving it. "Not at all, boy. His children could have come here before the wedding. They could have hired the staff for their father and provided them with the morphine that was used to drug him. The Crowers might be involved in the plot, or simply not have realised what it was they were giving him. Unless of course…" He turned his anger back upon the doctor. "What medicines did you prescribe your patient?"

The man still looked disturbed by the accusations against him but, some seconds later, he finally replied. "After he deteriorated, there was very little I could do. I gave Mrs Templeton-Swift an herbal treatment – a tincture of St John's wort and valerian. I thought it might at least make her feel as though she was doing something to help her husband. I provided a mild sedative too, for when he was at his worst. She rarely replenished the prescription, so I don't think she used it very often."

For every clue that pointed towards the widow's guilt, another appeared to turn us in the opposite direction.

He looked more serious all of a sudden. "I wouldn't have given him morphine, though. I don't believe in prescribing the stuff. It does more harm than good."

"Isn't it illegal these days?" I unhelpfully demanded.

"Not for medical purposes – pain relief and the like." Dr Merrick spoke as though he were imparting an important lesson. In fact, with his booming delivery, he rather reminded me of my school chaplain. "And though controls are tighter now than they were a few years ago, if someone wants to get hold of it desperately enough, they'll find a way."

These details did not appear to interest my grandfather, who tapped his fingers on the desk impatiently. "Tell me, doctor, for how long was the dead man your patient?"

Merrick's temper appeared to have cooled, and he answered in a calmer voice than before. "I moved here from Wales over a decade ago."

"And what can you tell me of Hugo's medical history during that time?"

He breathed in slowly, then shook his head a little as he exhaled. "It was the story of most men in their twilight years." The doctor hesitated; he was sitting before the living proof that not all elderly men end up in such a poor state. "By which I mean I saw a steady decline in both his mental and physical health. He'd been less mobile for some time before he remarried. If I'd seen any kind of deterioration the moment a pretty young wife appeared, don't you think I would have been suspicious? He was eighty-one years old. I believed he'd had a stroke. There really wasn't a hint of foul play."

I thought back to something that Vivian Highley-Summers had mentioned on our visit, and I'm certain that Grandfather recalled the very same thing.

"But when the pair got married, Hugo's speech was still functioning. And he had good periods of health."

"Before the attack, that's true. But over the last year, he's got increasingly worse. I know that Mrs Templeton-Swift tried various therapies, but nothing worked because Hugo was simply at the end of his life." The doctor leaned over the desk to whisper a secret. "Have you considered the possibility that it was out of kindness that someone in this household was dosing him with morphine? It would not be the first case I've come across where a loved one decided to put a broken old beast out of his misery."

I could see just how much my grandfather suffered to hear these words, but he stopped himself reacting, and Dr Merrick continued in his usual self-righteous tone. "I'm not saying it isn't a tragedy for the family, but if that's the only crime there is to investigate, perhaps you could find it in your heart to look the other way."

Lord Edgington gave no clue as to how he felt about such a possibility but took a moment to study the doctor anew. He had lost the arrogance with which he had previously addressed our witness and even found the humility to offer an apology.

"Dr Merrick, I must say that I am sorry for the tone I took with you at the beginning of our discussion. I can see you are a compassionate and conscientious practitioner, and I should not have suggested otherwise. Perhaps the situation was not as clear as I imagined. I had no right, therefore, to imply that your diagnosis of a stroke was prompted by either malice or negligence."

Merrick looked a little surprised by this volte-face. "That's very good of you, Lord Edgington. Very good of you indeed. And all that leaves me to say is that you have my word that I did all I could for Hugo. He was not only my patient but a friend, and a man I regarded with the utmost respect."

Grandfather bowed as the doctor stood up to leave. "There is one more thing I should ask you." He paused, teasing the final question but not yet delivering it. "I wondered whether you had any knowledge of the rift that emerged between Hugo and his children. Did you know their mother?"

He had reached the door by now and looked in a hurry to get home for his lunch. "With regards to the former Mrs Templeton-Swift, I'm afraid I can't help you. She was already dead by the time I moved here. As for the children, Hugo rarely spoke of them, and they only visited a few times in all the years I attended him. They always struck me as decent people, but I got the impression Hugo was a little ashamed of his offspring."

"How fascinating." The inquisitor joined his fingers together over the desk and nodded thoughtfully. "I feel that whatever drove the family apart may be more significant than we yet know."

CHAPTER SEVENTEEN

"That was really very good of you, Grandfather," I told him once we were alone. "Mending fences, I mean, after you'd taken the man to task."

In truth, I knew that there was nothing that made the old chap humble so much as his failure to foresee a development in one of our cases. Of course, I wouldn't have made such a claim out loud.

"It was wrong of me to antagonise him," he confessed. "He may have made an innocent mistake." He looked quite saintly and serene at that moment, before a devilish gleam sparkled in one eye. "And besides, he may yet be implicated in this conspiracy, and we wouldn't want him knowing that we suspect his involvement now, would we?"

"You were acting?"

He closed his eyes as though I'd paid him a great compliment. "In the words of William Shakespeare, 'All the world's a stage, And all the men and women merely players.' I was just playing a part."

"Do you really think he had something to do with the murder, though?"

He had a wicked side to him at times and enjoyed a few seconds' reflection before concluding, "Well, the morphine had to come from somewhere and he did explain, at length, just how readily available it is. Yet, to my knowledge, there are numerous intoxicants that are far easier to obtain were one so inclined. A country doctor wouldn't necessarily be privy to such information, though."

"Well, I'll be…" I declared, as he'd surprised me once again. "I would never have suspected a doctor of being anything less than an upstanding citizen."

"The good ones are." He pushed back his chair to stand up. "And the bad ones aren't. Now, Christopher. You know how I like to conduct my investigations; I think it's time you took the lead on this one. Who should we interview next?"

I stopped slouching, jumped off the shelf upon which I was leaning and tried to look the part of a detective's assistant. "That's a very good question, Grandfather."

"Thank you. I agree."

"Who should we interview next?" I repeated, in the hope it would spark a clever answer. "I would say that, now we have spoken to the medical man and examined the scene of the crime ourselves, it is time we turned our attention to…" I had started my speech most confidently but, by the end, was speaking in little more than a whisper. "Ummm, it's a toss-up between the merry widow and the dead man's children."

"That is correct."

"Excellent. Well, in that case… I think we should talk to… my mother."

He made no attempt to hide his confusion. "Your mother?"

"Precisely." I really don't understand how I could get myself into such twisted predicaments. "Mother has spent more time with our suspects than either of us. I think that she is best placed to point our investigation in the right direction."

He regarded me for a moment without moving a muscle. "You have an exceedingly unusual mind, Christopher. You presented an equation with one of two answers and solved it using a third." It was hard to know what he made of this, but then he placed his weighty hand on my shoulder. "I approve wholeheartedly. Lead onwards, dear boy. Lead onwards."

We left the study and walked back through the ground floor of the house. This gave me just enough time to put a further question to him. "Grandfather, you told the doctor that you believe that Mr Templeton-Swift might never have died if we hadn't come to Riverside Keep. Is that true?" I'd long since learnt to take what he uttered in interviews with an unhealthy fistful of salt.

"I consider it to be a genuine possibility." He continuously scanned the picture frames and photographs as we walked along. "It is quite possible that, when I told the various members of this household that I would no longer allow Hugo to take his medicine without one of us present, it precipitated his murder. If, as we've come to believe, the morphine was being used to keep him docile, the drug would eventually have worn off and he would have come back to his true self. The game would have been up then; he'd have told us all he knew. It could certainly explain why he was suffocated."

I should have considered such a chain of events myself, but something did finally stand out to me. "Of course, we have no evidence that was the case. Surely, with the amount of medicine Hugo had taken, he would have built up a certain level of tolerance. Perhaps our murderer couldn't be sure that the morphine would kill him, and so he resorted to other means."

"What a clever piece of supposition, Christopher." He stopped at the door to the lounge where we had left our suspects and looked slightly awed. "Bravo."

I felt apologetic myself then, as though I'd been caught cheating on an exam. "I don't know how to explain it, Grandfather. Really, I don't. Perhaps it's all the revision I've been doing. Perhaps I've finally expanded my brain, just as you are always telling me I must."

"Indeed, boy. It's another mystery." He jabbed me in the ribs with his elbow to show that he was joking. It hurt. "But one of which I approve." He let out a throaty laugh and opened the door, as an unexpected sound emerged from within.

> **"Perhaps you think of going for a day,**
> **Down to a place called Pegwell Bay.**
> **Put your togs all nice and trim, while you go and have a swim.**
> **In the water you feel funny when**
> **The kippers come and nibble at your toes,**
> **But don't you give a shout when the tide goes out**
> **And takes away your clothes!"**

I could not have anticipated the scene inside that sunny salon. Tiffin was banging away at the keys of the piano in the far corner as Christabel descended into floods of tears in the opposite one. There was no sign of the other siblings, but my dear mother was on hand to comfort the poor woman as her elder stepson started the chorus in a chirpy East-End accent.

> **"You can't help laughing can yer?**
> **Don't it make you laugh? Not half!**
> **You'll look like Adam, you're nice and cool,**
> **Then along comes a young ladies' school.**
> **They pass by, the sun comes out to tan yer,**
> **But you have to rush back in the water again.**
> **Well, you can't help laughing can yer?"**

"That's enough," Grandfather roared – though, I must say, he took his time. "What on Earth do you think you're doing?"

The song concluded with a clatter as Tiffin pulled the lid of the piano closed to hide his misstep. "I... Oh, yes, I see. It might not have been the suitable choice of song for the occasion. I was merely..." His eyes hadn't left my grandfather, and he looked quite mortified. "... merely trying to lighten the mood a little. I may have got carried away with my playing."

"You thoughtless fool." I could see just how close a bond my clever mother had formed with Hugo's widow. Standing beside her chair, she clutched the tearful woman's head to her side and sent a disapproving glance in Tiffin's direction.

I tried very hard not to jump to the conclusion that what we had just witnessed made him look like a terrible brute, which would make Christabel the unlucky victim of the whole sorry undertaking. As my grandfather never failed to remind me, the truth generally has two sides to it.

"Violet?" my grandfather used the very lowest register of his range to get my mother's attention. "Christopher needs your assistance with his schoolwork. I will wait here with Mrs Templeton-Swift until you return."

Mother looked quite confused by the interruption but did not complain as she extricated herself from her charge. Grandfather walked over to take her place. He did not wrap the woman up in his arms, as my mother had, but sat in the chair beside her and gently patted her on the back. It was a comparatively demonstrative gesture by his standards.

"What's the matter, Chrissy?" my dear mama asked once we were out in the garden, and I was sure no one in the house could hear us.

I peered back in the direction whence we'd come, just to make certain. "I need your opinion on everything you've seen since you arrived at Riverside Keep."

The sky was overcast, but the warmth in the air made me think that the sun would soon burn the clouds away. Mother pulled me over to a bench under a trellis canopy, and we both sat down. "But what about your exams, Chrissy? If you need my help, now is the time."

"That was just something that Grandfather said to get you out of the room." I was trying to speak quickly so as not to miss too much of the conversation that my grandfather was having with our key suspect back in the bright lounge. "If the truth be told, he's gone out of his way to stop me opening any books since we got here."

She missed my point and chose to berate me once more. "That's no good, Christopher. Really, it's not. If you don't study, you'll fail your–"

"Mother, I promise I have been swotting like a swot for weeks, but there are more important things to worry about just now. I need your help."

She pouted for a few moments before accepting my argument. "Very well. You're a good boy, and I trust that you will do your conscientious best when you return to school."

"I promise, Mother." If anything, this made me feel more guilty. I considered rushing to my room at that very moment to dive headlong into algebraic equations and karst geology.

"What would you like to know?"

"It's hard to decide where to begin. I suppose Christabel is the obvious place. You seem to have veritably charmed her."

Mother smiled then and put her hands together in her lap. "I can tell you that the feeling is more than mutual. To think of all the things that tragic creature has suffered causes me great pain." That infinitely compassionate woman collected her thoughts before continuing. "I can honestly say that I have seen nothing in her behaviour over the last day to suggest that she is capable of such wickedness as murdering her own husband. She is the picture of innocence in every imaginable way."

I'd spent enough time with my cynical grandfather to know that such perfection was often too good to be true. "Doesn't that make you at all suspicious?"

"No, it does not." She sat up a little straighter and tutted at her newly cynical younger son. "I have detected no guile or chicanery in her. No hint that she could be concealing her true intentions. Everything she has told me from the moment I met her suggests that she truly cared for her husband and is sorry that he died."

I didn't like to doubt her, especially after her wise old father had reminded me what a fine detective she was. I really wanted to believe that, if there was something to discover, she would have wormed the truth out of Christabel by now. And yet, every suspect I'd seen the inimitable Lord Edgington interview had been hiding something. How could this woman be any different?

"Are you certain, Mother? Are you totally convinced that the grieving widow isn't a sophisticated trickster, and you've fallen for her ploys?"

"Christopher!" she said, her tone rising across the three syllables to become as high-pitched as a station guard's whistle. "I would hope that you know me better than that. I can assure you; Christabel is no killer. It's her infernal stepchildren you should be investigating more closely."

I chewed my lip, still not persuaded as she plainly was. "Fine, then what about Hugo's offspring? What do you make of Tiffin, Lettice and Devyn, beyond the fact that they have a selection of truly unusual names?"

She adjusted her position on the bench so that her bright yellow pleated skirt lay more neatly across her lap. "I can't say that I've warmed to any of them. Tiffin evidently holds great faith in his own ability to entertain those around him, and rarely allows anyone a moment's silence. Lettice is morose and wary. She may not mean ill, but she has made little effort to endear herself to me. And, as for Devyn…"

Instead of replying, she shook her head and looked up at the sky as though she couldn't bear to think of the man.

I was about to ask her exactly what impression she had gained of the barbarous fellow, when someone spoke in Devyn's defence. "He ain't so bad, old Devyn," a voice from the bushes declared, and Ned Crower straightened up so that his head was visible on the other side of one of the colourful flowerbeds. "He treats us wiv a bit of respect he does. Not like that brother of his. Nor that sister. Stuck up, them is. Stuck right up, but not Devyn."

I wasn't just startled by his sudden appearance; I was downright mistrustful of what he was doing there. "Were you listening to our conversation?"

"Yes." He wouldn't even deny it.

I was incensed. "The very cheek! Don't you know it's rude to eavesdrop?"

He finally showed a little contrition. "That it may be, my boy, but I don't have no corks about my person to block me ears. There really was nothing I could do about it."

My mother touched my arm ever so gently to draw my attention to the fact I was behaving like a nitwit. I asked him another question all the same. "Then why were you hiding?"

"Hiding?" He wrinkled his nose up and disappeared into the bush before coming back to standing a moment later. "I weren't hiding, lad. I were planting these here tubers." He held up something that looked suspiciously like a potato, and I wondered if he knew as much about plants as he claimed. "Dahlias, they are. Should be lovely come the summer."

"Well, I suppose you've passed that test," I conceded, though, for all I knew of botany, he might just as well have told me they were the seeds of the Martian weed that covers London in H.G. Wells's terrifying work of 'fiction'. "Still, I don't appreciate eavesdroppers."

He somehow took this as an invitation to come closer. "It's not eavesdropping if you include me in the conversation!"

To my surprise, he navigated the twisting path and came to sit next to us. Mother seemed quite amused by his behaviour, but I was more than a little unsettled.

"As I were saying, Devyn really ain't so bad when you gets to know him. It was him what hired us in the first place. And, I reckon, if his dad had treated the boy with a bit of human kindness, old Hugo might not have needed the young wife for company who ended up killing him."

Despite his overfamiliarity, I was really quite heartened that he had taken my side in the discussion. "You see, Mother, another vote for my theory. Christabel is surely the person who would benefit most directly from her husband's death, and we can't rule out her guilt based on her gifts as a pleasant conversationalist."

"Christopher!" she vociferated once more. "Is that really what you think I was doing?"

Whoops. Curse my unending lack of diplomacy! "No… or rather… Ummm… I don't know how I should answer that question."

Ned found this hilarious and slapped his knee. "Children today ain't got no respect for their parents, madam. My kids are all just the same. If you think this one's bad, you should meet my boys."

I thought it might be best if I summoned a few words to soothe her temper. She was staring at me as though I'd just belched out the national anthem – which, as it happens, Simon Speight in the fifth form once did in the dinner hall at school. It was terribly funny, though I doubt my mother would have approved.

"I'm sure you're right," I began, my tongue finally untwisting. "But you know what Grandfather will say. If I explain that Christabel seems lovely and the Templeton-Swift children are all horrid, he'll ask me for proof. He's forever telling me off for presenting him with–"

"Vague suspicions?" She finished my sentence for me. "Yes, I remember it well. He's a terrible hectorer, my father, but a good teacher nonetheless."

I was glad that she agreed with me, but she hadn't responded to my main point. "And so? Have you come across anything significant that might help us solve the case?"

Ned leaned in to listen, as though he were settling down for the night next to his radio. Mother did the same, apparently keen to keep this information among the three of us.

She was about to speak when our accomplice had a thought. "Wait just one moment. We should have refreshments." He hobbled off through the garden towards his house and I had to pray that he didn't bring any of his wife's sandwiches. To my excitement, he returned a moment later with a bottle of lemonade and three glasses.

"Made it myself," he announced with pride and poured the sweet yellow beverage into the tumblers, which he held in one large hand. I could already tell it would be the most delicious thing I'd consumed since we arrived at Hanging Langford. "Go ahead, madam. I'm all ears."

Mother took a sip, nodded her thanks and obliged. "It's the elder two: Tiffin and Lettice. I've been watching them, and they're forever whispering together, forever scheming. I was sitting in the front salon with a book yesterday afternoon while Christabel napped. They paid me no attention, but whenever someone else entered the room, they would snap shut like oysters. They must have a secret they don't want anyone to know."

"What did I tell you?" Ned's great hand landed noisily on his knee once more. "If it ain't the widow, it's them two what did it." For perhaps the first time since I'd met him, he lost his joyful air and his face fell to frowning. "There's something not quite right about them. Something a bit off. I've seen them out here in the garden too. They go about cheek by jowl and yardarm to yardarm. I don't trust 'em."

Considering what my informants had told me, I knew who I wanted to interview as soon as Grandfather had finished with Christabel. My mother still looked uncomfortable with the discussion, but Ned knocked back the last of his drink and, standing up brightly, returned to his smiling ways.

"I'd better be getting back to work, but you mark my words. If the old fella really was murdered, it'll be them two frilly types what did it." He scratched his chin with the broken nail on his thumb. "Well, them or the pretty lass... or I suppose their brother might have been involved. But... No, no, my money's still on Christabel."

CHAPTER EIGHTEEN

"That wasn't the most helpful statement I've ever heard," I whispered to Mother once we were, more or less alone. I could hear Ned whistling from a few flowerbeds away and didn't want to roil him again.

"You should learn to be more subtle, Christopher," she told me in a didactic tone. "I don't know what's come over you, but you sound like a terrible snob sometimes."

"Me? A snob?" I considered telling her that I'd once intended to marry our housemaid but didn't think she would have taken the news too kindly. "I disagree entirely. And, what's more, if I am a snob, it's because of my upbringing."

Apparently enjoying my defence, she couldn't suppress a gentle laugh. "Well, I hope that's not the case. I hope we've brought you up to see that one's good fortune in life does not necessarily equate with one's worth as a human being. I rather thought you would have learnt that from your time with your grandfather. I remember when I went to the City with him when he was a superintendent. He used to introduce me to all sorts of people with whom I would never have become acquainted if I'd stayed at home in Cranley."

I thought back through the cases I'd investigated with the famous detective, and I realised just how right she was. "Gosh, Mother. You are clever." *And I'm not*, I might have added, though I felt this went without saying. "That's exactly what the old chap has been trying to show me, and I failed to see it. I've met murderous aristocrats and honest country folk, kind-hearted criminals and even the odd corrupt policeman or two." I was quite stunned by the revelation.

"It's not that the rules of society have no place in the world," she said to expand on the point. "But we mustn't rest on our laurels. The prim and properness of my grandparents' generation is not suited to the twentieth century. If we lived our lives believing that the old way of things is always best, we'd have no schools for the poor, no hospitals or modern medicine and women would be locked at home with no voice of their own." She may have gone off at a slight tangent, but I certainly appreciated her point.

"You're right, Mother. You're absolutely right." I placed my hand on her shoulder and stood up with great purpose. "Ned," I shouted across the garden, and the cheery, grubby chap poked his head above the plants, like a rabbit peeking out of his burrow. "I must apologise. I've been a terrible snob, but I honestly believe that your garden is delightful, and your lemonade is delicious."

"Right you are, young one!" He took off his sun hat and waved it at me through the air. He seemed like a forgiving sort.

Feeling quite lightheaded, and wondering what he'd put in the delicious libation, I marched back towards the house, before remembering that my mother would want to come with me and turning back to escort her.

When we reached the lounge where we had left my grandfather working his investigative magic, very little was happening. Christabel was in the bay window which overlooked the garden, gloomily browsing that week's edition of 'The Lady'. Grandfather was sitting at the piano, walking his fingers up and down the ivory keys. I had no idea the man could play a note, but he managed to produce a maudlin melody that was far more in keeping with the mood of the day than the jolly music-hall number that Tiffin had performed. His audience seemed moved by the performance as, every time she turned the page, Christabel would look out of the window for a moment and sigh despondently.

"How are you getting along in here?" my mother asked tentatively.

"Perfectly well, thank you." Grandfather finished his piece with a short flourish and turned to us. "I haven't touched a piano for nigh on twenty years, but it's just like playing chess or bowling a ball in cricket; it came straight back to me."

I tried to signal to him with my eyebrows to show that it wasn't the piano about which we wished to hear but his time with our suspect. He did not appear concerned over the matter and, as his dear daughter went to check on Christabel, I waved him over to the door and whispered, "Well? What did she tell you?"

"Nothing," he replied.

"You mean that she wouldn't answer your questions?"

"I mean I haven't asked her any." He really wasn't in any hurry to solve this murder and I decided he'd probably made the right decision putting me in charge of the interviews. "I didn't want you missing out on the fun." He rippled his bushy eyebrows with great glee and spun on his heel so that the tails of his long coat shot out behind him.

"Mrs Templeton-Swift," he projected across the room in that deeply resonant voice, "if it is not too painful, the time has come for us to have a conversation."

She shot up in her seat and snapped her paper shut. As I walked closer, I could see that her eyes looked sore from crying. I would have said that such anguish would be impossible to feign, but I'd been similarly fooled before. You know what they say, fool me once, oh, tut tut. Fool me twice, I'm a great raging dunderhead.

Unable to produce the necessary audible response, she nodded silently. My grandfather held his hand out for me to take the seat in front of her. I thought this was jolly nice of him to let me rest my weary bones until I realised what he expected.

"I... But... Why don't...?" I tried a few different sentences, but none of them quite took.

He folded his arms and came to stand at my shoulder, just as I normally did to him at such moments. "Christopher would like to ask you a few questions about yourself and your relationship with your husband."

"Would I?" I couldn't hide my surprise. "Or rather... Indeed I would."

"He has no wish to pry, of course, and will treat anything you tell us here today with the utmost discretion."

"Indeed, I will," I confirmed with some feeling, desperate to show that every word my grandfather had said on my behalf was truly heartfelt. "The utmost discretion."

There was a brief silence and, perhaps thinking I was waiting for her to say something and not the other way around, she closed her eyes gracefully, bowed her head a fraction and whispered a "Thank you."

Mother stood up from her seat beside her friend and sat in the chair next to mine. This gave me a little burst of confidence and I attempted to formulate my first question. "When... Which is to say, exactly where... Or rather, how is it that you came to..."

"I believe what my grandson is trying to ask is whether you could tell us a little about your life before you came to Riverside Keep." Grandfather put his hand on the back of my wicker chair as he spoke to show that we were acting as one. To tell the truth, I was incredibly proud of our work together. "I understand you were married before?"

Her eyes shot over to him as he asked this question and, seeing his stern expression, she immediately turned back to me. "That is correct. I have experienced great misfortune in my life. I am now thrice widowed." If there's any statement that is likely to make a person cry, it is "I am now thrice widowed." Her cheeks flushed red and great salty tears ran down them. "Hugo was my third husband."

"What happened to the other two?" I asked as, diplomatically, I'm on a par with a wild boar or perhaps a large goat.

Every new question made the poor woman jump in her seat. "They... died..." It was a perfectly accurate answer to a perfectly stupid question. "Alonso had never been a healthy man, and Harry... I don't know how else to say it, Harry killed himself shortly after we were married."

This sounded a particularly unlikely story to me. What kind of person would marry such a charming, beautiful (though potentially murderous) woman and then end his life?

Perhaps aware that I would think just this, she offered up an answer. "Harry had served in Flanders and never recovered from the horrors he'd witnessed. When I married him, I knew that he was plagued by demons, but I hoped that we could fight them together."

My next obvious question would have been how much money she'd inherited from each man. Luckily, she interrupted me before I could ask this undoubtedly rude question.

"I can imagine what you must be thinking..." she said, which was really quite incredible as I still didn't know what to believe. "You must think I was responsible for their deaths. But that is not the case. Fate has dealt me a cruel hand, and there is something you must know."

She took a ragged breath, and my mother spoke to soothe her nerves. "My dear Christabel, take your time. You are among friends here."

This intervention seemed to do the trick and Hugo, Harry and Alonso's widow started her tale once more. "I'm sure you are wondering how I came to be married three times at such a young age. The truth is that I had no choice but to remarry each time. Alonso and I had a son together. He is now nine years old. My second husband would have nothing to do with my David and sent him away to boarding school. I never told Hugo about him for fear he wouldn't accept me. If I hadn't married again, I wouldn't have been able to support my son. I have no money of my own. No wealth or property. I have spent my life at the mercy of others, and I am afraid that my dear son will do the same."

This was too much for Mother, and she knelt down before her friend to offer her support. Not knowing what else to say, I moved the conversation away from her first two husbands, who had died in potentially suspicious circumstances, to the one who had most definitely been killed.

"I didn't mean to upset you, madam." I hoped this sounded sincere. Despite my grandfather's training, I still couldn't bear to see our suspects in tears. "Perhaps you can tell us how your marriage to Hugo came to pass?"

She sniffled for a moment but set about answering to the best of her ability. "I found him in a newspaper." She managed a sad laugh. "Well, that's what we liked to tell people. Hugo thought it was so funny, as though I'd been searching for a lady's maid or a new car to purchase. In truth, he had placed an advert to find a wife. I know that may sound like a terribly strange thing to do, but Hugo was an unusual man, and he didn't have any other way of meeting someone. I replied to the advert and, a month later, I had the most charming letter back from him. We made the arrangements, and it was decided that I would come to visit."

Her story fitted with what Vivian had told us the day before, and it still sounded as though the old rotter had entertained the two women without care for their feelings.

"Were you living far away?" Mother was so much more practical than me. I always overlooked such simple matters.

"No, not at all," Christabel replied. "My previous husband's family was from Salisbury, and so it was only a few miles to come." I wondered if perhaps that was what pipped Vivian to the prize. Proximity would have been a useful bonus when searching for a new spouse.

"Was it long after that you were married?" I continued.

She shook her head, and a momentary smile crossed her lips. "It all happened incredibly quickly. We met two or three times, and Hugo told me he did not want to wait and wished to wed immediately. His previous wife had died over a decade before, and he regretted being alone for so long."

"And you said yes?" I tried to hide the surprise in my voice. I didn't do a very good job. "You married the old chap after you'd only just met him?"

Grandfather squeezed my shoulder, not so much in support, but to suggest I go a little easier on her.

"I was in no position to say no. I had been left with nothing after my second husband's death. His estate went to his family, and they'd made it clear they wanted rid of me."

To paraphrase 'Alice's Adventures in Wonderland', I was suspiciouser and suspiciouser!

"Do you know whether Hugo had considered any other candidates for the position?" I thought this a rather neat turn of phrase, but Mother looked quite judgmental for some reason.

"I couldn't possibly say. He was a private man in many ways. All I know is that he wanted to marry me, and I found him quite charming. I enjoyed his company and thought that, by living together, we could make one another happy."

"The man was twice your age!" Whoops, I was talking without thinking again. "I'm sorry. I'm so sorry. I had no wish to sound unkind. I just meant that... well... he *was* twice your age."

The interview wasn't going as I had hoped, but she wasn't nearly so offended as I might have imagined. Clutching her handkerchief tightly in one hand, she soon responded.

"That's right, and I'm sure you think I married him for nothing more than his money or the security he offered. But I can tell you that there was magic in Hugo, and we truly did fall in love. When I first lived here, he was so bright and full of energy. He spent his life in his wheelchair but even managed to walk a few steps some days, and I hoped he would get stronger with my support."

"But that's not what happened," Grandfather stated, his voice cutting through the still atmosphere in that room like an axe through a tree trunk.

"No. A few months after I arrived, his condition worsened. It was quite sudden, in fact. His speech became slurred, he couldn't concentrate in the way he previously had. He went from spending his days reading books to merely sitting in his chair, staring through the window. It was tragic to see his deterioration, and Dr Merrick said there was nothing we could do for him except try to lessen his suffering and confusion. The one mercy was that he was in no real physical pain."

I'd been hesitant to embark on the interview, but now discovered a list of questions in my head that needed answering. "What about his children? You said that they didn't come for your wedding. Did you write to them when he became ill?"

She hesitated, and the words got stuck somewhere within her. "N... no. Hugo wouldn't have wanted them to come. It was clear whenever he spoke of his offspring that their relationship was strained. I asked him about them from time to time, and he told me happy stories from when they were children but would say little on the death of their mother, which he admitted had created the rift in the family."

"Do you know how she died?"

She peered at Mummy then. The encouraging look she received in reply must have animated her a little, as she summoned the strength to answer. "I never discovered what happened when Margery died. That was her name, Margery Templeton-Swift. I believe she was an adventurous woman. She travelled all over the world with Hugo before the children were born. I'm sure she was an amazing person, but I always felt that I had taken her place here. The photos of her about the house have haunted me ever since I arrived."

I wondered if this was the sign of a nervous disposition or a guilty conscience but decided to move on from her deceased predecessor to more current events. "Perhaps you could tell us what happened this week?"

She nodded and I could tell that the present was easier for her to relate than a distant, misty past. "Lettice was the first to arrive. She made a big fuss of her father as though she had only left the day before. She was particularly hostile when he wasn't near and accused me of seducing Hugo to rob her children of their inheritance. I tried to convince her that I had no such intentions, but it was like talking to a piece of furniture. She was immovable in her convictions and, when Tiffin arrived, she found an ally. They were convinced I was poisoning their father."

She had to stop herself then; her anger had risen, and her lower lip quivered. She put her fingers to both temples, and Grandfather rang the bell for refreshments to comfort her. A minute later, Cook stuck her head around the door.

"What?" was all she would say.

"Tea for four, please, Betty."

She nodded and disappeared again, looking more furious than I'd seen her that weekend.

When the silence of the room had been restored, I attempted a softer question. "I'm sorry to press you, Mrs Templeton-Swift, but can you tell us your impressions of your third stepchild?"

I think she must have appreciated my good manners as, though still shaking, she gathered her wits and responded. "Devyn is the harshest of Hugo's three children, but he has not treated me nearly so violently as his siblings. Though he clearly has a temper when roused, he has not directed it towards me and, for the most part, keeps his own counsel."

"From what he said in the dining room yesterday evening, it seems that he was particularly cut off from his father. Do you know anything of their disagreement?"

She was more resolute this time. "Yes, in fact. I managed to glean certain facts from Hugo before his stroke. Devyn had wanted his father to support him in a business venture, but Hugo deemed it a risky investment and said that he would need to prove himself first. It made the boy quite furious, and that was when he sailed to America, believing that, if his father wouldn't provide for him, he would have to make his own fortune.

"Though Hugo didn't speak about his family in much detail, this was the one topic we did discuss. I think that Devyn was his favourite child. The Joseph to his Jacob, if you like. He was disappointed in his son and often railed against his decision to move abroad. I got the impression that he felt quite deserted by all three of his children."

We were finally getting a fuller picture of the family and it made certain possibilities more likely. I still couldn't decide whether the delicate woman before me was a devil or a saint. The luxurious golden tresses of her hair, which fell in ringlets at the side of her face, and the sparkling green of her eyes made me want to believe every word she said. Her murky past and the mountain of circumstantial evidence we'd collected suggested otherwise.

Perhaps it was my grandfather's composed, steadying presence there beside me, but I felt that I must have grown into the interview. When I was ready to ask my last question, I did so with far more patience and sensitivity.

"Please don't feel you have to answer this if it upsets you, Christabel, but do you have any idea to whom your husband left his estate?"

She looked quite alarmed but swallowed and answered in a fragile tone. "He changed his will soon after we were married. Aside from a small provision for his servants and a fixed sum for each of his children, he left the majority of his wealth to me."

CHAPTER NINETEEN

While I could have argued that I was capable of occupying the role of a detective, that did not in any way imply that I was adept at the art of detection. Practically every other sentence that Christabel uttered forced me to change my perception of her.

> **Her three husbands died in circumstances which did not rule out foul play?**
> **Lock her up!**
>
> **She loved Hugo for the person he was?**
> **Oh, that poor woman!**
>
> **Nearly every last penny of the Templeton-Swift fortune had been left to her in his will?**
> **Send her to the gallows!**

It was like watching a tennis match except that, with every point that was scored, I changed the player I was supporting. By the end of the interview, I was exhausted and didn't feel as though it had got us any closer to identifying the man's killer.

I'd finished my job, but there were a few details which my grandfather still wished to address.

"If it is not too personal a question, could you confirm that you slept in a separate bedroom from your husband?"

She looked a little shy then, and I was reminded of the innocent young girl of whom Vivian had spoken. "That's correct. Hugo often talked as he dreamed and, as a light sleeper myself, I took the room across the hall from him. He didn't seem to mind."

"Did he ever say anything useful?" I asked, somewhat optimistically.

"Not that I recall." She smiled at my question. "I think he used to dream of his time abroad. I would occasionally hear the name of distant places that I would have to look up in an atlas to identify."

Grandfather did not object to my interruption but had more to ask. "When I inspected your husband's body, I discovered a bottle of morphine under his bedclothes. Can you tell me how it might have got there?"

"Morphine?" She was apparently quite unnerved by the mention of that wicked substance. "I haven't a clue what it was doing there. Perhaps the killer tried to subdue him before the attack?"

I thought this unlikely, considering old Mr Templeton-Swift's condition during his last year on Earth.

"And you've never seen any such substance here in the house?"

"I swear I haven't. As I said, Hugo was limited in his abilities but in no great pain. Why would he have needed such strong medicine?"

Before my grandfather could answer, we heard a rumpus and several raised voices from the other side of the house. The sound was audible even through the closed door of the lounge and the long winding corridors of Riverside Keep. Perhaps unsurprisingly, the old man responded quicker than I could. Lord Edgington shot across the room and out into the hall to see what had caused such caterwauling.

"I've said my piece," were the only words I caught with any certainty, and, ten seconds later, Devyn rushed past us and up the stairs. He'd come from the direction of the kitchen. My mother, grandfather and I hovered for a moment in the hall and, when the others didn't look as though they would investigate, I decided to head towards the kitchen to see what had occurred.

"I'll return forthwith," I said with some confidence. If I was to make a go of this detective lark, it was about time I stood on my own two feet.

I followed the gloomy corridor along to a comparatively meagre kitchen for such a large house. It had no worktable in the middle, but merely an old wooden sideboard with a butcher's block and two marble counters on either side of the sink. That being said, the place was equipped with all the modern conveniences one might require. There was a mechanical dishwasher, a Miele rotary washing machine and an electric kettle. I probably shouldn't have been paying so much attention to these appliances, though, as sitting on the floor in quite a state was poor Betty.

"Young man, you shouldn't be in here." She flapped her hands and peered about as though she expected someone to tell us off for some unfathomable misdemeanour.

"It's all right, Cook. Nothing bad will come of this." I reached one hand down to help her up. She was not the daintiest of women and I was not the strongest of boys, so it was something of a challenge.

"You're fine now."

"Thank you, Chrissy lad." She held her hand to her lower back as though she'd hurt it in the fall. I was surprised she even knew my name. "I'm sorry to have troubled ya. There's really nothing for you to worry yourself about."

"What was all that commotion I heard?"

I could tell that she was nervous, and I had to think that the youngest Templeton-Swift boy had been up to no good.

"Really. It was nothing at all. I lost my footing, that's all it was."

I wanted to prove to her that I could be trusted. "But I saw Devyn running away. If he has hurt you, I can assure you that Lord Edgington will deal with him without mercy. You must simply tell me what occurred." I wonder if I was the first boy in history to threaten someone with the full might of his grandfather.

Perhaps I'd been a tad too earnest in my entreaty, as she laughed at me then. "It weren't nothing of the sort, lad. I only slipped!" She shook her head in puzzlement. "It must have been wet on the floor from when I was washing the dishes."

I wouldn't let her lie for him, and so I pressed her more information. "I know that's not the whole story. I heard Devyn shouting. He said, 'I've said my piece.' So what exactly had you been discussing?"

Her eyes flicked out of the window to the garden where her husband was still working. "All right, lad. You've got me. I wasn't going to say nothing, but I made a fool of myself with Master Devyn. I mentioned his father, and he said I were wrong to do such a thing so soon after the poor chap was killed. I hadn't meant nothing bad by it, but he took it the wrong way. He's a sensitive one that Devyn. I should have known to watch my words, but he means no harm."

"Did he push you?"

She spoke in that same amused tone. "No, lad, I really did slip. The force of his words mighta sent me head over tip, but he never laid a hand on me."

In all the excitement, I hadn't noticed that two figures had come to stand in the doorway. One of them was Betty's daughter Wilhelmina, and the other was my curious grandfather. It was he who now addressed the steadfast domestic.

"You've had a shock, Cook." He came into the kitchen to check on the poor woman. "I insist you rest for the remainder of the weekend."

"I couldn't possibly," she said, her voice finally showing a little of the panic that she'd managed to suppress. "Who will make the meals if I don't?"

"You needn't worry about that. I'll call some of my people to come." He looked at his watch and did not seem deterred by the rapidly latening hour. It had already gone midday, and I was starving. I felt just as unnerved by the thought of going without food as Betty clearly did about there being no one around to make it.

"But it's my job, M'Lord. I'm no shirker."

Grandfather was unmoved by her response – and no doubt eager to have an excuse to send for a proper chef! "Go back to your cottage, madam. Should we find ourselves short of staff, we will call for you. Though I'm confident it won't come to that."

Torn between fulfilling her duties and avoiding any insult to the gentleman before her, Betty nodded and hobbled through the kitchen towards the back door without another word.

"She'll be all right," Wilhelmina promised. "Mum's made of sterner stuff than most, and it will do everyone a world of good to have a break from her cooking." It was a relief to hear someone say these words, though I was glad it was her daughter speaking and not me. I still hadn't got the taste of last night's quail out of my mouth (or my nightmares).

"Christopher," Grandfather began, his eyes still watching the woman through the kitchen window as she picked her way across the elaborate garden, "go out to the car and tell Todd to call Cook and Halfpenny. Tell him we'll need their services, posthaste."

I wondered why he didn't ask me to ring Cranley myself, but I did as requested. I found Todd sitting in the Rolls, which was parked in the shade of a wide weeping willow. To my surprise, he was reading the very same H.G. Wells book that I had up in my room.

"It's a real winner, don't you think?" I asked and I could tell that he agreed.

"'War of the Worlds'? Oh, absolutely. I only started it this morning, and I've been gripped ever since."

"You lucky thing. I wish I could read it again for the first time." I stood staring gormlessly, and he eventually queried what was wrong with me. Well, those weren't the words he used, but I think we both knew the underlying meaning.

"Master Christopher?" he asked, and I continued grinning. "Was there a reason you came out to see me? Or was it just to talk about books?"

I was knocked from my daze. "Oh, yes. Grandfather says you're to call Cook and Halfpenny and get them here at once." I thought I should add an important caveat to this. "In fact, if they happen to have any food already prepared, you had better tell Cook to bring it with her. I may very well waste away before she arrives."

"Very good, sir."

Hmmm, it wasn't like him to call me 'sir'. I must have sounded terribly authoritative in my commands.

Despite the emptiness of my stomach, it was Todd's welfare for which I was most concerned at this moment. "You surely didn't spend the night out here in the car, did you?"

"I certainly did." He spoke most tenaciously on the matter. "And if the young maid here is to be believed, it was a real slice of luck. Someone was *murdered* in there!" Still rattled at the thought of the killer in our midst, he clearly wasn't his usual self, and I wondered if it was due to the terrifying books which he so enjoyed reading.

"It was an old man with a great deal of money who was murdered," I attempted to reassure him. "I can't imagine you would be a target."

"You're probably right." He sighed as he considered the possibility. "And now that the murderer has struck and we know what kind of fellow he is, I'll kip in the house tonight."

I struggled to make sense of his logic as he marched into Riverside Keep in search of a telephone.

Having returned to the spacious entrance hall, with its macabre burgundy walls, I noticed something that I hadn't spotted when I'd run through a few minutes earlier. There were muddy boot prints on the floor. I could see that they came from the doors that gave onto the garden at the back of the house, so I only needed one guess to identify who had left them. But that wasn't the most interesting part. What drew my attention to them was not where they began but where they ended.

Listening for a moment to the sounds of the house, to make sure no one would surprise me in my task, I followed the prints to a door under the stairs. It was only small, and the top descended at a diagonal to match the cyma moulding and blend in with the wooden panels around it. It was just the kind of door that people find in mystery stories which can lead to all sorts of hidden secrets. In my case, it led to a gloomy cellar.

On flicking a light switch at the bottom of the stairs, I instantly knew why that rascal Ned Crower had been down there, and I very much doubted it was his first trip. You see, I'd just discovered Riverside Keep's collection of wine and spirits, and there were any number of spaces where bottles had been removed and not restocked. For some reason, this knowledge made me like the mischievous gardener even more.

The space was cold, dusty and cobwebby – three qualities of which I'm really no admirer. I was about to mount the stairs and return to more important business when I noticed a shape in one corner, hidden by an old white sheet. Admittedly, for the briefest of moments, I was worried it was a ghost. But once my heart rate had returned to normal, I whipped the covering away to discover a number of wooden crates underneath.

I rummaged about in the nearest one and found another large selection of photographs. There were pictures of the Templeton-Swift offspring in their adolescence this time. The decades in between had done their work, but I could just make out who was who. They couldn't have been more than eighteen, and Lettice had certainly got a great deal more attractive since then. From the look of her in the photographs, she'd been a real tomrig in her youth. There was a picture of her on a boat, another of her playing cricket, and even a shot of her fishing. She had none of the elegance she would develop in later life and, perhaps to her horror, I discovered she was not a natural blonde. Even in the sepia photos, I could tell that her locks had once been mousy brown.

I wondered what other (more useful) secrets I could discover about the family by rooting through their old possessions, but my examination of Tiffin's photographs offered little reward. He had always looked a little obnoxious, posing as an admiral on a rowboat or pretending to be super strong, with his muscles bulging. As for Devyn, who was a good few years younger than the other two, he was clinging to his father in every frame. It was clear that, once upon a time, he had held Hugo in far higher esteem.

The one interesting feature I noticed was that their mother must already have been ill at this point. In every last one of the photographs, she was sitting or lying down, her skin pale, her expression pained but resilient. It made me wonder if this, more than the rift in the family, was the reason that the photographs had been stored in the damp, musty cellar – which, as everyone knows, is a terrible place to keep photographic material. Had they been removed from display for the simple reason that it was painful for Hugo to see his deceased wife suffering? Or was there yet more to discover about the fallout between the patriarch and his children?

These thoughts were still bouncing about my brain like footballs when, having passed a good bit of time with the once happy family, I put the last of the photos back in the box, turned the light off and climbed the stairs.

CHAPTER TWENTY

Returning to the entrance hall, I found Delilah coming down from her master's bedroom looking particularly hungry. She peered about the room as if to say, *what's been going on here without me?*

"Have you been sleeping all morning, you lovely lazy beast?"

She didn't respond, not only because she was a dog, but because that other beast, Devyn Templeton-Swift, rushed down the stairs at that moment. "Are you talking to that animal again?" he growled. "You're really not the full shilling if you think she's capable of an intelligent reply."

He sneered at me, and I had a good mind to tell him what I really thought of a man who went scaring his staff and apparently lacked the capacity to smile. I didn't, of course, as I was afraid he would hit me, but I was sorely tempted. Instead, I made a small, scared noise and ran off to find my mother.

There was no sign of her in the lounge we'd previously occupied and, by the time I'd finished looking for her downstairs, Halfpenny and Cook had arrived.

"How on Earth did you get here so quickly?" I marvelled. "It's been less than half an hour since Todd called you."

Our footman, Halfpenny, turned to stone and could think of no possible explanation, whereas Henrietta pushed straight past him with a brief, "Afternoon, Master Christopher. We were lucky with the traffic, that's what it was."

Halfpenny nodded nervously and dashed after his colleague. I suppose that, to be a cook, Henrietta must have required an intrinsic knowledge of architecture; she knew where the kitchen would be without asking. I went outside to look for my family, and the truth finally hit me. "They didn't come all the way from Cranley." I walked a little further through the immense forecourt of the house. "They must have been staying nearby." A few more steps and I'd dismissed the possibility that our footman and our creative chef were conducting some kind of illicit affair before a more realistic explanation finally presented itself. "This was Grandfather's doing!"

It was at this very moment that Lord Edgington, the paragon of virtue and truth, appeared from the house with his daughter at his side. They had changed into walking clothes; I believe it was the first time I'd seen my grandfather in anything but grey wool and cashmere since he'd dressed up for a treasure hunt in the winter.

I stood at the stone entranceway to the estate, waiting for him to arrive and, when he finally strolled over, I had an accusation to put to him. "You've been keeping two members of your staff in Salisbury. You sneaked out of the house under false pretences yesterday evening to dine with them, isn't that correct?"

"I don't know what you mean." He selected his most indignant tone for this statement.

Sitting on the running board of the Silver Ghost, our chauffeur was only a few feet away. I knew that *he* couldn't lie. "Todd, tell me the truth. Did you drive my grandfather to see Halfpenny and Cook last night?"

He scratched his head and looked up at the bright blue sky. "Ummm… did we go… I'm not sure that I…"

"Todd?" I prompted him.

"Halfpenny and Cook?" He thought a little harder. "Now that you mention it, we might have come across them in Salisbury. I didn't think anything of it at the time, and I'm sure it was just by chance." Of his numerous skills, acting was not the strongest one.

"What did Cook make for dessert?" I knew this would get him.

"Apple crumble with custard and whipped lemon mousse." The words burst out of him, and he immediately covered his mouth in shame.

"Ah ha!" I turned to the deceitful chap who could have saved me from *Betty's Burnt Quail Surprise* but had, instead, kept his culinary treats to himself. "You've been caught, old fellow. I knew you were up to no good when you left here yesterday, but I never suspected you of such treachery."

My mother didn't look too impressed either and, for once, I wasn't to blame. "What have you been doing, Father?"

His cheeks glowed like a stove in winter. "Ahh…" He struggled to muster an explanation but emitted a sheepish laugh. "Well, you see… the truth is…" He could summon no excuse and finally confessed to his scheming. "The truth is I knew you'd both mock me if I travelled with so many servants, and so I booked a hotel for them in town and planned to pop down there whenever the grey gristly grub here got too much for me. I've stayed at houses such as Riverside Keep before, and I knew that the food on offer is rarely to my standards."

"And when you say, 'so many servants', do you mean the three who have already arrived? Or are there–" Before my mother could finish the question, a car pulled through the arch and our maids, Alice and Dorie, were driven onto the estate by another of Cranley Hall's long-serving employees.

"Good afternoon, M'Lord, M'Lady, Master Christopher," the Irishman said as he climbed out of the stately blue Lagonda from Grandfather's automobile collection.

"You brought your gardener?" My voice was thick with wonderment. The ground in front of Riverside Keep had been turned into a veritable car park by now. There were four of the blasted things, plus three which belonged to the Templeton-Swifts, and the two inspectors' Vauxhall was still there too.

The old chap instantly turned defensive. "You see, this is why I kept it a secret. I didn't want the pair of you ganging up on me." He adopted a most forlorn expression. "Is it really so terrible that I like to enjoy a few home comforts when away from home? Am I really such a dreadful person that I deserve your censure?"

"I'm not sure I'd call six members of staff 'a few home comforts', Father. By the time we take our summer holiday, you'll insist on dismantling Cranley Hall and transporting it, stone by stone, across the country."

"Stuff and nonsense," he said and marched towards the open gate. "Are you coming for a walk or not?"

Mother moved to follow him, but I was more reluctant.

"Come along, boy. A short constitutional will surely assist you in building an appetite."

"I don't need a walk to help on that score. With all the brouhaha that went on this morning, we quite forgot about breakfast." Through the piqued tone I adopted, I tried to make it clear that I held him responsible for this terrible outcome.

He did not reply but rolled his eyes and whistled for Delilah to join us.

It was almost lunch and, from the look of the hampers in the back of Halfpenny's Austen Twenty, there would be plenty of food to go around. I knew that the only time Grandfather indulged in a little ambulatory exercise was when he had something he needed to contemplate. I couldn't miss out on the discussion that he and my mother were about to enjoy so, when Delilah drew alongside me, I set off after them to leave the estate.

We followed the road around a little way and took a country path between two fields. The weather was mild, the sun kept finding holes in the clouds through which to shine, and the world looked a little brighter than it had that morning. I might have made use of this time to consider my own dilemmas in life, but Grandfather drew our attention to some significant pieces of evidence that I would otherwise have overlooked.

"The doctor was correct this morning when he said I could have tried harder to protect the man who requested our presence here." He sounded humbled, though I wondered how much that had to do with the subterfuge I had just uncovered. "I should have stayed in Hugo's room with him at the very least. I left him to the wolves, and I can't forgive myself for such a mistake."

I knew this was only half true and that, as soon as one of us told him it wasn't his fault, he'd perk up again.

"It really wasn't your fault, Grandfather. As you stated to the doctor, the police wouldn't have listened to you if you'd told them of your suspicions. And how were you to know that Hugo slept alone?"

He gave one last sigh and did as I'd predicted. "You're absolutely right, Christopher. There was nothing I could do for the man. Yet I must try all the harder to find his killer. That will surely help him rest more easily… wherever he may now find himself."

This sparked all sorts of interesting questions that I would like to have put to him. Did he believe in an afterlife? Was heaven a physical realm or just a spiritual one? Would each person be assigned his own personal angel on passing through the pearly gates, or would we have to share them out between ourselves? Before I could broach such a topic, my mother had something more pertinent to ask.

"Are we absolutely sure that the morphine you found in Hugo's bed was being administered to him? If you were wrong about not sleeping in his room to protect him last night, isn't it possible that you're wrong about this, too? He was a very old man, and you are not a doctor. It seems quite possible to me that he really did have a stroke."

Grandfather wore a look which seemed to imply, *now wait just one moment. I believe that Christopher has already proven that I was not wrong, after all.* But instead of making such an argument, he considered her points. "It is theoretically possible. And I concede that it seems highly unusual that the bottle would be under his bedsheets. But I'm resolute in my judgement that, as Hugo had periods of lucidity and improved abilities, the stroke was a misdiagnosis."

"Unless it was all just wishful thinking," I said, and they looked at me appraisingly as though they had not expected me to say anything useful. "Perhaps he really wasn't so much better from day to day. Perhaps that was merely his loved ones' attempt to reassure themselves. Remember that the only evidence Wilhelmina could give of his occasional miraculous recovery consisted of the waves across the room he would sometimes issue."

They both nodded then, and I felt quite proud of myself. I'd made two distinguished detectives nod!

Delilah took the break in the conversation as a sign that she should canter ahead of us up the lane to chase a sparrow into the high hedges on either side of our route. There were blackberry bushes, but no fruit upon them and I occasionally heard wrens, greenfinches or maybe bluetits singing from within the thick branches – I've never been particularly good at identifying birdsong.

It was my mother's turn to be clever. "So let's say someone wanted us to believe that Hugo was being drugged to render him incapacitated. Why would they have done such a thing?"

"To make it look as though Christabel was responsible for his condition, obviously," I said, as, for that hour at least, I was a great believer in her innocence. Don't worry, I'd soon change back the other way and paint her as a heartless murderer.

"It's possible." This was as substantial a concession as Grandfather was normally willing to grant. "And there are certainly elements to the story she told us which shine a positive light on the unfortunate widow. But think back to when we first arrived. The argument that Lettice and Tiffin were having did not appear to have been staged for our benefit. They genuinely seem to believe that Christabel is responsible for their father's condition."

The three of us trundled along quietly for a few minutes, chewing over our thoughts until we came to a wide meadow that was full of wildflowers of every description. There were poppies and ox-eye daisies, bird's foot trefoil and hound's tongue, cornflowers, cowslips, cranesbills and corn chamomile. I wanted to go dashing through them with my fingers extended to soak in all that life and colour. I think my normally sensible mother would have joined me – after all, she was the one who taught me about flowers in the first place – but we fought such an urge. Instead, we followed the path around the side of the field and began the walk up the gentle slope towards the village.

"What did you make of the drama in the kitchen earlier?" Mother asked. "Was Betty all right?"

"She certainly claimed to be." I took a moment to relive that scene and could still make neither head nor tail of it. "It strikes me that we're wasting our time with much of our investigation. If we simply tell the police what a beast that chap Devyn is, they'll be able to get in contact with their counterparts and find out what the unsavoury fellow has been up to in New York. He'll have a criminal record out there; you mark my words."

"He is a prickly fellow. I'll grant you that." The path had become narrower, and Grandfather stopped to let his daughter go ahead of him. "But why would Devyn have travelled halfway around the world to murder his own father? No matter what passed between them all those years ago, it seems strange that he would have heeded Hugo's call to return home in the first place, especially considering the expense of a trans-Atlantic voyage."

"Perhaps that was just an excuse and there really was no letter." Have I ever mentioned that my mother is a genius? "If Devyn decided to sail home to settle scores, he might well have written to his brother and sister and told them to come to the house. Perhaps he wrote the second letter to you, too."

Grandfather turned his head with a look of puzzlement. "If he was planning to murder his father, why would he have wanted the man that The Pall Mall Gazette once described as 'London's foremost tracker of cunning criminals' on the premises?"

It's quite incredible that he managed to utter these words in a comparatively modest tone, considering the fact he had gone to the effort of memorising the quote for just such an occasion.

"In order to frame his stepmother, of course," I said, with a click of my fingers. "From everything I've read in the English papers, America is a wild and lawless land populated by cowboys and vagabonds; surely it would have been easier to come by the morphine over there. He must have brought it with him to hide in his father's bed and wrote those letters to make it look as though Hugo suspected his wife of poisoning him."

"The first letter was sent before he entered the country," Grandfather was quick to remind me. "He couldn't have written it."

"How do we know when he arrived?" Mother copied me with a gleeful click of her own. I thought Grandfather would soon follow suit, but he refrained.

"You're right, we do not. Which is one of the reasons we're going on this excursion. When we get to the village, I hope that my contact at Scotland Yard will have gathered some significant information on the three would-be heirs to the Templeton-Swift estate."

"Say hello to P.C. Simpkin for me," I said, which admittedly robbed a little of the mystery of his "contact at Scotland Yard".

He ignored the comment but explained his thinking. "I could have phoned from the house, of course, but I didn't want anyone overhearing me. As far as they know, Christabel is our primary suspect. That is one of the reasons I have delayed interviewing any of them in depth. I have observed them, I have heard what they have to say, but I will not turn the screws until I am sure of my facts."

"And are you? Sure of any facts, I mean. It seems to me as though we've a real mare's nest in front of us, with evidence pointing in every direction at the same time."

He smiled but still wouldn't click his fingers. "Precisely, my boy. And that simply makes it all the more joyous. Solving a case like this will be a real feather in my cap."

My mother looped her arm through her father's, and I could tell that she was about to tease the delightfully conceited fellow. "What's to say that Christopher and I won't solve it first?"

He was not quite so fond of his own legend that such an eventuality appeared impossible to him. "What indeed, my dear? If either of you get to the killer before I do, I will be over the moon." It was his turn to tease us. "And besides, who would your success reflect most kindly upon if not me?"

"Well us, obviously!" I had to argue.

"Oh, no, no. When a pupil surpasses his teacher, it is thanks to the teacher." Even when that impish smile was plain on his face, it was sometimes hard to know whether he was joking. "Just think that, but a year ago, Christopher here believed that every pretty lady we came across could do no wrong and that every great hulking chap was bound to be a killer and now..." He hesitated for a moment. "Well, now, he at least considers the evidence to the contrary before coming to that decision."

"You're incorrigible, Father," my mother told him with a laugh, thus very much encouraging him to remain exactly how he was.

A burst of optimism rushed through me. "Perhaps it will be my turn to solve a case. Yes, I think I have a good chance this time."

As the village came into view, we increased our pace and the three of us bounded along with such enthusiasm that we nearly caught up with Delilah.

"Didn't you just say that it is quite unsolvable?"

"Indeed." I wasn't nearly so confident as I pretended to be. "Which will make it all the more spectacular when I accomplish the impossible!"

"That's the spirit, Christopher." My mother put her free arm around my shoulder which, admittedly, made walking along the narrow footpath rather difficult.

I continued with my display of bravado. "In fact, now that Cook has arrived and I no longer have to subsist on Betty's excuse for sustenance, I imagine I'll have everything neatly tied up by the morning. Yes, it will be a real feather in my cap!"

Grandfather was most magnanimous in response to my unlikely prediction. "I wish you the best of luck."

"That's very good of you. And to celebrate my future success, you can buy me a bun in the bakery before we head back to the house."

CHAPTER TWENTY-ONE

The only new information that Simpkin had discovered for us was that, according to the ship's manifest, Devyn Templeton-Swift really had arrived on a passenger liner from New York a few days earlier. It was hard to know what Grandfather made of this, but I didn't spend too long worrying about it as I had something more interesting on my mind.

O lunch! How I love thee.

I should compose poems to your very existence, sing songs to convey your wondrousness and name my firstborn child after you. Along with your gorgeous sisters, breakfast and dinner, you are the friend who never disappoints, the servant who is always on hand, the lover who–

"Christopher?" my mother asked as, apparently, I'd been daydreaming.

"Sorry?" I was sitting in the dining room with all of our suspects around me and almost as many servants to boot.

"Gravy, Christopher. Halfpenny was asking whether you'd like gravy with your meal."

"Gravy?" I bellowed out a truly unnatural laugh. "Would I? Not half!"

I noticed that several brows furrowed in my direction. I think I might have put on a cockney accent for some reason and everybody there, from devilish Devyn to adorable Alice the maid, looked really quite worried about me. I would have felt quite touched by their concern if I hadn't been dying of embarrassment.

Despite my idiotic performance, we were all in good spirits. Betty's concoctions were a distant memory, and Henrietta had been installed in her rightful place as the head of any kitchen she deigned to enter. A scrumptious roast dinner had been laid before us and I could only imagine that our dear cook had been halfway through preparing it when she was summoned, as it was ready in record time. That did not, however, explain why she had been whipping up a dinner for seven. I know my grandfather had a healthy appetite, but even he couldn't have eaten that much.

The food and wine worked their way into each of us, and the

experience was only enhanced by Halfpenny and Todd, serving us in full livery. Their roles were supplemented by the two maids who brought the food in from the kitchen. It felt like something of a party and, despite the obviously tragic circumstances, everyone seemed to be enjoying themselves.

Tiffin was the first to toast our absent host. "It's what dearest Papa would have wanted. I'm sure he's looking down on us now, wishing he were here to enjoy this feast."

I was a little surprised to see that even his sister agreed with the sentiment. "That's right. Daddy would have loved to be here indulging in such delicious food."

Devyn did not join in with the reminiscing. I thought he might have rebuked Lettice for her inadvertent criticism of Betty's cooking, but he was too busy shovelling potatoes into his mouth to complain.

Perhaps noticing the path by which my gaze had strayed across the table, Grandfather leaned closer to whisper into my ear. "As Oscar Wilde wrote in one of his plays, 'After a good dinner, one can forgive anybody, even one's own relations.'" He let out a surprisingly high-pitched giggle at this slice of witticism, and there were yet more raised eyebrows.

"My apologies," he said to the party at large, "I remembered something really very droll."

"It's rude not to share." Devyn had thankfully finished his mouthful of food by now. "You'd better tell us what was so funny."

Grandfather lost his carefree expression and thought up a more tactful response. "Well… I was thinking of an old story from my days in the Metropolitan Police. I hadn't been on the force for long when I arrested a young chap who had ordered a suit from a tailor near King's Cross. He got into a spot of trouble when, instead of going to the shop to pay for his clothes, he broke in and stole them. I was out on my beat that night and caught him red handed. He had a hammer in his pocket, the suit under his arm and specks of glass all over him where he'd smashed the window. I'd never encountered such a guilty fellow; it was an open and shut case." He started laughing again and could not finish his tale.

"I can't say it's the funniest story you've ever recounted, Grandfather," I had to confess. "Surely such events occur quite frequently to police officers."

"No… no." He tried to speak again, but it was no good. His

body was racked with laughter. "That's not the humorous part. I'm laughing because…"

He had to wrap one arm around himself and hold his side as the waves of snickering that passed through him were too painful to bear. His eyes were watering, and this set off the others around the table. Tiffin predicted a real corker of a joke and began to chuckle away to himself, which made Lettice titter in that delicate manner of hers. Even Christabel couldn't resist a soft exhalation that served to express her amusement.

"Father, you're terrible." My mother looked adoringly at the old thing.

"I'm laughing because, when we got him in front of a judge, the young lad claimed there were extenuating circumstances that simply had to be taken into account. The judge looked down at him from the dock and said, 'Oh yes, young man. And what would they be?'"

"'Well, you see, your honour,' he duly replied. 'I'm due to come here next Thursday on another charge. I only stole that suit so I'd have something nice to wear. I didn't want you thinking badly of me!'" Grandfather only just managed to get the last words out before he broke into fits of table-shaking guffaws.

To my genuine astonishment, Devyn did much the same. His laugh emerged as a staccato, "Ya ya ya," and it spurred the others on around him as Tiffin turned to point at his brother and, in joyful voice, exclaimed, "Oh Dev, it's wonderful to hear you laugh. To tell you the truth, I'd concluded that you'd forgotten how."

Lettice found this just hilarious and put one hand on Tiffin's arm and buried her head in his shoulder. I'd never seen such blissful tears in my life and couldn't help but participate. It wasn't just the story that was funny, though it was good for a few chuckles. It was my grandfather's reaction that united the table and sparked that happy cacophony. Standing to attention beside the door, even Todd and Halfpenny were unable to hide their amusement at seeing their normally upstanding master descend into howls of joy.

"To Papa and the brevity of good living." Tiffin raised his glass once more and, this time, we all did the same.

"To Hugo," I said, and the words echoed back to me.

It was an incredible moment; a break in tensions after all the hostility we'd witnessed since we'd arrived at the house. Clearly, what had been missing this whole time was adequate nourishment. Not just of the stomach, but of the soul. The frivolity that my grandfather had inspired was as important as the beef on my plate, and it made me rather introspective.

You see, most people decide what they want to do in life based upon financial considerations. Some men follow their parents into the family business, be it as a baker, a fruiterer or a criminal. Many will start a job at eighteen and still be there forty years later. My father, for example, had spent his adult life working as a stockbroker because his father told him that it was a dependable way to make money. And yet, did any one of them ask what would be the best, not just for the balance of their bank account, but the well-being of their eternal selves?

Perhaps this is an arrogant question of me to pose, seeing as many people don't have the luxury of not knowing what they want to do. Most fellows don't have rich grandfathers to take them off around the country on jolly holidays while they contemplate how best to spend their days. And yet, I believe the world would be a better place if we thought a little more about what purpose each of us might serve, rather than simply accepting what is handed to us. I think that, in such a scenario, the happiness we find would be spread around a little more evenly.

And, while I was reflecting on the matter, the mood in the room had changed once more. Lettice had reverted to her usual circumspect self – the intense fear I had witnessed behind her eyes that day was present once more. Christabel was gazing at her plate and would not look up again until dessert was served, and Devyn's scowl had reconquered his face. He fired his gaze around the room and nothing there appeared to cheer him. Even Grandfather's chattering stories couldn't restore a sense of harmony.

I realised then that all the mirth and cheer and jubilation that had flared up around us so joyfully only served to underline just how grim that house had become. There was something not entirely right in that family, and it wasn't just the presence of a pretty young stepmother that had rendered it asunder. Although, when we first arrived, the three siblings had put on a show of solidarity for our benefit, Hugo Templeton-Swift's children had a secret to hide, and I was determined to discover what it was.

CHAPTER TWENTY-TWO

I'm getting ahead of myself, of course, as, before I could do any such thing, there was an assortment of delicious food to eat. After I'd mopped up the last remaining traces of cook's honey and plum gravy from my plate with my extra helping of Yorkshire pudding, a lighter vegetable course was delivered. This was something of a relief as I'd had far too large a serving of roast dinner. We had haricot bean pie with rice balls and spicy stuffed marrow, followed by a cheese platter with several French *fromages*, and slices of fruit to go with them.

It had been a whole half-a-day since I'd last eaten a tasty pastry – excluding the Bath bun I'd wolfed down at the bakery that morning – and dessert did not disappoint. Whatever dark thoughts were passing through the head of the savage who had murdered Hugo Templeton-Swift would have been momentarily forgotten as the scent of that delicious creation wafted about the room. In keeping with my conclusion that all cooks must possess an instinctive knowledge of space and structure, Henrietta's Apple Charlotte with butterscotch sauce and Chantilly cream was impressively architectural in its construction.

Its name really didn't do justice to the work of art that was placed before us, and I feel I should add some extra detail. The central portion of the dessert was shaped like a fort, complete with ramparts and a butterscotch moat. Around the outside was a ring of sponge that was decorated with neat triangles of sugared pear beside a further defensive perimeter of cream. I couldn't decide whether I wanted to explore it or plunge my face into it. Evidently, the latter option was always going to win, and I stormed the battlements.

I have never overindulged on drink to such an extent that I have no memory of what occurred around me. In fact, the most alcohol I have ever consumed was when my father attempted to make his own cider, and he insisted that we tried every batch. After my fourth glass, I became very giggly and then fell asleep in my chair, but it did not compare to how I felt when polishing off my second portion of Cook's quite masterful pudding.

I really can't explain what happened, but when I looked up from my empty bowl, Christabel had already left the table, the plates had been cleared away and the other diners were getting up to congregate in a neighbouring room. It was most uncanny.

"That was delicious," I stated, unashamed of just how much I'd enjoyed the meal.

"You've already said that, Christopher." Quiet concern was my mother's standard tone for the day. If I don't describe anything to the contrary, you can assume that was how she spoke to and regarded me.

"But it was the most exquisite dessert I've eaten in perhaps my whole life."

"Yes… You said that too. Are you quite all right?" Standing over me, she put the back of her hand to my forehead. "You're sweating and your pupils are really rather large. Perhaps we should call Dr Merrick to take a look at you."

I sighed a happy sigh. "Really, Mother, I have never felt better." I licked the corners of my mouth to savour the incredible taste. I even considered popping to the kitchen to ask Cook for a third helping and, conceivably, her hand in marriage.

My grandfather had maintained a happy-go-lucky attitude throughout lunch and even he looked a little concerned, though it turned out that I was not the cause of his worries.

"Interesting," he said. "I wonder…" He did not explain any further but followed the others into the front lounge.

"I love you, Grandfather," I called after him and my mother had to take a step back to contemplate me.

"Christopher, what in heaven's name has got into you?"

Her shocked tone made me sit up a little straighter and consider exactly what *had* got into me. "I don't know… In fact… Oh my goodness, I think I'm drunk on apple Charlotte!"

"You can't be drunk, Christopher. There's nothing intoxicating in apples, flour, bread, sugar and egg."

I had a good think. "Perhaps the apples had fermented?"

"I very much doubt it." Shaking her head in bemusement, she helped me up to standing. "And besides, your grandfather had quite as much as you, and he's as sober as a judge."

I couldn't move very fast, as I'd clearly eaten far more than was good for me, but we eventually made it to the front lounge – or, as I'd come to think of it, Delilah's salon. When she wasn't dashing around outside or upstairs asleep, this seemed to be the room that the friendly beast enjoyed most. It was the brightest in the house, for one thing, and the only one not filled with portraits, photographs and sketches.

As it was free from such personal touches, I could only assume it had been kept for entertaining. There was yet another piano in there, only this one was far bigger. A baby grand dominated the space in the centre of the room and provided our golden retriever with the perfect canopy under which to rest her weary bones. There was enough seating to accommodate a sizeable audience too, and I half hoped that one of the Templeton-Swifts would be putting on a concert for us.

My mother deposited me in an armchair in front of one of the high windows, which looked over the drive and up the grassy hill that I'd accidentally driven down the day before.

"So, who plays the piano?" I asked, still not quite myself.

"I certainly do," Tiffin responded from his position beside the fireplace. He couldn't hide just how eager he was to perform again.

"Not you, you dolt." Lettice rose from her seat to poke her brother in the ribs. "He's talking about Mummy."

"That's right. It was our dear old mother who taught me how to play." Tiffin looked a little chastened by his sister's punishment.

"I suppose musical instincts often run in a family." My grandfather had found a sunny spot in the corner and looked as though he had settled down for another "long think with eyes firmly closed." I should have known that his senses would still be firing when there were suspects around.

"Yes, I suppose so," Tiffin said in a strangely dreamy voice. I wondered if he was thinking back on his childhood, his beloved mother at the piano, the house full of music and laughter.

"Do you mind telling me about her?" the wily old detective enquired.

Lettice had a long look at him just then and, though I expected Tiffin to be the talkative one, it was she who answered. "Mummy was special. There was something so joyous and gentle about her. I remember when I used to come home from school, and we'd walk along the river together and talk as old friends." A single tear ran down her left cheek, and I could see how hard it was to come back to this place with all the memories it contained.

"She was a lovely old girl, that's for sure," Tiffin added, sounding as though he was talking about a former pet rather than his mother. "A real dazzler of a person. You know, kind, friendly, outgoing. All the things one could want in a parent."

"That's very touching to hear you talk about her in such a way," my own mother replied. She was the nicest person in the whole of England, so of course she'd be moved by their story.

"What about you, Devyn?" Grandfather's voice boomed across the open piano to a shadowy spot in the far corner of the room where, apparently, the third sibling was concealed. I couldn't see him through the great beams of sunlight which cut through the windows in diagonals. "Were you close to your mother?"

As soon as he was addressed, I heard his breathing and could imagine the glowering expression on his lips. "Everyone's close to their mother, aren't they?"

Grandfather shook his head doggedly. "I wouldn't say that. In fact, I knew men from my days working in London who were happier to see me strolling through their neighbourhood of an evening than the women who bore them. I once arrested a man for pushing his poor old mother into the Thames."

There was a gasp from Lettice and Tiffin at this point, but my own dear mater was used to such stories and barely reacted.

"Could she swim?" There was a jocular tone to Tiffin's question, but it was undermined by the serious expression he wore.

"Let's hope so." Grandfather crossed his arms, and I realised at this moment why he had chosen that precise spot. From there, he had a view of the whole room. "Let's hope that she swam the length of the river, right out to sea and across the channel to France. That is perhaps the most optimistic conclusion, as no one ever saw her again in England."

Lettice looked away then, and I bet she wished Lord Edgington would return to his hilarious patter from lunchtime.

He would not oblige. "Tell me, now that I've got you all here, what exactly caused you to move so far from home? What drove you out of your father's life so dramatically, and why did you come back now?"

I was interested to see that, even though he was hidden, Devyn's two siblings turned in his direction, clearly deferring to his judgement on the matter.

"You go first," the big chap's voice seemed to materialise in the space between us, as though he had run across the room.

"I'm sorry?" Grandfather responded, and I wondered whether he was just as unsure who Devyn had addressed as I was.

"You heard me," the bruiser shot to his feet so that the light now shone upon him. "You go first, Lord Edgington. Tell us what you've worked out about our dear dead dad, and I'll tell you why he didn't like me anymore." I'd never heard such a well-spoken man infuse his speech with such aggression.

I could trust my grandfather not to be intimidated by this behaviour. Though he would have lost in a physical fight with Devyn, in a battle of wits, the feeble-minded chap didn't stand a chance. "Fine. As, in one sense at least, I came here for your benefit, I will reveal everything I have discovered."

Devyn walked around the piano and sat on the stool to listen. "Go on, then. I'm all ears."

That same hesitance passed over his brother and sister whenever he spoke, and I saw Tiffin help his sister down into her chair once more and place his hand on her shoulder as though for protection. They truly were an odd bunch.

Never one to snub the offer to take to the stage, Lord Edgington seized his amethyst-topped silver cane and rose to his full, imperious height. "I came here this weekend having already carried out some preliminary inquiries. I discovered that your stepmother had grown up in a very poor part of London, which I had patrolled during my days on the force. It struck me as interesting that she would have married a man of some wealth and standing, though I cannot say this is the first such case I have encountered."

"You see, I told you she was nothing but a ragamuffin parvenu," Tiffin announced with some pride. His brother raised one hand to silence him, and it worked.

"Christabel Quintin had been married twice before. Both gentlemen died at a comparatively young age, which was another point of curiosity for me. Such coincidences are no guarantee of a wicked nature, though, and I would need more evidence to condemn the woman as a murderer."

Slowly and conscientiously, Devyn rolled his sleeves up as I imagine he had so many times when working as a butcher. He must have had more muscles in his forearm than I did in my whole body, and I wondered if this little show was another attempt to intimidate the famous detective.

"A murder was predicted and has now taken place, but that only makes me wonder whether whoever wrote me the letter to summon me to Riverside Keep knew about the killing in advance."

"Daddy wrote to you," Lettice began, but she'd lost her confidence before the words were out and glanced at her younger brother.

"Yes, that's what I was led to believe. But how could that make sense when I'd already received a letter in your father's hand that was barely legible? How could he have recovered from his stroke to such an extent that he could compose and transcribe a comparatively comprehensible epistle? The writing was a decent imitation, but I am certain that the letter that accused your stepmother of wicked intentions was not written by Hugo Templeton-Swift. What I still cannot say is why it was sent. Did the person who wrote it intend to harm or protect your father? Was it written out of fear for what might happen to a vulnerable, elderly man, or to shift the blame onto his young wife?"

"So then who wrote the darn thing?" Tiffin spat across the room, his nerves showing.

"I'd like to know that myself," Devyn agreed, with his fist wrapped up in the palm of his other hand.

Grandfather just smiled. "Fear not. We will know all before too long." Rather than continue with his explanation, he made them wait and went for a short stroll over to the window. I noticed the two detectives were sitting outside in their car having a sandwich and now gave their emissary a wave. He couldn't acknowledge them in such a fashion as it would have broken the tension he'd so skilfully orchestrated – though I believe he might have winked so as not to appear rude.

"I also discovered a small bottle of liquid morphine in your father's bed. I have spoken to his doctor, and he informs me that he had prescribed no such medicine, which leads me to two inevitable doubts. First, we must discover from where such a dangerous and addictive substance could have come and, second, why it was left behind when your father died."

I was busy considering a third point at this moment. As Grandfather's assistant, was I expected to contribute anything to the discussion? I'd barely said a word since my pudding-induced funny turn. So, what exactly was my job in this scenario? And furthermore, how could I become a good detective myself without being able to summarise the facts of the case in such an efficient manner as my mentor? Perhaps I should have been taking notes.

Grandfather turned back from the window to shake his head at me. I could only conclude that he knew exactly what I was thinking. He had a habit of reading my mind – or perhaps just my over-expressive facial displays.

"And so, in conclusion," he said, facing the three siblings once more, "I have discovered quite as much in this intriguing case as that which there is still to discover. But discover it, I will. Before very much longer, I will have a clear sense of how the different players in this household fit together, of who is innocent and who stood over your father last night to press a pillow to his face until his life was extinguished. This shared interest between us is surely enough of a reason for you to tell me everything you know."

Standing in the natural spotlight in the middle of the room, he straightened his imperious form and pulled on one cuff to tug a crease from his long grey jacket. With his eyes fixed on the three suspects, he had thrown down the gauntlet.

CHAPTER TWENTY-THREE

"Dad and I did not have the relationship for which a son would hope." It was rather remarkable to see the closed-book that was Devyn Templeton-Swift finally open. "It's no secret, and I haven't tried to hide it. The fact is that I wasn't like him. He wanted me to work in the City or become a lawyer, but I had other ideas." I hadn't expected Devyn to speak with such passion, and I could certainly relate to his sad tale. "Even when I was an infant, I think I knew deep down that I wasn't like the rest of the family. I wasn't smart or creative. I didn't have any instincts for business or mathematics."

Goodness me, these words could have spouted from my very own mouth, and I was tempted to stand up and clap. The power of the man's speech was remarkable; he'd stunned his brother, sister and even the eminent lord into silence. I really should have been taking notes!

"Things came to a head when I was due to go to university. I didn't see myself fitting in at Oxford, or wherever he wanted to send me, and I told him just that."

"He didn't take it well?" Somewhat predictably, Grandfather looked at me as he asked this question.

"You could say that…" Devyn paused, and I was moved to see that the big, brutish man was just as susceptible to emotion as any of us. He couldn't speak for a moment but, still sitting at the piano, glanced down at the swirling patterns on the Shiraz carpet at his feet. "He said I would have no future without a proper education, and I told him I'd rather make my own way in the world."

Grandfather allowed the chap a few minutes to gather his thoughts. "Your stepmother mentioned that you wanted him to invest in your business proposal. Was that when things came to a head between the two of you?"

The mention of the young interloper in the family seemed to trigger a brief flare of anger, but he fought it off and managed to find his composure. "No, that was a few years later. It took me some time to get to that stage. After school, I admit I wasn't myself. I spent time with people with whom I shouldn't associated. I acted like an imbecile and ran up debts I couldn't pay."

I was trying to connect the story he was telling with what we'd already seen of him that weekend. His spiky personality, less than perfect manners and occasional dialectal barbarities made more sense in the light of his youthful indiscretions. What I took most from the monologue, though, was that, if I didn't devise a plan for my life soon, I could end up just like the rogue before me!

"And to give Dad his due, he forked out each time. He liked me a little less with every new transgression, but he continued to support me. I must have been twenty-three when it got too much for him to abide. I'd spent all those years listening to his diatribes against my wicked ways, but the point at which he couldn't stand it anymore was when I actually tried to make something of myself."

He ground to a halt again, and his brother came to stand closer in support. Tiffin didn't say anything, but he made his presence felt, which I thought was jolly brotherly of him. I realised then that, for all that we bickered, my brother and I were just the same. Perhaps that's why we have siblings in the first place. They're not so important when times are easy, but we can always rely on them to catch us when we fall.

"What of the war?" Grandfather asked. I was surprised by his change of topic, but he was generally aware of every date, fact and piece of evidence as I daydreamed about birds and buns, so I imagine he knew what he was doing. "You served abroad, surely?"

"Right." Devyn nodded to himself and took a deep breath to relate something from that terrible period. "Though I'd rather forget it, you're correct. I spent the best part of two years in France. I think that Dad hoped it would make a man out of me, but I was just as dissolute afterwards as I had been before, if perhaps a little more cynical about the men in charge. It doesn't matter if it's my good old dad, some toffee-nosed policeman or my commanding officer, I've spent my life being ordered about by someone."

"That seems to be how we shape our societies. It's true." There was an apologetic note in Grandfather's voice, but he said no more, and Devyn soon picked up his thread.

"When I was in Arras, I met a bloke who told me that he had a tip on how we could make some money once the fighting was over. He reckoned things would change and that the bankers and old rich families of the past would be swept away by a broom of our own making." This sounded distinctly like communism to me, but I wasn't about to make a squeak whilst he was holding forth. "He'd heard about a great stretch of land near Baku where the prospectors believed there was oil."

"Baku?" Grandfather asked. "That's in Azerbaijan."

"Well, the Azerbaijan Soviet Socialist Republic these days, but, yeah, close enough." I noticed that the longer he spoke, the more slang and argot had invaded his speech. Perhaps he was back in those trenches in his head just then, with all our airs and graces far away. "After the war, there was a brief window when we could have made a fortune, but Dad wouldn't give me the capital I needed, and the Russians invaded two years later."

"So that's why you really fell out with your father; it was all over money."

The fierce, animalistic expression claimed the man's face once more, and I thought he might attack. "It wasn't just money. It was pride. That was the one chance I've had in my life to make something of myself, and he let it slip from my grasp."

Despite being a younger son himself, Grandfather apparently couldn't see the pain the man had suffered and, instead, tried to respond with a rational argument. "You just admitted that the Soviets went into Azerbaijan in 1920. You'd have lost your investment."

"That's not the point," Devyn wailed and, throwing his brother's hand off his shoulder, stood up from the piano stool. "I told you, it wasn't about the money, it was about my own father believing in me."

No one made the faintest noise at this moment as the interviewer and his subject locked eyes on one another. My mother had almost disappeared, Lettice was a statue and even Delilah seemed to be holding her breath as she lay in the sun, her tail wagging silently against the carpet.

"So then you moved abroad?"

It took Devyn a few moments to calm down again. He puffed out a breath like a dragon exhaling a channel of fire. "I didn't know what I'd do when I got there, but yes. I went to New York. I had no love left for Dad. In fact, I hated this whole damn country. I took the lowliest job I could find, spent time with criminals and *women of ill repute,* as my father would have called them, all to spite him. I've done things of which I'm not proud – hurt people when I shouldn't have. But can you really blame me?"

Even normally talkative Tiffin didn't say a word. I could see that he wished to comfort the wounded animal his brother had become, but he held his peace.

"You came back twice, though, isn't that right? In the last eight years, since you left Britain, you came to visit your father in order to help choose his staff, and you came again now."

He sneered at this, perhaps impressed and infuriated by the quickness of my grandfather's mind. "That's right. I came under false pretences the first time. I played the good son when Tiffin wrote to say that Dad's health wasn't at its best. I thought I could squeeze him for a few quid, but he was as stubborn as ever. So I set him up with the worst cook I could find and an old drunk for a gardener then left him to their mercy. If I'd known he'd end up marrying some floozy, I might have stuck around to protect my inheritance."

Grandfather allowed the room to fall silent before addressing the other siblings. "And neither of you saw your father any more often in all that time." The claim went unanswered, and so he moved on to another accusation. "Perhaps Devyn isn't the only one who came this week to protect the legacy you believe you are owed."

"How dare you?" Lettice's response was a quiet scream. A long, drawn-out declaration at high pitch but low volume. "All anyone has told us our whole lives is how lucky we are to be born into such luxury. The great Hugo Templeton-Swift was a wizard with money but a pitiful father. He never hit us, but he didn't know how to love us either. We existed in his orbit until we no longer had to, and I–"

I had hoped that we would now hear the only daughter's chapter of the story, but it was not to be. Her voice broken, she peered briefly at Tiffin then ran from the room.

Grandfather watched her leave with an unreadable visage. He was cold and resolute, much as the woman's father had been depicted by his youngest child. Nobody spoke, and I struggled to imagine how this deadlock would be broken until Lord Edgington signalled to me with his hand. I needed no more prompting and went running after Lettice.

CHAPTER TWENTY-FOUR

This felt more like the work of a detective; I was pursuing a suspect, determined to uncover her secrets. While it was true that I could only keep track of her thanks to the regular sobs she emitted, and I felt like a cad for doing so, I would not abandon the task my grandfather had set.

She sped off through the hallways of Riverside Keep and I caught sight of her for the first time when I reached the garden. There was no sign of old Ned as I navigated the riotous flowerbeds and twisting paths. I passed the fountain on the central terrace and knew where she must be going.

"Wait," I called out. "Lettice, I just want to talk to you. I don't believe you're to blame for your father's death."

I don't know why I felt the need to reassure her. Unless she planned to jump into the river and escape downstream, it wasn't as if she could get away from me. In the end, she came to a stop on the little jetty, the furthest point she could get from the house without soaking her long dress.

"I'm sorry to bother you," I said, sounding as though I wished to enquire where the nearest bus stop was or ask a shop attendant if she could direct me to the menswear department. "I know how hard this weekend must be for you. I've never lost a parent, of course, though I did once have a–"

"You can't understand." It was probably a good thing she interrupted me before I mentioned my deceased rabbit, Betsy. "You can't possibly understand."

I'm afraid to say that I rather took her word for it. I was awfully close to turning around and heading back to the house, in fact. What right did I have to comfort a woman twice my age at such a difficult time?

"You don't know how impossible this all is for me," she began before I could walk away. "I thought I would be able to stick it out, but no amount of money is worth this suffering." I was taken aback by her frankness.

"So Grandfather was right. You came here because of your inheritance?"

"Of course I did." Her sobbing had subsided, but tears still fell from her half-closed eyes. "I'm sure you think I'm a terrible mercenary, but you'll realise one day just what money can do to change a life." She looked across the water and then, in a whisper that I think was meant for herself more than me, she added a short refrain, "I was going to start afresh."

I wondered for a moment what such a change would look like for a woman her age with two children and a husband in tow, but then she had already said less than flattering things about the man she had married, so perhaps he wouldn't be going with her.

"I can imagine how appealing that must seem," I said, not knowing how else to respond. She sat down on the dock and, slipping her flat shoes from her feet, put her legs into the water. There was no sign that she objected to my presence, and so I did the same.

The water was cool, fast-running, and it tickled my toes. I'm happy to say that I successfully suppressed a laugh.

"I should never have returned to Riverside Keep."

I thought this would be the time to nudge her towards the conversation I really wanted to have. "Is it because of your mother that you found it so hard to come home?" I realised that this comment was a little sudden and so I explained my thinking. "I noticed that there are no images of the three of you after you were children and found photographs in the cellar from the time your mother was ill."

"My mother…" she began, in something of a daze, as though the words made no sense to her. She peered around at me and studied my face for a few seconds before continuing. "My mother was a good person. I loved her very much."

Rather than unlocking the secrets of this flighty character, my question appeared to have sent her into hiding. Something came over her at this moment, and she donned a new mask with which to carry out the conversation. I must have seen twenty different versions of Lettice over the last day, but the one thing they all had in common was the fear that occasionally peeked out from inside of her.

"Do you mind me asking how she died?" I prompted in my most polite Oaktonian voice. If there was one thing my school had taught me, it was how to be obsequious.

She turned back to the water and shook her head. The

vulnerability she had previously displayed had been replaced with an indescribable void.

"Mother was ill for several years. I was practically an adult, and I suppose I took a lot of the burden on myself. Daddy was still working then and would be away for long periods, and so it was just the four of us here. It broke my heart to see her so sick."

My brain raced off in search of some connection between the death of Margery Templeton-Swift and our investigation that weekend. "What about your father, then? Did he still love your mother?"

She shrugged and allowed her fingers to dance across the surface of the water. "I suppose he did. I've no reason to believe otherwise. But it was his money to which he was truly married. He was a creature of business; family is an abstract concept to such men."

I had expected more emotion from her. Those photos had made me think that the deceased mother would be the key to all the anguish and drama that had passed between Hugo and his three children, but only Devyn had shown much attachment to her. Lettice was strangely distant as we spoke, as though her mother's illness and demise had happened in a different life altogether.

So if not the first mother, perhaps the second… "When we arrived yesterday, you said that you couldn't bear to see Christabel slowly killing your father. But I wondered whether, perhaps, it was seeing her here in your mother's place that you couldn't tolerate."

She raised her chin and seemed to grow into this idea. "Yes, that's nicely put. You're cleverer than you look." I really tried to take this as a compliment. "Seeing one's mother replaced cannot be a pleasant experience for anyone. In fact, that's just it."

"In which case, you had no particular reason to believe that your stepmother was responsible for your father's deteriorating health?"

She hesitated then, and I could see that she was torn between these two stories. On one side, she was a grieving orphan, lost without the anchor her mother had provided and, on the other, a jealous stepdaughter, automatically suspicious of the new arrival in the family. She spent a few seconds balancing this equation before presenting her response.

"You're forgetting that Daddy had written to each of us. He expressed his belief that Christabel was poisoning him. It was the only reason I returned to Riverside Keep."

Feeling increasingly uncertain of my previously sound logic, I devised another question. "But have you witnessed anything to suggest that your stepmother really is responsible for his death?"

Lettice looked along the river to the wooded island where I'd seen the (almost definitely) geese the day before. "Well, it's simple, isn't it? Daddy predicted that someone wanted to kill him, and he died soon after. Unless he suffocated himself, I'd imagine that most people would accept the idea that the home-wrecking, money-hungry trollop who had recently forced her way into the family is to blame."

"But she wasn't the only one in the house at the time your father died."

"She was standing over him with a pillow in her hand. If your interfering grandfather hadn't turned up when he did, the police would have done their job and arrested her."

I thought that her impression of the case was a little simplistic. This made me terribly happy as it suggested that, after a year of my grandfather's tutelage, mine was not!

"There is no solid evidence that your stepmother is responsible for the murder. And if she really is to blame, Grandfather will prove it." I realised that what I was about to say would not please her and chose my words carefully. "Have you considered the possibility that your brother was involved?"

She immediately snapped out her answer. "Tiffin would never do such a thing."

"Not Tiffin." Why on Earth had she assumed I was talking about Tiffin? "I mean Devyn."

She wasn't convinced by this possibility either and shook her head.

"You must admit that, of everyone here, he has the most to gain. He has not discovered the promised land for which he left Britain. It sounds as though he has little money and has only managed to secure a job at the very lowest level of society. What's more, in Christabel, he had the perfect cover. A young wife, recently arrived in the household? Of course everyone would think she was responsible for her husband's death. Who's to say that Devyn didn't make the most of the situation and murder your father?"

When she responded, I could see just how nervous she was. She searched her pockets, presumably for cigarettes, but found nothing.

"Devyn…" this was as much as she could mutter before she had to look away across the water to the other bank. "My brother isn't a killer." She dug her nails into the wooden planks of the jetty. "How would the morphine make any sense if that were the case? Why would he have allowed you and your grandfather to stay for the weekend? And furthermore, why wouldn't he have waited for you to leave before dispatching the old man?"

These were the sort of questions that my grandfather could have answered in the time it took to count to one, but they were all too much for me. I thought perhaps there was still a route through the evidence if Devyn were trying to frame Christabel for the murder, but it seemed like a risky path to take.

"You're scared of him," was the best response I could compose. "I see it every time he speaks. You're terrified of your own brother."

She breathed in through her nostrils to steel herself. "I'm scared of the change in him. He was little more than a boy before he went abroad, and now he's this huge, fierce man. I've never said that he's perfect. Devyn is so sure of his own virtuousness, so convinced of the fault of those around him, that he does scare me at times, but that doesn't mean he would murder a helpless old man."

Even with her brother far away inside the house, she was still trembling as she spoke of him, and I knew there was more to the story than she was willing to share.

"Is it something that happened when you were children? Is that why he unnerves you?"

"Oh, Christopher, you are so young." She spoke as though she was suddenly much older. She sounded eighty, one hundred, a thousand years old. "Not everything in this life can be explained via a quick peek into an unhappy childhood."

She'd become quite superior, but I knew this was yet another persona she had adopted to deal with my questioning. It was my turn to become emotional. In fact, I was quite angry that she would speak to me in such a manner. I'd been polite and understanding. I'd even refrained from accusing her of complicity in a terrible crime.

"I overheard the conversation you had with Tiffin when you were smoking below my window." My diction was clear, the words carefully delivered. "You said your appearance before us yesterday was an act. You said you were sure my grandfather would see through it. And then your brother reassured you that it would all be worth it for the money."

I'd expected her to cry out in pain as my knowledge became apparent, but instead she just laughed. She tipped her head back and, for the second time that day, she absolutely howled. "Oh, Christopher, you really are too funny." She put her arm on my shoulder to support herself, as she couldn't control her body for the spasms passing through it. "And you thought that meant we were going to kill Daddy for the inheritance?"

"Well, yes!" I had to admit.

It would be another minute before she could acclimatise to the hilarity I had unleashed upon the world. I spent this time looking glum and feeling sorry for myself. It reminded me of when I was much younger, and my mean brother Albert would rag me rotten and laugh and laugh as soon as I showed how upset he'd made me. In fact, with this in mind, I take back every nice thing I'd thought about my cruel sibling just a short time earlier.

"Of course I didn't kill Daddy," she finally said with tears in her eyes (though of joy this time). "What you overheard was my fear that I'd be recognised as the selfish, unloving daughter that I really am. You see, your grandfather was right. Perhaps I shouldn't utter such words during a murder investigation, but we only came back here to protect what was ours. I have no love left for my father and only care about this estate, which may one day pass to my children."

Her amusement had been replaced by a steely determination. She pushed herself up to standing, slipped her wet feet into her shoes and, with one last shouted declaration, marched from the scene. "I'm no killer, Christopher. That is one thing which you simply cannot say."

CHAPTER TWENTY-FIVE

I was knocked for six, I can tell you that.

While, on the one hand, I had expected there to be a rational explanation for the conversation that I'd overheard – if for no other reason than the fact that I would never be so lucky as to stumble across a confession – the sudden fury that Lettice had displayed at the accusation seemed out of proportion.

Much as she had admitted to her brother, there was something performative about her whenever she spoke. Though she claimed she had only concealed her negative feelings toward her father, this didn't explain her shifts in mood. It wasn't just the fear of being implicated in a murder that had rocked her; I was certain that she was afraid for her life.

I knew then that there was only one way to discover whether the story she'd told me was the truth. She was halfway through the garden when I realised that I'd have to beat her back to the house. I sprang to my feet and ran as fast as they would go. I charted the shortest, straightest path through the Carrollian garden and shot between the sweet williams and roses, past a bed of thin, reedy plants and all the way to the Crowers' cottage before I drew level with her.

Presumably realising what I had in mind, she increased her pace. Her arms and legs pumped in that namby-pamby manner in which adults run without really running. I was on a parallel path to hers, and she kept darting glances over at me, seemingly aware that she couldn't match me for speed. This was another revelation, as but a year earlier, I'd struggled to run more than a few hundred yards in the school cross country race.

What had my grandfather done to me!? I was barely out of breath and hadn't even broken a sweat when I reached the lounge, where several of the others were still assembled.

"You," I said, pointing to Tiffin as I entered. "I need to speak to you."

He was back at the piano, gently bothering the keys in a low octave. He immediately stopped and looked around in a panic as I approached.

"What's got into you, boy?" my grandfather demanded from his seat in the corner.

I had no time for him; I knew that Lettice would be close behind.

"I need you to come with me this moment." I laid my hand on

Tiffin's shoulder and pulled him off the stool. He didn't resist so much as go limp in defence, much as a rabbit would in a fox's mouth.

Finding the strength to walk, he finally supported his own weight. "Steady on, lad. I'll go with you. Just don't rip my shirt. I bought it at Harrods!"

There was a door in the far corner of the room, beside which Devyn had previously been sitting. I had no idea where it might lead, but it seemed like the place to go to avoid his approaching sister. I flung it open and pushed my next suspect inside, just as I heard her footsteps.

Slamming the door behind me, I found myself in a room the size of a W.C. There was barely space for the two of us to stand in what turned out to be the family's drinks room. There was a cabinet filled with cut-glass stemware, a table for preparing libations and a shelf covered in bottles. We had such a room back at Cranley Hall, but there was enough space to swing a proverbial cat in ours. Well, a proverbial kitten, at least.

Tiffin looked quite bamboozled. "Urmmm, if you don't mind me asking, lad," he began, his face approximately seven inches from my own, "what are we doing in this cupboard?"

I would not be cowed. "It won't take long. I have some questions for you, and I need the answers right this moment."

"Jolly good! Well, there's nothing like a dose of alacrity. That's what I always say."

He'd distracted me from my purpose with his usual carefree tone. "Right… well, thank you."

"You're very welcome."

I twiddled my thumbs for a moment as I tried to remember exactly what questions I'd intended to put to him. I had never realised before that this was anything more than an expression, but I quite literally made my thumbs twiddle.

"Your sister!" I finally remembered.

"Lettice!" He pointed his finger at me then to show that he knew exactly to whom I was referring. As there was very little space around us, he knocked a bottle as he did so. It wobbled but did not fall down and I thought that a rather perfect metaphor for myself that day.

"Yes, Lettice. I heard you talking to her."

"Well, it is something I indulge in from time to time." He was far too jovial a chap to interrogate with any ferocity. Perhaps my grandfather would have managed to put the fear of God into him, but I'd merely made him smile.

"No, I mean… I heard Lettice say that she was worried my grandfather would see through her act. And you told her to calm down and think of the money."

Perhaps I was some sort of sophisticated humourist, as he had a good laugh at this. "Oh… whoops. It looks as though you've caught us red-handed!"

I gasped. "You mean to say that you're the killers after all?" Optimistic, I know.

"No, my boy. Lettice was merely saying that she felt like an imposter here. She didn't have much love for our dear papa. I felt much the same way, of course. Though, now he's gone, I can't help missing the old hound."

My stomach sank at the confirmation of his sister's story, but there were still elements of their conversation that didn't sit right in my mind. "'Laughing all the way to the bank,' is the phrase you used. I'm sorry, but that doesn't fit with your sister feeling a tad guilty over her relationship with her father. What were you really discussing?"

He tried to stand back to get a better look at me but only succeeded in rattling the glasses behind him. "My dear boy, you have a very suspicious mind. It's true that I could have used a more diplomatic turn of phrase, but it's nothing so sinister. As your grandfather established, my brother, sister and I came here on quite the most mercenary grounds. We didn't want that silver-tongued Jezebel stealing our inheritance out from under us. Father was old. Even if someone hadn't decided to murder him, he would have died before long. When that happened, if we could show that Christabel had been poisoning him as our father himself had written, we would have been sure of receiving the estate. There is nothing more nefarious in what you overheard than that."

Their stories were perfectly aligned. It almost made me wonder whether they'd spotted me eavesdropping and planned for just such an eventuality. But, no, that would have been quite impossible. I was floored by his response and struggled for anything more to say.

He attempted to put his hand on my shoulder, but there really wasn't the room. "I can understand why you'd think such a thing." He reflected on the misunderstanding for a moment. "Obviously, you're here to help your grandfather as best you can, but I can assure you that my sister is no killer."

"So what about you?" I thought I'd give it one last attempt.

More laughter ensued. "I couldn't kill a goat. Not even an old one that had been sick for a long time."

"But you said you go hunting in Scotland." I'd got him!

"That's a very different matter altogether. Shooting something from a long distance is nothing like looking an innocent creature in the eyes and snuffing the life out of it. I'm no savage."

I hadn't got him.

I was trying to understand the difference between killing an animal and, well… killing an animal, when he added a short explanation. "I know it might sound contradictory, but, with hunting, the thrill is in achieving my goal, not hurting the beautiful beasts I take as trophies. To be perfectly honest, I don't have much to do with that side of things. I have a beater who picks up the carcases and sends them to the taxidermist. A few weeks later, I get the mount back for my wall with the creature looking just as alive as if I'd gone to have a chat with him in the valleys and glens of the Highlands. Now, if you don't object, I'd rather like to…"

He pointed towards the exit, and we shuffled around one another for him to leave. It was a tight fit, but he managed to push past.

"Shall I close the door after me?" he asked once he'd escaped. I shrugged in reply, and so he did just that.

Stored away in there like an old bottle, I couldn't fathom how I'd been so wrong about them. If Tiffin and Lettice weren't involved in their father's death, and we still hadn't discovered any real evidence on Devyn, didn't that mean that Christabel was guilty after all?

I knew I should return to the land of open spaces and other humans, but my time in the gloomy cupboard – which had nothing but a small window above the door for light – was oddly illuminating. I mean, I had no idea who the killer would turn out to be, no new theories of why Hugo Templeton-Swift had been killed, or why we'd been summoned to Riverside Keep, but a bit of peace and quiet made me feel a great deal less frustrated by these failures. And that was surely something worth celebrating.

CHAPTER TWENTY-SIX

As tempting as it was to spend the rest of the day in my private, though poky, sanctuary, I knew that my grandfather would only tolerate me hiding away from the world for so long.

"Ahh, Christopher, there you are. I was intending to send a search party to look for you if you hadn't returned within a few minutes. Is the drinks cabinet a worthy destination for one's travels? Would you recommend it for our summer holiday, perhaps?"

I was glad to see that none of our suspects were present to hear his witty routine.

"Yes, it's quite lovely."

"Leave the poor boy alone, Father," my mother scolded him. "Let Christopher tell us what he's discovered."

I couldn't abide the idea of disappointing my mother – which, now that I thought of it, explained why I hadn't told her about my lack of future plans – but there really wasn't much to tell. I sat in the chair beside hers, and Delilah immediately jumped on top of me. I swear she still believed she was a puppy and had no conception of the fact that she weighed almost as much as I did.

"So, boy, what did your interviews reveal?" Grandfather raised his eyebrows so that they practically merged with his hairline as he awaited my answer.

"Nothing."

"Full sentences please, Christopher."

I was truly surly by now and responded accordingly. "I have discovered nothing of interest whatsoever."

Far from criticising me, as I'd expected, he pulled on his long beard and said, "Hmmm, that's interesting. Very interesting, in fact."

"I know nothing more now than when I left this room half an hour ago," I added, to impress him further. "Nothing at all!"

"Perhaps you should tell us what happened all the same." The old fellow was surprisingly contemplative on the matter. "Just to ensure that your concept of nothingness matches my own."

I rose once more. I felt that I would need all my faculties about me if I was to recall every last detail that I hadn't discovered during my interviews. As I had learnt from both my grandfather and Sherlock Holmes, a good pace back and forth helps clear the mind. Delilah jumped over to the neighbouring chair and I set to work.

"I left here with three key questions that needed answering." Pace, pace, pace. "First, I wished to discover more about the exact relationship between the three siblings and their parents. On a trip downstairs to the cellar this morning, I spotted a box of photographs of the family from when Mrs Margery Templeton-Swift was dying. There are no images from that time on display in the house, and I wondered whether it was her departure from this earthly plane which had led to the rift between Hugo and his offspring."

"I had made a similar observation." Grandfather crossed one leg over the other and leaned back in his chair to enjoy my speech. "But time is of the essence, Christopher. Perhaps you could summarise a little more concisely?"

"Oh… right, yes. Will do." I tried to remember where I'd got to and couldn't, so I started again. "There were three questions to which I wished to know the answers when I–"

"You're repeating yourself, Christopher," my mother helpfully informed me.

"I'm aware of that. Thank you, Mother, and if you could both refrain from interrupting, I won't have to start a third time." I huffed out a disgruntled breath and realised I'd lost my place again. "Where was I?"

"The second question on your list!" Father and daughter declared as one, and I gathered my thoughts.

"That's right, the second question with which I left here was…" I had to remember the first item on the list and go from there. Even Delilah let out a censorious bark, proving that, these days, everyone is a critic. It went, *woof woof woof,* which presumably meant, *Hurry up, Christopher!* "…well, it concerned the conversation I'd overheard between Lettice and her older brother."

"And the third thing?" Grandfather asked with some relief that we were getting towards the end of my very short but surprisingly time-consuming list.

"The fear that Lettice has shown around in the presence of her younger brother."

"A fine summation, indeed, Christopher." My mother really is an angel and clapped appreciatively.

Grandfather was looking contemplative and allowed himself a few moments before prompting me for more. "You've isolated three points which I myself have been mulling. Yes... I did well to send you after Lettice." He seemed very pleased with his delegating once again. "Now, tell me exactly what she said on these matters."

I tried to recall her wording and the way in which our conversation had developed. I came back once more to the simple truth that she'd said very little. "Well, that's the thing. She had a good excuse for all of the suspicious behaviour I put to her. To my surprise, the death of her mother does not appear to be the cause of the rift with Hugo. In fact, though I overheard her saying that she was guilty of duplicity, she claims she was merely worried that we would notice the lack of love she felt for her father. As for her relationship with her brother, Devyn, she admits that he is an intimidating fellow. She even says that he has returned an altogether rougher character after his time abroad. But she resolutely denies that he could be the murderer."

"She really did tell you nothing," my mother muttered with a note of astonishment.

"Yes, but she said it all with great heart. Though there were moments when I doubted that she'd entrusted me with all the details of her story, I cannot say that I ever concluded she was lying outright."

"I have no doubt she spoke with deep conviction." Grandfather kept me focussed on the matter at hand. "What happened after that? You ran back here in quite a state."

I stopped my walking and smiled at him. "That is because I did something rather clever. I returned to check that her brother Tiffin's version of events matched her own."

Delilah looked up at me from her spot by her master's feet. "And did it?"

She didn't actually say these words, but I could tell that's what she was enquiring with her big brown eyes. Perhaps this was another skill I'd learnt from my grandfather. I'd soon be able to converse with the canine just as he could.

"The two stories were presumably identical," Lord Edgington said, to answer his faithful hound's question. "Going by the fact that the two of them told you nothing worth knowing whatsoever." He brought his bony fist down on the arm of his chair and the windows behind him shook.

"Nothing whatsoever," I confirmed. "And I'm certain they can't have known that I'd heard their conversation, so it isn't as though they would have thought to make up an excuse for it in advance."

Mother leaned forward to escape the glare of the sunshine that had reached her seat opposite the window. "Isn't it possible that you're overlooking something, Christopher?"

"No, I promise. I really learnt nothing useful in the slightest."

Grandfather did not reply for a few seconds. I could tell from his pose that he was thinking very hard. This might sound like an idle claim, but he had his fist raised to his chin, his ankle held over his knee and his back hunched. "As I said before, that really is very revealing."

I could only imagine that my mother was wondering, much like me, what was so revealing about nothing. The only thing it told me was that I wasn't such a genius detective after all. Before we could ask our distinguished leader what he had discovered, he was up on his feet and headed to the door.

"Come with me."

My mother could be far more impudent to the eminent detective than I dared and did not immediately do as he'd instructed. "I'm sorry, Father. But was it the dog you were talking to or us?"

He peered back into the room to apologise most graciously... not really. He stuck his head around the door and said, "The whole damn lot of you, obviously. There's someone we still haven't interviewed." And then he wandered off ahead of us.

I couldn't imagine to whom he was referring. It seemed to me that we had finally crossed off the suspects on our list of potential interviews. Whoever it was, I would have to wait to learn his name as this plan was soon abandoned.

"Oh, goodness!" my mother said on my behalf, as I was quite speechless.

We'd got halfway across the garden when Grandfather rushed forward to the fountain in the middle of the elegant terrace where a well-dressed woman had been dumped headfirst into the water.

Putting his finger to her neck in search of a pulse, he confirmed my fears. "I'm afraid she's quite dead."

CHAPTER TWENTY-SEVEN

I couldn't understand how such a thing had happened right under our noses. It had only been half an hour since I'd spoken to her, but Lettice Templeton-Swift was no more. My temptation was to mourn the poor creature. Though not as warm-hearted a character as some I'd known, she seemed like a decent person. I could also now conclude that she was innocent of the crime which we had come to Riverside Keep to investigate.

But why would someone have killed both the patriarch of the family and his second-born child? If it had been Tiffin we'd found, that might have made sense as, being the oldest child, he was next in line to the family fortune after Christabel. Rather than making our task any easier, Lettice's murder added to the mystery of our killer's motives.

These were the thoughts that were passing through my head as we fell into a hazy stasis before Grandfather decided the best course of action. "Both of you, search the house for the others. Try to remember where you find everyone and what they are doing."

My mother and I exchanged a brief glance and bolted back inside. We separated at the stairs, so that I could search the ground floor while she went up to the bedrooms. I found Tiffin in the back lounge, playing an old music hall song once more.

"What is it?" a voice enquired as I thundered over to him. It was not Tiffin but the maid, Wilhelmina, who addressed me. "What's happened?"

"It's Lettice…" It was normally my grandfather's job to break bad news, and I didn't know what to say. "She's… Well, I'll get the police first, but perhaps you should both come with me."

By the time we got back to the hall, my mother was descending the stairs with Devyn and Christabel in tow. I opened the door to wave to the police, and the two inspectors looked lively and came rushing over. Like a tour guide at some famous monument, my mother led the party out to the garden, and faces soon fell.

Grandfather must have gone to collect the missing members of the Crower family as Ned and Betty were standing beside him; they looked just as distraught as the dead woman's siblings. I watched our suspects one by one to decipher some sign of guilt. I noticed that the good widow was in a bathing robe and that her hair was wet. This could have explained what she was doing at the time when Lettice was killed or, alternatively, be another sign of her culpability. What better way to hide evidence than a quick wash and a change of clothes?

Devyn tensed his muscles as though appalled at the sight before him. He peered about at his kin, perhaps looking for the killer, or attempting to disguise his own part in the crime. But it was Tiffin whose reaction was most pronounced. He fell to his knees on seeing the body and let out a heart-wrenching scream. It was painful to watch and triggered some sort of attack in the poor fellow. He fanned his hands in front of his face, and his head snapped from right to left and back again. I wondered what he was looking for at first, then realised that it must have been his sister for whom he searched – for Lettice, alive and well.

"No!" was all he could say, but he repeated it over and over again until it lost all meaning and became little more than a sound.

Devyn waited in the hope that someone else would deal with his brother, but with Lettice gone, it fell to him now. It was interesting to see the stark difference in the two siblings' reactions: one angry, one terrified. Even as Devyn pulled his elder brother up to standing, Tiffin reached his hand back to us. It was as though, caught in the clutches of the grim reaper, he was desperately trying to avoid his final journey to the grave. Well, perhaps that's a little over-dramatic, and he simply didn't want to be parted from his sister, but that's what occurred to me as I watched them leave.

"This is not on, Lord Edgington," one of the inspectors said to break the hush that had seized us. "We left you in charge of the house. We did not imagine you would allow another person to be murdered."

I had expected Grandfather to react with his usual superiority and vitriol, but he could summon no response. He stared at our second victim, who now lay on her side on the paving stones. Lettice had her eyes open and drops of water from the fountain still decorated her fine lashes. Her lips were parted as though she had something she wished to say, and her arms had fallen closed around her body. I noticed that there was still a large wet patch on the ground around her, where the water from the pond had splashed out of the basin as she died.

I couldn't help feeling that we had failed the tragic figure, and my grandfather clearly agreed.

"I never thought…" he began, but his voice was weak, and his normally stentorian tone trembled. "I couldn't have imagined that the killer would strike again in broad daylight. He was so careful when carrying out the first murder that I thought we would be safe."

I could tell that he was in no fit state to lead an investigation at that moment, and so I did something rather out of character; I stepped in front of the group and took charge.

"Did any of you see or hear anything in the last…" I looked back at the famous detective for the time of death.

"I'd say she died no more than ten minutes ago; there was still blood seeping from the wound on the back of her head when we arrived."

"…in the last ten minutes?" I allowed my voice to rise and looked into the faces of our remaining suspects.

"I was in the shower in my room." Apparently seeing the need to explain her absence over the last hour, Christabel looked quite defiant. "I took a nap after lunch as I always do, and it's been so hot today that I decided to wash."

"Wilhelmina?" I asked, turning to the maid. "When did Tiffin come into the room you were cleaning?"

I noticed then that she looked almost as nervous as the elder Templeton-Swift son had. She turned to her parents in the hope that they would offer her solace, but they could do nothing but gaze back with the same sad expressions on their faces that they had worn since spying the body.

"I…" she tried and, when that didn't work, she started once more. "He came in just a little while before you did."

"In what sort of state was he?" Yet more energy appeared to have drained from my broken grandfather. His face pale, he sat with his back to the hexagonal base of the fountain.

Again, the maid needed a moment to compose her thoughts. "He was a little agitated, maybe." She looked up to the perfect blue sky and cast her memories upon it as a shadow puppeteer uses a paper screen. "Yes, he didn't see me at first. He stood beside the piano looking quite unnerved until he rolled his sleeves up and sat down to play."

"And how long ago exactly was that?"

She looked straight at me, and I could see how she hesitated. Her eyes raced over to her parents once more before she replied. "Around ten minutes. He seemed worried, but not like he had just done anything terrible. And the music he played was incredibly jolly."

"Ladies and gentlemen," one of the D.I. Simpsons began. "This is a terrible situation, and it might be best if anyone who feels unsafe in this house stayed elsewhere tonight." He paused and looked down at the man they had put in charge. "Former Superintendent Edgington is still best placed to solve this terrible crime, and we will now discuss the correct way to progress with our investigation."

"It would be my recommendation," the second D.I. began, "that you all stay together in one place until the killer is identified. I will have a word with the kitchen staff to see whether they can provide afternoon tea while we examine the scene of the crime."

Grandfather was heartened by their further show of trust in him. He pulled himself up on the stone wall and to his full height, rose like an elderly phoenix. "Violet, Christopher, one of you should go with the others and make sure that everyone is safe. You will also have to collect the grieving brothers from wherever they have disappeared."

I was torn between staying to help my grandfather in his time of need and heading inside with the others to enjoy a spot of afternoon tea. It was a rare moment in which my heart won out over my stomach.

We waited for everyone to funnel inside the house, and my grandfather's usual investigative instincts came to the fore. "There's no sign of strangulation around her neck, but she appears to have suffered some trauma to the back of the skull. It would seem, therefore, that the victim was attacked from behind and fell forward into the basin of water where the killer held her down to finish the job."

The fleur-de-lis fountain continued its gentle trickle as though nothing terrible had occurred. I always find it rather tragic that the world keeps turning at such moments. The garden was just as beautiful, the sun equally bright, but Lettice lay on the ground, a mere husk of the person she had been minutes earlier.

"Can we rule out a woman's involvement this time?" the second Simpson enquired. I do wish they'd told us their Christian names so that we could have differentiated between one and the other. I couldn't even describe them as Tall Simpson and Short Simpson. They were nearly identical in every way! Perhaps they were pulling our legs, and they were actually brothers.

Grandfather appeared sceptical of their suggestion. "Not at all. If the initial blow had been delivered with force, the victim would have been quite incapacitated. Little real strength would have been needed to maintain her head beneath the water."

"So who do you think the culprit is?" asked, let's call him… 'Simpson on the left'.

Lord Edgington's expressive visage froze for a count of five. "I thought I had him. I really did. But this presents me with a whole new collection of doubts. I am no longer certain of the evidence I had previously gathered. It seemed so simple before, but now…" He didn't finish this thought but stared down at the body at his feet.

Delilah decided she would try to be of help by sniffing around the base of the fountain. She found nothing, but it gave me an idea, and I walked over to peer into the murky pond. I saw the lily pads and even a frog, its eyes poking above the surface of the water, but it was the faintest glimpse of something in the depths that most interested me.

"Grandfather, the weapon. I think it's in there."

The three men crowded around me and 'Simpson on the right'… no, hang on. They'd shifted positions! 'Simpson on the right' had become 'Simpson on the left'. So that really didn't help things. Perhaps I should number them?

Simpson One pointed to the metallic object that was just visible, and Simpson Two put a glove on to retrieve the item.

"A candlestick," I said, just in case anyone failed to recognise the… ummm… candlestick.

"There'll most likely be a matching one somewhere in the house," said Simpson Two.

"We'll call the doctor to inspect the body and then set about finding it," said his colleague, and the two men nodded to one another efficiently.

"What should I do, Grandfather?" I knew the answer to this question would not be, *Go inside and indulge in some of Cook's Poor Knight's Pudding!* But I'd hoped for some clear instructions at least.

I could see that Lettice's death had made the great Lord Edgington doubt not only his hypothesis for the case, but his own ability to solve it. His whole being had become muted. His charisma had hidden away, his force of presence diminished, and I didn't know how to make things better again.

"Grandfather?"

He no longer looked through me but studied my face as though he was seeing me for the first time in years. "I suppose you could look around the house with the inspectors. I need…" I didn't think he would finish the sentence as he'd already begun to float away from me towards the river. "I need time by myself."

It was a phrase I was unused to hearing fall from his lips. Ever since he had chosen me as his assistant, he'd been the one pushing us on towards new experiences, but now he couldn't even be with me.

I didn't stop him. I simply stood there and watched him go. He grew smaller in my vision as he crossed the wide garden, before finally disappearing beyond a row of hedges.

CHAPTER TWENTY-EIGHT

I was at a loose end. I could go wagging my tail after the inspectors and follow them about the house like Delilah, but I knew that wouldn't help us catch the killer. So I decided to do something that, until now, propriety had forbidden.

I collected a set of keys from the hooks in the servants' dining room and went poking about the place for myself. It was no stroke of genius that had told me where I would find them, Halfpenny kept the keys to every room in Cranley in a box on the wall of the very same room back in Surrey.

I selected the ones I thought would be the most interesting and stashed them about my person in different places so that I would remember which was which. As I only had three pockets on my white linen trousers, I had to tuck a few keys into my leather Oxfords. It made walking about quite uncomfortable.

I thought I'd start with the first floor and work my way upwards, only I'd already been to most of the rooms there. I also knew that, had I gone anywhere near the dining room, my will would have crumbled, and I'd have been seduced by the scent of tea and fresh cake.

Limping a little, as the keys had now slipped down under one foot, I headed upstairs to the bedrooms. It turned out that most of them weren't locked, and so I'd suffered for nothing, but was quite pleased with my forethought, nonetheless.

I went to Christabel's bedroom first. She was still the greatest enigma to me. Beyond the question of who was a murderer, and who was innocent, I felt that I had a good understanding of each person in the household by this stage. Devyn really was a swine – even if he'd never laid a hand on another person. Tiffin was a fop and clearly loved nothing more than entertaining those around him. But Christabel could still be an angel or a devil, and I didn't know which I thought more likely.

I also couldn't be sure whether I was relieved or disappointed when I confirmed that the scene she'd left behind in her bedroom, where my mother must have found her, fitted precisely with her testimony. The bed was unmade, the bathroom mirror showed signs of condensation, and there were soap suds beneath the shower in the bathtub. It didn't rule out her involvement in Lettice's death, but neither did it prove she'd been lying.

She had no personal possessions in her room except for a photograph of her with her son when he was little more than a toddler. It made me wonder just how far a woman would go to be reunited with her child. Could little David be the reason that two members of the household had died?

I moved along the corridor to the rooms of the three siblings. Lettice's was the easiest to identify. It still had the periwinkle curtains and riding rosettes she had stuck to her wall when she was a child. There were more photographs missing and, yet again, no trace of Margery Templeton-Swift in later life. The same was true for the two brothers' rooms, though they lacked the floral fabrics and horse paraphernalia.

Tiffin's room was full of fishing equipment, which rather surprised me. There were cases full of hand-crafted flies, old tackle boxes and a selection of rods in a glass case above the bed. It reminded me of the pastimes in which he indulged up in Scotland, but I still couldn't imagine that jolly, effete fellow with a rifle or fishing rod in his hands.

Devyn's room was yet more puzzling. There was really nothing personal about it. There was a suitcase with various paper labels from American ports, a rather shabby, plain green rucksack and the long leather coat he'd worn, hanging behind the door, but that was all there was to it. It was in every other respect a nondescript guestroom. This only made sense when I tried the door opposite and discovered the bedroom he'd had as a child.

Football! That's what young Devyn had apparently loved. Before the war and his argument with his father, he'd covered his room with cigarette cards, cuttings on various F.A. Cup finals and even a signed photograph of the great outside forward Billy Meredith – I knew nothing about football, but even I'd heard of him.

Perhaps more pertinently, there was a picture by the bed of Hugo with his youngest boy upon his shoulders. The two of them couldn't have looked closer, and it rather broke my heart to consider what had passed between them as Devyn grew up. I came to see that the room had been preserved exactly the way it was when he had left home all those years before. Was that the reason that he had slept in a spare room instead of his own? So as not to mix the past with the present?

The two Simpsons were rifling through Lettice's possessions, still looking for the fabled second candlestick, but I had my mind on other things. I looked in every last remaining bedroom in that wing of the house, and there was little of interest. The only thing that struck me was that those which were not in use that weekend were quite filthy. This reminded me of the room that Wilhelmina had been cleaning to accommodate my mother. She'd only joined our travelling party at the last minute, after all, so the staff couldn't have been expected to know of her arrival. Though I suppose that meant someone had told them to prepare for my grandfather and me.

I found a dark-room with all of Hugo's photographic equipment and, just next to it, a small office that I hadn't entered before. It was not as grand as the one downstairs, where Grandfather had interviewed Dr Merrick, and looked like it could do with some tidying. It was a small, stuffy space, presumably used more for storage than work, and the desk which took up half the room was covered with books and papers. Though it was almost as dusty as the cellar, I noticed some cleaner spots.

A few books had seemingly been opened quite recently. There was an atlas, the third volume of an Encyclopaedia Britannica (covering Austria Lower to Bisectrix) and a book on oil production in modern day Europe. I could have looked for a bookmark to see what page had last been read, but I didn't want to leave my fingerprints anywhere.

The rooms on the other side of the house, where my mother, grandfather and I were staying, were even grimier than the ones I'd just inspected. It was clear that no one had tended to them in years and the impression they gave, not to mention the large population of spiders who had set up home there, was quite at odds with the neat presentation of the rest of the house.

And yet, when I climbed the narrow stairs to the top floor of the property, I was still shocked by the state of things. There was a nursery up there which looked like it was probably haunted. The wallpaper was peeling from the walls, and the paint on an old wooden cot was chipped and flaking. A platoon of tin soldiers had been scattered across the floor and the whole place smelt like mould and fungi. In fact, it was worse than that. There was a stench of something ever so nasty coming from a cupboard in the corner of the room.

A blackboard and chalk had been situated in front of it and there was a stack of old schoolbooks piled on top of a wooden chest that was blocking the door. I noticed signs once more that someone had been up there. There were no footprints, which would have been terribly useful, but there was a large channel which ran through the dust from one side of the room to the other, and I could see that the large toy chest must have been moved.

I held my nose and cleared a path to the cupboard, which was trapped in under the sloping roof. This was no easy task to accomplish one handed, I can tell you. The blackboard was light enough to move, and I made short shrift of the schoolbooks – though they did make me feel guilty for not returning to my studies that day – but when it came to the chest, I huffed and puffed and almost accepted defeat.

I considered emptying the contents, but I had shifted the thing just enough to squash myself between the chest and the wall and, from there, push it into the middle of the room. Before I could grasp the cupboard handle, the door swung open as though some spirit wanted me to find something inside. My eyes processed the contents, and an uncanny frisson of fear passed over me. I must admit that the macabre sight was so terrifying I had to take a step backwards. It's amazing I didn't scream out, but then, some things inspire such chills that we are entirely robbed of our faculties.

The cupboard was empty except for a Victorian doll that looked identical to one that my mother had owned since she was a child. Though mother loved 'Baby Jennifer', I've never seen such an ugly thing and still had nightmares about it whenever I returned home. Not wishing to spend another second there, in case the tiny porcelain devil should come to life and eat my soul, I trotted back through the nursery and was about to walk downstairs when I realised that the smell had disappeared once more.

I ran back to the cupboard and peered beneath the floorboards in case that would reveal the source of that acrid odour, but there was no sign that they'd been disturbed since the house was built. I took one more trip around the perimeter of the room, without luck, before remembering that I was a first-class nitwit and opening the chest I'd been dancing around for the last ten minutes.

That was where I found him, tucked up in the box like Houdini. He had his knees folded uncomfortably, his skin was purple and there was a ligature mark around his neck where someone had choked him. He was a tall, well-dressed fellow with hair to his shoulders and a neat black beard. I didn't have the first clue who he was, but I'd been working with my grandfather long enough to know that he was dead.

CHAPTER TWENTY-NINE

"Lord Edgington, this is becoming a nasty habit," Simpson One said. Well, I assume he was number one. He was certainly the first to enter the attic, though I cannot be certain he was the same Simpson One whom I had so christened out in the garden.

"This man was dead before I arrived in Wiltshire." The old detective sounded quite indignant. "You can't blame me for this."

I was beside myself with excitement. "Three bodies, Grandfather! In the same investigation! That's a record for us."

"Yes, boy, it's simply marvellous." He was not nearly so enthusiastic on the matter as I was.

"We'll get the doctor from the garden to have a look and then call the members of the household up here to see if they can identify the chap," (approximately) Simpson Two announced and shuffled back downstairs to do just that.

"Do you realise who this is, my boy?"

I was tempted to lie. "No. Do you?"

"I believe so. In fact, I believe I've been a prize fool for some time now. Come along, Christopher. There's no sense in standing about up here. You can be sure that the others won't tell us the name of the unlucky fellow, especially if they were the ones who killed him."

To say I was confused would be an understatement. "So, what now?"

"I told you before Lettice was murdered, there are still two people whom we haven't properly interviewed." Grandfather had left the musty attic before he finished the sentence, and we walked past Doctor Merrick with a civil nod. The poor man had his work cut out for him that day.

We went first to the sunny salon, which was deserted, and then to the kitchen where there was a case of too many cooks spoiling the atmosphere.

"Nah, that's not 'ow you cook pa-tay-tas. They need a good hour's boiling before ya serve 'em." Betty had returned to her kingdom to reclaim her throne.

Henrietta of Cranley Hall had more to say on the matter. "I can assure you, my dear, that overcooking is a guaranteed way of robbing all flavour from the vegetable and ensuring that no one will want to eat the pile of mush you've served."

Our gigantic scullery maid, Dorie, was on hand in case things got out of hand. She positioned herself next to the two women, ready to pounce.

Betty took a step closer to stare down her nose at the rival cook. "People in this house like my piles of mush. Thank you very much."

"Betty, what are you doing back here?" I thought this was an odd question, considering that Grandfather had clearly gone there looking for the woman. "You must rest after your shock this morning. Henrietta will prepare the meals. You should put your feet up (and never set foot in a kitchen for as long as you live)." He didn't actually say these last thirteen words, though I, for one, was definitely thinking them.

It was Betty's turn to sound indignant. "I was only tryin' to help!"

Henrietta turned back to her work as a smile blossomed on her face. Grandfather, meanwhile, had a favour to ask from the usurped queen of the kitchen.

"Betty, would you happen to have time for a brief conversation?"

She sized up the esteemed lord for a few moments, then shrugged her sizeable shoulders.

"If you wanna waste your time with me, that's your business." With her piece said, she marched through the side door of the house.

It was lucky the weather was so nice; I seemed to have spent an inordinate amount of time outside that day. We returned to the garden yet again and Mrs Betty Crower led us across to her family's cottage. An ambulance had presumably come to take poor Lettice away as there was no sign of the body.

Delilah had been sitting on the terrace in the sunshine, waiting for some company, but she would be disappointed. The first thing Betty said on opening her front door was, "No dogs!"

The poor creature looked heartbroken. Delilah, that is, not the fierce domestic.

"I don't know what I can tell you," she said, as she directed us into the living room where I'd seen Ned sipping his whisky the night before. In fact, he was in the exact same spot when we entered and raised his glass in celebration.

"Evening, gents. I hear there's bad business afoot. Billie just popped in to say there's been another body found. Who's dead now?"

I took a seat beside the cheerful chap, but Grandfather remained on his feet, looking at the bric-a-brac that was displayed on a Welsh dresser. There were hunting horns of various descriptions, old clocks that didn't appear to tick and a photo of the Crower family in full. It featured several burly sons, portly wives, and grinning grandchildren. They were clustered together at the seaside, in front of Brighton Palace Pier.

Grandfather snapped his heels like a soldier and answered the question. "Identity unknown, for the moment. Though I'm hoping you'll be able to help resolve some of the mysteries that we've uncovered this weekend."

"Him?" Betty bustled over to demand. "What would 'e know? It's Billie whats you want to talk to. Our Wilhelmina has got more brains than the rest of us put together. This one can't even read and write."

"True," Ned replied with some pride in his voice. "But I can tell a darn good story if anyone's willing to listen."

"I've heard toads in a pond who have more to say for themselves than you have, you old–"

My grandfather wisely interrupted at this moment. "I wish to talk to both of you."

A curious silence descended upon that cosy room just then, and I thought he might have won them over with his explanation. It didn't last long.

"Her?" Ned asked with pure wonder in his voice. "What does she know? She's a cook who can't even cook!"

Seeing the dispute that was about to engulf us, Grandfather stepped between the quarrelsome couple. "Why don't you sit down, and we'll begin?"

"Don't you want no tea?" the woman barked.

My grandfather couldn't help wincing in reply. "I'm sure we'll be fine without it."

Betty looked bewildered by the idea but plumped herself down on the sofa beside the rather elegant radio set.

Standing at a distance to view the whole room, Lord Edgington regarded his witnesses for a few moments before he began. "I've come to speak to you, as I believe you are the best placed to tell me about the past of the Templeton-Swift family."

"We don't know much about no ancient history." Ned seemed to lose some of his usual mischievous energy and sat a little lower in his chair.

"My Ned don't know much about the present neither!" Betty's joke led to some chortling across the room, but Grandfather would not be distracted from his task.

"As I understand it, you came to work here two years ago. Is that correct?"

The old gardener smiled again. "That's right, I can remember that much."

"And it was Devyn Templeton-Swift who hired you?"

"That's right. We'd seen an advertisement in 'The Lady' and moved over here from Wimbledon."

Betty had something to add to this. "It was just what we was after cos it's not often a family like the Templeton-Swifts takes on a whole team of staff in one go. All three of us needed jobs, you see?" She asked this as though it were some Gordian knot that Grandfather would have to unravel.

"I do. And can you tell me how you found Devyn at the time? Was he calm, aggressive, welcoming?"

Ned looked at his wife, and the ruddy-cheeked cook spoke for him. "Well, he's no charmer. That's for sure. But he treated us well enough. He was trusting us to oversee his father, like. So that was good of him for a start."

"Were his brother or sister here at the time?"

It was Betty who now looked hesitant. "No, we only met 'em this week. But they seem like a nice pair. Higher manners, you might say."

Grandfather turned and stared at a clock above the mantle, as though wishing time would travel faster. I wondered what was frustrating him so, but, as he hadn't given me any clue as to why we had entered that pretty abode, there really was nothing I could do to help him.

"All I can say on the matter," Ned began in a rather punctilious voice, "is that the old fellow, God rest his soul, treated us ever so nice. This cottage is a palace compared to the dark rooms we shared in the attic of the last place we lived. He furnished us with all the most modern conveniences we could have hoped for. Even gave Betty and Billie money for nice clothes. Hugo Templeton-Swift was a true gen'leman, and long may he be missed."

He concluded his tribute with a staunch nod of the head. His wife looked as though she'd rather her husband would stop blathering, while Grandfather glanced around the living room with fresh eyes.

A thought occurred to me and, as the genius present wasn't saying anything, I thought I might just as well have a go. "Do you know why Devyn came back here when he hired you?"

Ned looked at Betty, Betty looked back at Ned. It did not appear that either of them knew the answer, and so I rephrased the question.

"Or rather, do you know what happened to the last people who held your posts?"

Betty smiled at last. Well, perhaps *smile* is too strong a word for it. She grimaced with a little less force than normal. "I believe it was a combination of factors." I could only imagine they had learnt such formal expressions from Ned's radio. "The master was getting a little long in the tooth to live at Riverside Keep without proper help, and the old couple what lived here before us retired to Broadstairs."

I couldn't see how this illuminated the matter, but Grandfather seemed interested in the response. "It's rather odd that he employed so few staff for such a large residence. Did you meet your predecessors?"

"Oh, no no." Ned extracted some tobacco from a tin and stuffed it into the end of his pipe. "They were long gone when we arrived. We only ever met Devyn."

"And in what state was Hugo himself when you came here? Did he require a wheelchair?"

"Not at the very beginning. He was all right when we arrived, but things went downhill for him. Ain't that right, Betty?"

"That's right." Betty peered out of the window and had a quick yawn, apparently now bored with the conversation. "He was the age that he was." She spoke this last sentence as though it were some profound and ancient truth.

"And when Christabel arrived?" Grandfather's eyes were ablaze with curiosity.

"Well, things went even further downhiller then, didn't they, Ned?"

Her husband tapped the pipe on the small table between his chair and mine before replying. "That they did – right down into the ditch at the bottom of the hill, in fact. At least he could have a conversation before she came. At least he made sense."

"Why, of course he could." Grandfather was quite cheered by this news and even released a high, airy laugh. "You know," he began and then stopped himself as though he'd had a better idea. "The two of you may well be the most helpful people I have spoken to all weekend."

Ned looked ever so pleased at this and wiggled his bottom in his seat. "We do what we can, guv'nor. We likes to help them folks what need it."

It was at this moment that Wilhelmina appeared. She stood in the door to the living room, looking quite petrified. I could only imagine she was afraid that her parents had spouted any amount of nonsense.

Betty didn't look too pleased to see her, either, and tossed a command in her direction. "Don't go gawping at the nice gen'lemen. Get in the kitchen and start making dinner. Lord Edgington has told me I must rest after my shock, and I intend to do just that." She nodded her thanks to her guest and the ends of her mouth turned up a little.

Before we left, Grandfather had an invitation to issue. "As it happens, I was thinking of holding a small tribute to Hugo and his poor daughter this evening. What would you say to nibbles and cocktails in the garden before dinner?"

That loveable rogue Ned Crower was beside himself with excitement. "I'd say, thank you very much, M'Lord, and I'll start with a whisky flip!"

"That's the spirit!" Grandfather replied, a little flippantly considering that we were investigating our third murder of the weekend and we would soon have more dead bodies than suspects. "Ha ha… Whisky… Spirit!"

He really burst out laughing at this point and Ned copied him. "Ooh, you're a wicked one, M'Lord!"

I suppose it was an amusing enough pun. Though I hadn't even broken a smile at the similarity between *flip* and *flippantly*. I wasn't the only one who seemed surprised by the old lord's behaviour. Wilhelmina remained bolted to the spot, and her mother had raised one mole-speckled lip in confusion.

"So, it's decided, I'll see you all at seven o'clock." Grandfather was still laughing as he beckoned me to follow him back outside.

Then, the moment the door was closed behind us, and he was certain they could no longer hear, his face became deadly serious again.

"The time is almost upon us, Christopher. I have few doubts left to resolve and can say with some certainty that our killer will be spending tonight in the Devizes County Gaol."

CHAPTER THIRTY

"You don't mean that it's Betty… or Ned?" I asked as we strolled back to the house with Delilah beside us.

"No," he replied, stretching out the O like a musical note.

"Devyn then?"

"Keep guessing."

"So it must be Christabel, after all."

"I thought you said you would identify the killer before I did?"

"Wilhelmina? Tiffin?" These two had not seemed like obvious choices, but I didn't see who else could be involved.

"No and no." He was inordinately pleased with himself, and I was struggling to think who was left.

"Or, what about the inspectors? Or Dr Merrick? Or your friend Vivian?"

He crumpled his face in dismay. "None of those people were even here when Hugo was murdered."

"You've just ruled out every last suspect." I barely managed to conceal my exasperation.

Taking pity on me, he put one hand on my shoulder. "My dear boy, it would be foolish of me to give the game away now. However, I will provide you with all the information you need to reach the right solution."

We had come to a stop at the large French windows that gave access to the rear lounge, where I could see my mother sitting with the remaining Templeton-Swifts. Before Grandfather could continue, Simpsons One and Two, appeared from the side of the house.

"Lord Edgington," One (or Two) called. "We've found it."

The superior officer took a few steps away from the window and held a finger to his lips to urge discretion.

The other Simpson was holding a long metal object, which he now lifted it up for us to inspect. The *other* other Simpson held an identical one.

"The second candlestick was wrapped in a yard of cotton, hidden in a drawer in a wardrobe on the first floor of the western wing of the house."

They made a superb double act. "The room belongs to Mrs Templeton-Swift herself."

"Excellent work, men. I think it's time you called for a few constables to assist us. Our investigation is almost complete," the cheerful old sleuth revealed. "If you could find the doctor up in the attic and tell him that I will require his expert opinion this evening, I will make the necessary arrangements." Dramatic pause! "In half an hour's time, I will deliver my verdict."

The two inspectors looked most grateful for his praise and bustled into the house, patting one another on the back as they went.

Grandfather returned to his previous point. "As I was saying, Christopher, there are very few things you need to know in order to be able to identify the killer. The first is the simple fact that–"

Before he could finish the sentence, there was another interruption.

"M'Lord," Alice, our lovely Irish maid, said with a curtsy. "I'm sorry to interrupt, but we just received a telephone call from Scotland Yard. P.C. Simpkin has received the laboratory results you requested. He asked me to tell you that the sample of medicine you sent has been confirmed as containing morphine."

Grandfather finally clicked his fingers. It had been a long time coming, and he really enjoyed it. The sound it produced was so loud that it made Delilah stop her excited circling and look up at him.

"That is wonderful news. Thank you so much."

"You're welcome, M'Lord."

She gave another bob and was about to leave when Grandfather spoke again. "Oh and, Alice, I'll be revealing the killer here in the garden at…" He pulled his watch out to check the time. "Yes…seven o'clock. Seeing as this is something of a holiday for everyone, if the staff would like to watch, you would be more than welcome along." The old braggart couldn't resist an audience! "You must find Todd and tell him that we will require his skills with a cocktail shaker this evening."

Alice nodded with every new instruction, and I could imagine that this capable young lady was keeping a meticulous list in her head. I have no doubt that she'd made more sense of all he had just described than I had. I was still trying to imagine who the killer might be. The best I could strike upon was that it was my grandfather himself who had committed the terrible crimes for the simple pleasure of foxing everyone.

"Oh, and…" This was his second "Oh and," in the space of a minute! "…once you've done all that, I'll need someone to set up some chairs and tables in the sunken garden. I think that will be the perfect spot–"

"…for you to show off how clever you are." I hadn't meant to say this out loud, and they both turned to me in surprise. Grandfather was horrified, but I'd made Alice smile, so it was well worth inciting his wrath.

"Christopher!"

"I meant *show*… not show off. My tongue tripped in my mouth." I gave him my toothiest grin in the hope he'd forgive me, and he waved away my excuse and returned to more pressing matters.

"Is that clear, Alice?"

"Yes, M'Lord." She gave one last curtsy and hurried off in excitement. I don't think she'd ever had the chance to be part of our investigation before, and it was nice to see my grandfather involving the widest range of helpers possible. This did nothing to make me feel better about my own lack of wisdom, but I did like seeing dear Alice so happy.

"And now I require one last word with Tiffin." Grandfather turned to walk through the French windows, but I stopped him before he could disappear.

"You were supposed to give me my clues."

He hit his forehead with the ball of his hand. "Of course, how forgetful of me. You know I've a simply filthy memory these days." I never believed him when he made such claims. "The first thing you must consider is that Devyn, Lettice and Tiffin called their father by different names. One called him Dad, one Daddy and the other Papa."

"Righto!" I said with great gusto, though I couldn't imagine for a moment what this indicated.

"Second, as Alice has only just relayed, the medicine that Christabel was giving her husband really was morphine and not a mild herbal remedy, as she would have us believe."

"Very interesting." This at least seemed like clear evidence, but I wouldn't form any further conclusions until I'd heard the final clue he had selected.

"And, last but not least, Devyn used to work in an abattoir." He nodded his head sagaciously, and I copied the gesture in the hope that, by staring into his eyes and really concentrating, some significant detail might transmit itself from his brain to mine. I don't think it worked. "That is the case in the nutshell. The real mystery is that it took me so long to understand the plot that has already claimed three lives."

"A mystery indeed." I had stopped talking like a human by this point and turned into a gramophone record that played nothing but vague platitudes.

"Come along, Christopher." He clicked his heels once more and led off into the lounge.

It was odd to see our depleted band of suspects together. I suppose they were following the inspectors' advice from earlier – safety in numbers and all that. Devyn was sitting at a desk in the corner playing jacks. Christabel and my mother were on the sofa, speaking about... well, I'm not certain what, but I've no doubt it was some very suitable ladylike topic. You know the sort of thing: female emancipation, the plight of the working poor, the simultaneous allure and limitations of communism. Now that I say this, it does occur to me that my former suffragette mother may not have had the same interests as most ladies of the day.

But it was Tiffin who caught my attention. He was pretending to play the piano with the lid closed and jumped at every sound he heard. I thought this a good metaphor for his personality that weekend. He was clearly a man who lived to make others laugh and enjoy themselves but was constrained by the fact his father and sister had been murdered and there was an unidentified body in the attic. Though he couldn't play and sing for us, he continued practising his fingering on the silent piano until my grandfather spoke.

"Tiffin? Could I possibly have a word?"

He nearly fell backwards off his stool. "Eh? What?"

He wasn't the only one to take notice. The others all turned to look, and the small Indian rubber ball from Devyn's game went bouncing off the desk and across the carpet.

"A word," the wise old chap repeated. "I need one... with you."

Much like a nervous groom at the fateful moment the priest asks the congregation whether there is any lawful impediment to the couple being joined in matrimony, poor Tiffin looked around the room as though he was waiting for someone to object.

"A word? Yes, you can have as many as you like." He attempted a smile, but I could see how shaken he was. "I've honestly no use for them."

Grandfather looked a little worried about the man. "Would you perhaps prefer to go somewhere private?"

"Private! Me?" He let out a laugh. "I've never heard anything so ridiculous. I'm an open book, a man of the people. You can say anything you very well like in front of my beloved family." The pronouncement of this last word seemed to knock the wind out of his sail. He hunched his shoulders and looked even more desperate.

"Excellent, well, it's really not such a complicated matter. I simply wish to know whether, on your hunting trips in the Highlands, you came across a tall fellow with long brown hair about his shoulders and a rather devilish beard. Went by the name of Pocklington."

"Pocklington?" He considered this for a moment before shaking his head. "I can't say I did, but Scotland is a big place. Why would you think I'd know the man?"

Grandfather leaned in closer, as though he wished to share a secret. "Well, he spent most of his time at the Ruthness hunting lodge above Loch Gerald, near the Muir of Invergussie. You must know the place. Every hunter worth his salt has been there."

"Know it? I practically lived there." Tiffin looked up at a painting of a pack of hounds on the wall above the piano, as if wishing himself back to the glens of Scotland. "The shooting is fine, and the whisky is even better."

Grandfather smiled at the riposte. "Pocklington was a regular there. Quite the sportsman he was – known for his skills with a bando stick, both on and off the pitch." When people spoke about sport, my mind wandered at the best of times, but my knowledge of Celtic pastimes extended to… well, nothing. "Now, this Pocklington was a dangerous chap. He was involved in any number of criminal enterprises and had several run-ins with the Highland police. The locals turfed him out in the end, but there are often rumours of sightings of 'Big Jock'. I just wondered whether he could have followed you down here."

Tiffin had already been on edge when the conversation began, but with the unexpected introduction of a tall, menacing stranger, I was worried he might go running into the garden and paddle downstream to escape this new danger.

"You think he could be the killer?" His eyes bulged.

"Perhaps not. You know, it was really just a presentiment I had. I'm sure there's no need to worry." I looked at my grandfather more closely then. He was the last person to talk about anything so unscientific as a *presentiment.*

"It sounds as though I was lucky to have missed him." Tiffin emitted another fretful laugh.

"Thank you most sincerely for answering my questions." With a gracious bow, Grandfather swept towards the far door. "I will see you all in the garden in a short time to raise a glass to the poor figures we have lost this weekend."

As I moved to follow him, my mother gazed at me in a baffled manner, as though to ask, *What on Earth is Father saying?*

I haven't the first idea, I responded with a pair of raised eyebrows. That's as far as the silent conversation went because, it turns out, it is far more difficult to communicate using small movements of your facial features than one might think.

I found Grandfather waiting for me in the entrance hall. "Christopher…" He spoke in the solemn voice which he reserved for such momentous occasions. "I am going to ensure that all of my instructions have been carried out to the letter, but I require you to do something equally important for me."

Though I'd intended to ask what the blazes Big Jock Pocklington had to do with anything, I was just as eager to discover my task. "Anything, Grandfather."

"Wonderful." His porcelain-white moustache curled up at one end like a pig's tail. "Before our little gathering, I am relying on you to find me a cushion. Garden furniture always gives me a bad back."

CHAPTER THIRTY-ONE

So, there you go.

This would not be the case where good old Christopher Prentiss would triumph against all odds and identify the mass-murderer before my experienced grandfather could. This was the one where I searched about in the various lounges of Riverside Keep to choose the most comfortable cushion to prop up the lead detective on the case – should he decide to sit down, which was unlikely as he rarely did. And yet I went about my duty with just as much commitment as if he had asked me to spy on a suspect or collate the evidence we had amassed.

I sat on just about every cushion I could find! Some were too lumpy, some too hard. Several seemed to disappear beneath me as though they were filled with nothing but air. The density of the item was not my main concern, though. Knowing my grandfather, I was certain he would look for firmness in a cushion above all other qualities.

The thing that really challenged me was the size.

I'd been in some pickles in my life, but this was a true stinker! He was a large man, and yet he disapproved of anything which might be deemed hedonistic. That surely meant that a huge, rectangular example, in purple and gold rococo fabric, was out of the question. Meanwhile, the small, round tartan jobbie was equally unsuitable, for it was simply too petite.

And then I found it. The perfect cushion. Square, firm, medium-sized and in an unimposing grey and blue cambric material. If I'd been asked to encapsulate my grandfather in only one cushion, this would have been my choice. It was the Holy Grail of cushions! Though I did bring the other two, just in case I was off the mark.

Yes, I admit, considering that I still hadn't divined a solution to our bloodiest and most taxing case yet, I spent an inordinate amount of time focusing on cushions. But there may be some method to my madness – or rather, my grandfather's. You see, as I carried out that peculiar task, I was not really thinking about fabrics or cushion densities or even rococo patterns. My head was full of the investigation.

I started with the three clues that Grandfather had given me. His observation of the fact that each of the Templeton-Swift children called their father by a different sobriquet – Dad, Daddy and Papa – was surely meant to show the differing relationships Hugo Templeton-Swift had maintained with his offspring. We had seen any amount of evidence to suggest that Devyn had fallen out of favour with his father. This was all the more alarming when considering the photographs that showed just how close they had once been. Lettice and Tiffin had also spoken of the distance that existed in the family, though it was clear they did not possess the same degree of anger on the matter as their younger brother.

As for the herbal medicine which turned out to be morphine, I wondered whether grandfather had given away more than he should have there. Soon after we arrived at Riverside Keep, he'd told me that we had driven all that way with the specific aim of discovering whether Christabel was guilty. It seemed somehow too obvious that the beautiful second wife – so much younger than her rich, elderly and increasingly infirm husband – could be the killer. For one thing, everyone suspected her, so why would she have gone through with the crime when London's most famous detective and a number of furious relatives were in the vicinity?

And then – as I had placed my derrière upon approximately the seven hundredth cushion – inspiration struck. What if Christabel had been relying on that very fact as her alibi? Perhaps she thought she could make herself such a likely suspect that we would doubt the very possibility of her guilt. Grandfather had commented on just how convenient it was that we should find a bottle of morphine under Hugo's bedclothes. So what if she had planted it there herself, knowing that the insightful mind of Lord Edgington would conclude that someone was attempting to incriminate her?

Her presence at the scene of the first crime with the feather-filled murder weapon in her hand served a similar function. Not to mention the candlestick in her room, which matched perfectly with the one that was used to kill her stepdaughter. Every last detail had made us think that her husband's children had set out to entrap her when, really, she was the one to blame. What's more, we never knew for certain who wrote the second letter that summoned Grandfather to Riverside Keep. That was surely the very first part of her vicious scheme.

That cruel-hearted savage of a woman had planned to poison her husband but suffocated him instead after Lord Edgington took away the supposed tincture. I could only imagine that Lettice had subsequently found evidence of her stepmother's wickedness and paid the price. As for the man in the chest in the attic, he was the very image of the Scotsman grandfather had described and… well, I couldn't say how Big Jock Pocklington had ended up dead in Riverside Keep, but perhaps he was Christabel's accomplice before he fell afoul of her. Or maybe he was one of her many husbands.

Yes! That had to be it. The woman was a bigamist!

Oh, how the pieces of the puzzle fell into place as I searched the house. My fabulous forebear had known the very thing to get my grey cells working. Cushions! The man was a genius. And though he'd flatly denied that Christabel could be the culprit, he'd said the very same thing about everyone else. I finally understood his thinking; he'd simply wanted me to consider all the different possibilities before coming to the right solution.

While it was true that I had not unpicked the conundrum of the third clue, I'm sure that would come in time. Devyn had worked in an abattoir, and what of it? How could his past career slaughtering animals have anything to do with Christabel's wicked crime? Killing livestock is not the same thing as murdering a human being, and I'd been wrong to equate the two.

Yes, that must be it. It was a red herring Grandfather had included in order to rule out Devyn's part in the mystery, not incriminate him. The poor man had spent his adult life being battered by the cruel winds of modern existence, and I had come to the wrong conclusions on his character. Devyn was no more a killer than Lettice or Tiffin. They had returned home to protect their inheritance but never wished their father dead.

With these thoughts neatly filed in my brain, I had to get those cushions to my grandfather or the whole case would fall apart. Oh, fine, it's possible that I was investing a little too much importance in my find. But I was sure he would be happy with my effort.

As I ran back to the garden, I went through the various questions that I had accumulated over the last two days. Perhaps it was all the work I'd been doing for my imminent school examinations, but I found that I remembered each piece of evidence just perfectly.

There were so many doubts which I could now solve. I already understood who had sent the second letter to my grandfather, though I was less sure why Christabel would have written to her three stepchildren. And admittedly, I still couldn't understand why Lettice had shown such fear before she died. If she'd suspected that Christabel was the killer, why hadn't she simply informed the police? And, now that I came to think of it, why was Tiffin acting so terrified? It really was a puzzle.

So, yes. There were still a few minor points which I looked forward to hearing my grandfather explain, but the bulk of my case was watertight. A good ninety per cent watertight at the very least.

As I navigated the path back to the garden, there were people everywhere. In addition to the gang of servants, a few uniformed officers had arrived in a police van, and I had to wonder whether Grandfather had invited them in order to provide an even more appreciative audience for his big moment, or they were needed to help with the imminent arrest of that devious murderess Christabel Templeton-Swift.

Outside on the terrace, Halfpenny, Driscoll and Alice were moving the furniture out to the sunken garden. I would have helped them, of course, but… well… cushions! I led the way before realising I wasn't entirely sure which part of the garden was sunken, but Todd soon directed me. I suppose my grandfather must have had a poke around when I was busy with something else, as he'd found the most exquisitely Arcadian spot to unmask a murderer that one could imagine.

Tucked away out of sight, behind a high privet hedge that circled the space, was a miniature meadow. Much like in the one we'd visited before lunch, flowers of yellow, pink, deep blue, and fiery orange blazed in the sunshine. Lines of apple trees provided a neat border and, in the middle of four petal-shaped beds, there was a sundial with several chairs already in place beside it. Todd had discovered the collection of alcohol in the cellar, and there was a table set up with any number of bottles and glasses. He was already hard at work mixing his libations.

It looked as though we would soon be enjoying a real garden party. Delilah was running to and fro, her tail wagging as she gave each new person who arrived a good sniff. Our maid, Dorie, turned up, carrying a sofa across her broad shoulders. The woman was stronger than a boxer, and I was certain that Grandfather employed her for her skills as his occasional bodyguard as much as anything else. Even creaky old Halfpenny had a spring in his step whilst he milled about getting ready.

Once we'd arranged all the chairs and tables that we would need, the guests and suspects started appearing. Inspectors Simpson and Simpson were the first to arrive. Stepping down into the elegant plot, they took their bowler hats off in quiet appreciation of their surroundings. I cannot say I was surprised to see that they had matching bald heads underneath.

Dr Merrick was next and took his place beside the inspectors in the crescent of seats. Tiffin was the first of our regular suspects to arrive and he was just as pale and nervous as when we'd left him in the lounge. I think it's fair to say that the hunter looked quite hunted at that moment. He glanced about the scene with no wonder at the joys of an English garden in the springtime, but a definite sense of terror about him.

The murderess herself appeared, looking dainty and demure on my mother's arm. She'd changed her attire since her ablutions. She now wore a white, barrel-shaped skirt, a simple matching tunic and held a frilled parasol in her free hand. She was the picture of innocence and sat down in the middle of the stalls, waiting for the main act to arrive.

She was not the only one who had dressed for the occasion. The Crower family had taken the chance to spruce up their appearance. I had never expected to see old Ned in a smart suit. Meanwhile, Betty wore a gown that was almost as fine as my mother's. She sat down beside the doctor, much as Queen Mary would take her place in the royal box at the opera.

In her crinoline skirts and tight bodice, Wilhelmina looked less confident than the others. She pulled at her collar as though it were choking her. I suppose these were the fancy clothes with which the late master had indulged his servants. I'd always thought my grandfather showed special kindness to his staff, though he stopped short of choosing their wardrobes. Our cook, Henrietta, had put on a wonderful spread of hors d'oeuvres and tiny bites, beside which I would spend the duration of the event, pecking away to my heart's content. She finally turned up to see the show for herself, and Mother insisted she take the spare seat beside her.

Perhaps unsurprisingly, Devyn was the last to arrive. He stalked onto the scene in his long, black jacket, which made me think of the old newspaper cartoons I'd seen of Jack the Ripper. Murderer or otherwise, he was a woesome fellow, and I was still a little scared of him. He stood behind the line of chairs, always lurking, always nimble on the balls of his feet.

I have a sneaking suspicion that Grandfather had been skulking in the fruit trees until his whole audience had arrived. Mere moments after Devyn showed his face, our star entertainer for the evening strolled onto the scene.

I held up my pick of the best cushions, but he did not seem interested after all.

CHAPTER THIRTY-TWO

He walked over with a confident salute to the other officers, and Halfpenny handed him one of the cocktails that Todd had mixed. Everyone else had one by this point, but I'd stuck to the pork pie and apple juice I was enjoying. Grandfather did not start with the topic in which we were most interested. He thought he'd ramble on about something completely unrelated for a while first.

"Over the last year, I've come to appreciate cocktails for their range and flexibility. The one you are currently drinking is known as a Jack Rose. It comes from America, like so many of the finest examples of the craft, and is made using applejack, grenadine, and lemon juice. Only I don't really know what applejack is, so our barman Todd suggested we use French Calvados brandy, and the result is quite stimulating. Don't you think?"

He held up the thick, red liquid in its long-stemmed glass, much as a sommelier would examine a fine wine. "Have you drunk them in New York, Devyn?"

The uncouth fellow at the back couldn't answer because he was swallowing the beverage down in one gulp. He wiped his mouth off on the back of his hand and said, "I prefer something a little harder. But this sort of thing is all right for the ladies." He wasn't the type of person who made much effort to endear himself to those around him.

Grandfather took a delicate sip of his drink and set it down on a small table beside the sundial. He reminded me of a magician I'd once seen at the Alhambra in Leicester Square. I half expected him to pull a rabbit out of his shirt collar or make my mother disappear. There was a large stone clearing in the middle of the cultivated meadow which would act as the old ham's stage, and he leaned with one elbow on the sundial as a brief eruption of silence caused the tension to rise.

"I'm not here to talk to you this evening about apple brandy or popular new tendencies in American culture." With a dreamy smile on his face, he shook his head. "Oh, no. I'm here to discuss the murder of three different individuals. Hugo Templeton-Swift was found suffocated in his room this morning by his devoted wife, Christabel. His daughter Lettice was beaten about the head and then drowned in the garden without anyone hearing anything suspicious, and before either of them had taken their last breath, another man was killed here. A man whom I suspect only two of you, including his killer, would recognise."

This brought about a real murmur of curiosity in the crowd. Dorie, who was occupying two seats at the end of the row, even clapped her hands together in excitement. I must say, I was enjoying the show myself and appreciated the intimation that our culprit was not quite so "devoted" a "wife" as she would have us believe.

"But even before those terrible events, I was summoned here by Hugo himself. I already knew who he was, of course. The name Templeton-Swift had become inseverably connected to finance and the pursuit of great wealth in this country. He was a one-man empire and would not have possessed this fine house and all its luxuries without his immense success in the stock markets and through foreign investments. And yet, his name was one of the few things I understood in the letter he sent. It was a messy, ugly thing, covered in spelling mistakes and smudged words as though it had been written by a drunken child."

Our speaker stood up straighter then, perhaps to draw attention to this frankly disturbing image. "My interest was piqued, and I contacted a colleague in Scotland Yard to find out exactly what had happened to the once famous investor. I discovered a little about his three children, who had all left the family home here in Wiltshire. I learnt that he was widowed, and that he had re-married a much younger woman, the knowledge of which made one phrase from his letter stand out to me."

Oh, this was going to be good. Christabel would be in chains in the local gaol before the cocktails had got too warm to drink!

"It said, 'She's the one. She's trying to kill me.' And due to the suspicious mind I possess, I immediately thought the worst of Christabel Templeton-Swift. I soon discovered that she had been married twice before and that both men had died. I had rarely stumbled across so simple a case. The woman was clearly a succubus of the most terrible variety. A deadly creature, moving from man to man to suck the life and wealth from them. I was reminded of Samuel Taylor Coleridge's famous poem, 'Christabel', which spoke of just such a malicious force."

This was the stuff. Every last person in attendance was captured by his tale. We were glued to each word and unable to look away. His slightest twitch of a muscle or blinked eye could reveal so much.

"However, I had forgotten something in this analysis. You see, Coleridge's unfinished masterpiece did not take its name from the supernatural being that haunts its lines, but the innocent and virtuous young woman upon whom the creature preys. I was mistaken in my assumptions and, upon receiving a second letter and coming to Riverside Keep, I realised my error. Christabel was a victim in the lyrical ballad, much as in real life."

I couldn't believe what I was hearing; he'd got it all wrong. I must have let out an involuntary, "This is ridiculous," as everyone turned to glare at me. "Oh... sorry. I just meant... well, this is ridiculous how well my grandfather's mind works. It's truly... ridiculous."

No one believed my explanation, but that didn't matter as he picked up the story again and they forgot all about me. "Ultimately, if our Christabel was not the killer, I was forced to question who had summoned me here. I still believe that the first letter was penned by Hugo, but the second was a mystery. The sentence structure and overall composition were too competent to be Hugo's and the message pointed to Christabel's guilt far more explicitly than the first missive had. Still, I could not be sure whether it was written out of fear for the patriarch's safety or to frame an innocent woman for a crime she never intended to commit."

I had to smile then, as I knew what he was doing. Grandfather was forever taking us down such twisting paths when summarising our cases. I'd doubted myself for a moment, but I was sure now that, before long, he would take us back to where he'd started and prove that the scarlet woman really was responsible for these heinous crimes.

"It was a question that, once answered, would change my understanding of the curious course of events that we have witnessed this weekend. Before Hugo was even dead, I had to consider who might wish him harm. His three children were the obvious culprits, as they would benefit most directly from their father's demise. If they could prove their stepmother was guilty of murder, they could claim the full estate as their inheritance. And yet there was a problem with my theory."

He paused then to make us hunger for the next part of the story. "If the prodigal children were to blame for the conspiracy, I had to wonder why Hugo himself would have been so afraid. When I spoke to him, he repeated his prior claim. 'She's the one,' he said, which might have referred to his daughter Lettice if she hadn't arrived here several days after the first letter was sent."

"And so I considered alternative routes to find the killer. I wondered whether, in his dotage, Hugo could have mistaken the innocent care his wife provided for some more sinister machination. Did he believe that the herbal remedies and sleeping draughts she gave him were the cause of his malady?"

Yes! This was another classic Lord Edgington gambit. At any moment he would reveal that such a supposition would have been correct as the medicine Hugo had been taking was, in fact, a strong opiate. I took a peek at Christabel as the pressure heightened, but she looked disappointingly calm. A little sad maybe, but not nearly as alarmed as I might have expected.

Grandfather indulged in a spot of pacing. "Or were Hugo's words merely the ravings of a sick mind? Such questions are difficult to answer in a case like this, especially when someone had attempted to obscure the picture that lay before me. At the first crime scene, in Hugo's room, a bottle of morphine had been planted beside his body. Lettice was struck about the head with one half of a pair of candlesticks, and the other was found neatly wrapped in a drawer in the new widow's room. With so much misdirection at play, I was willing to believe, therefore, that the second letter I received was nothing but a red herring."

He'd abandoned his post in the middle of the terrace by this point and came to walk around the semi-circle of white metal chairs where every last suspect and all of his most portable staff were seated. I noticed that Grandfather stopped before each of the most suspicious characters. Tiffin was first, then Devyn and finally Christabel herself. He smiled and patted her hand affectionately. That sneak! He was setting her mind at ease, laying a trap.

"Which means that the killer wished to have me here on the premises to follow the trail of clues they believed that the great Lord Edgington would follow. There was a conspiracy at work; a complicated plot to condemn an innocent woman and steal the Templeton-Swift fortune from its rightful owner." He paused in front of his beloved cook and raised his eyebrows as she was smiling at him rather broadly. "What is it, Henrietta? Have I given the game away?"

Her cheeks turned red, and the poor woman looked quite shy. "I wouldn't like to precipitate anything, M'Lord. It's just… well, you have rather made it sound as if Mr Templeton-Swift's children are responsible for his death. They would be the ones to inherit if Mrs Templeton-Swift were out of the picture."

You dear sweet woman, I wanted to shout but kept the thought in my head. *That's just what he wants you to think! Before long he's going to turn this whole explanation back on itself and prove that Christabel is the only conspirator.*

"Well, yes, I admit. It does appear that way," he replied with a respectful nod of the head. "But before I explain who is responsible for these sickening crimes, I must pose another mystery. Why was Lettice murdered?"

He looked around the group then, and I'm certain we all hoped that it was a rhetorical question. Perhaps inevitably, he shot his hand out in my direction.

"Christopher? Why did she have to die?"

"She knew too much," I replied rather ominously. "I mean… well, she discovered something that the killer didn't want her to know." Why was it that my ideas always sounded so ingenious in my head and then, when I said them out loud, I lost all confidence?

"An excellent idea." He was undoubtedly the best grandfather in the known universe. "Truly, my boy, that is very clever thinking. But if that was the case, who killed her? Surely her own brothers wouldn't have done it. As we've seen this weekend, the three siblings have supported one another through this tragic time. Violet, have you any idea what happened?"

It was my mother's turn, and I was surprised to see that she looked just as uncertain as me. I saw her glance along the line of chairs to where Devyn was standing in the shadow of an apple tree.

"Perhaps it was to remove another rung on the ladder of inheritance." I suppose it only made sense that she was nervous; she was accusing the man of murder.

"I see. And so, respecting the normal order of things, that would mean that Tiffin would also have had to die in order for his younger brother to gain the estate. Interesting." He put his tongue against his cheek, as though carefully considering the possibility. I admit he wasn't the worst actor, but he'd already told us that he knew who the killer was, so this can't have been too taxing for him.

"It struck me as unusual that, having gone to such lengths to murder Hugo at night, so as to avoid anyone else chancing upon the crime, the killer would despatch the second victim in the daytime. There were any number of people here at Riverside Keep when Lettice was killed, including two serving police officers." He motioned to Simpson and Simpson, and his restless swaying came to a stop. "Tiffin, you've been very quiet. Might you have any idea why your beloved sister was murdered?"

The typically nervous fellow couldn't sit still by this point, and he replied in clipped sentences. "None at all. I don't know anything about it."

"Then perhaps you might hazard a guess as to why your father was murdered with a pillow rather than poisoned as the bottle of morphine suggests the killer had intended." The detective increased the pace of his words as he delivered this sentence.

It was clear that, for once, Tiffin had no wish to be in the spotlight for any longer than necessary. "I... ummm... Or rather, perhaps he... yes, perhaps the killer changed his mind."

"He changed his mind?" Grandfather can be terribly cruel sometimes.

"That's right, he'd planned to use a large amount of morphine, then decided that a pillow would be... quieter." This was the kind of nonsensical conclusion that I would have drawn just one year before. "You know, all those feathers must keep the noise down."

Instead of pointing out the idiocy of this statement, Grandfather peered over at the doctor, as though just having the natty physician there added gravitas to the proceedings.

"Tell me, Dr Merrick, how difficult would it be to obtain such an addictive and dangerous substance today?"

As Tiffin continued his quaking, the good doctor sat up straighter and consulted the medical encyclopaedia in his brain. "Well, as I told you this morning, morphine is no longer available to the public. But I have no doubt that some illicit drug peddler would be able to get hold of it."

"And in your years working in Wiltshire, have you come across many 'illicit drug peddlers'?"

Merrick had to laugh at this. "Not one. And I was about to say that the most likely explanation is that whoever brought the medicine into this house had possessed it for some time. It was really not so very long ago that you could buy the stuff widely in Britain. Even without a prescription."

Grandfather nodded and turned back to his real target. "Do you know how the morphine came into this house, Tiffin?"

He had to place his hands together on his lap at this point to hide just how much he was shaking. "Of course I don't. I don't know anything about drugs, or pillows, or even candlesticks." I noticed that he kept his eyes straight ahead of him at all times. Even when Grandfather wasn't talking to him, the elder Templeton-Swift boy barely shifted his gaze.

"And rightly so," Lord Edgington replied a little opaquely. "In fact, since my arrival here at Riverside Keep, I've been amazed at just how little anybody knows about anything. In his interviews with you and your sister, my grandson succeeded in learning absolutely nothing whatsoever." He gave me a warm smile to suggest that this was no failing on my part. "However, I've got another question for you, Tiffin. And I believe you'll have no difficulty with this one."

I think that the suspect nodded at this point, but he was vibrating so much it was hard to tell.

Grandfather knelt down so that his eyes were at the same level as his quarry's. "Did you love your father?"

"Of course I did." His reply was one indignant rush of sound. "He was a wonderful old chap. He achieved so much in his life, and I owe him a great deal."

"Oh, I see." Grandfather pretended to be confused – as though such a thing were even possible. "I merely ask because that is what you implied when we first met but, by the time your father was dead, you'd changed your story. Both you and your sister told Christopher that you possessed no fondness for Hugo, and the only reason you came back here was to protect the inheritance which Christabel would claim for herself."

This was as much as Tiffin could take. He threw his hands in the air and jumped to his feet. "Of course I said I loved my father. He'd just been murdered but–" Without warning, he threw his cocktail glass in his inquisitor's direction, pushed the nearest table over and went dashing back towards the house.

The scene suddenly came to life as the Crowers and the other servants cooed with excitement. Todd was always more practical than the rest of us and immediately shot across the sunken garden. He launched his cocktail shaker through the air like a javelin, narrowly missing the escaping suspect, whose panicked run was less than direct.

Shaken by this unforeseen development, it even took my grandfather a moment to react. "Catch the fool before he can escape."

Our athletic chauffeur leaped over the fallen table, sprinted straight through the long grass and nabbed the runaway as he reached the steps to the main garden. He seized Tiffin by the collar and hauled him back towards the crowd of excited onlookers.

Grandfather laid one hand on the fellow, as though to keep him from blowing away in the breeze. "Why on Earth did you run, man? You're not even the killer."

Tiffin was suffering through a fit of nervous tears. "I don't know what to think anymore. Your interrogation left me so discombobulated I had to wonder whether you knew something about me that I didn't. I thought perhaps I'd murdered them all in a trance."

"No, of course you didn't. Just sit down and stop making a fuss."

The police officers who had (slowly) left their seats returned once more, and Dorie disarmed her lethal knuckles.

"So Tiffin's not the one after all?" Ned Crower was greatly enjoying the spectacle and, from the napkin full of savoury treats on his lap, he took a handful of food to load into his mouth. "That's a shame."

"I never thought it would be him, to be honest," Betty revealed. "My money's still on the widow. I've never trusted 'er."

Grandfather reclaimed his spot in front of the sundial and held his hands in the air in an act of contrition. "I am sorry, ladies and gentlemen. I should have corrected my cook, Henrietta, when she mistakenly assumed that one of the Templeton-Swift children murdered their father. That is not the case, and it was wrong of me to have played with your expectations in such a manner."

This would surely be the moment when he revealed that, as the three siblings were not to blame, their stepmother, Christabel, was the killer after all. I couldn't wait to see the realisation dawn upon her that her plan had failed, and that she would pay for her crimes.

"In fact, I told my grandson that none of the names he put to me – none of the suspects we've investigated – are guilty of these murders. At several moments this weekend I myself was convinced that Hugo's youngest boy, Devyn, had suffocated his father and drowned his sister, but I could not have been more wrong." He looked at the unkempt gentleman and pursed his lips in an apologetic frown. "Such an explanation is quite impossible, as Devyn Templeton-Swift was found dead this afternoon in the attic of Riverside Keep."

CHAPTER THIRTY-THREE

Oh, for goodness' sake.

I was so sure of my theory. So certain that the thread of suspicion I had chosen must be the right one, but as soon as Grandfather revealed the truth, I realised my mistake. The abattoir! Devyn, or at least the man we had known by that name, had worked in New York in an abattoir. I still couldn't say why that fact was so significant but, evidently, it was the key to the whole case.

All eyes turned to the imposter at this moment as I, for one, attempted to work out what the revelation implied. If he wasn't Devyn, who was he? The police decided not to take any more risks and, though they did not yet put him in handcuffs, they got up off their behinds and spread out around the garden so that no one else would think of running away. The counterfeit Devyn remained his typically inscrutable self, and he held his anger in reserve.

Grandfather was in his element, though, and began his gentle swaying dance once more. It was rather a shame he hadn't had his top hat and cane with him, as he could have put on a performance for us. I've always thought he would have made the most sensational adagio dancer on the London stage.

"I'm going to take you back to the beginning of this whole saga and tell you the story in full. Approximately ten days ago, I received a letter from a man who believed he was being kept incapacitated against his wishes. For a long time, I was not certain that Hugo had written it but, upon close inspection of his handwriting, I am satisfied that was the case. Though the letter intrigued me, I did little about it until a week later. In the meantime, a woman claiming to be Lettice Templeton-Swift and a man claiming to be her brother appeared here in Hanging Langford and presented themselves to their father as if they were his children."

Well, this proves I was not cut out to be a detective. I had failed to realise that, if Devyn wasn't Devyn, his brother and sister could hardly be who they said they were either. I tried to jump ahead to consider what other impact this might have, but he was too quick for me and continued his tale.

"All photographs of the siblings beyond their early childhood have been removed from view and so, at first, I found no visual evidence of their ruse. It was my grandson Christopher who discovered the vital clue. I have just returned from a trip to the cellar where boxes of photographs show three adolescents on holiday with their parents. The two boys look quite similar to the men here today, but Lettice's hair colour had changed, and her features were far less traditionally beautiful than the poor woman who died in the fountain this evening.

"So then, what happened to the real Tiffin, Lettice and Devyn? In his search, my assistant at Scotland Yard has been unable to locate either of the eldest children, and the addresses I found here in Hugo's office are no longer correct. It seems that the two of them had cut their father from their lives completely after falling out with him over their mother's death. Hugo's favourite son, Devyn, meanwhile, really did come back from New York upon receiving a letter from Riverside Keep. He came to the house – just one day before we arrived – and was shown upstairs, where his imposter murdered him and hid the body somewhere he believed no one would discover it. But my dear grandson can always be relied upon to root about in the places in which most others wouldn't think of looking."

He walked over to me then and put his hand on my shoulder. It made me feel the tiniest bit better about getting every single possible fact in the case wrong. In our last few investigations, I thought I'd been making real progress. So this felt like a huge step backwards.

But don't worry, there was still time for me to be mistaken once again. "Are you saying that the three fake heirs worked together to kill Hugo?"

"Not quite." He un-squeezed my shoulder, gave me a supportive smile and returned to his audience. "Christopher had also overheard Lettice telling the man who was playing her older brother that she was sure that I would see through her act. Tiffin said that if they could get through the weekend, they'd be laughing all the way to the bank. My grandson naturally assumed that they were referring to the inheritance, but it struck me as odd that they'd only expect to keep up appearances for the weekend. Such a fixed period put me in mind of a specific job they were undertaking, but it was only when I heard Tiffin playing the piano – most insensitively, I must say – shortly after his father had been murdered that I perceived another interpretation of their conversation. He sang a song of which I've seen far less enthusiastic performances on Shaftesbury Avenue."

"It was Harry Champion's 'You Can't Help Laughing Can Yer?'" Tiffin couldn't help but explain. "It was always one of my favourites to sing with my Cathy."

I think he would like to have said more, but Grandfather didn't want him giving away any secrets and took over again. "My attention had first been drawn to their duplicity when I noticed that each of Hugo's children called him by a different name. In my experience, one form of dad, daddy, father or papa is preferred in a family, and it struck me as unlikely that there would be three.

"What's more, there was something too perfect about Lettice's performance. Though she may have been frightened of the man who had hired her to play his sister, when it came to answering questions, she was a consummate professional. I knew she must be lying, and yet it didn't appear that she was. In my book, this could only mean one of two things. Either she was psychologically deranged, or she was an actress."

The phony Tiffin broke into tears once more, and I noticed that his accent had become a little more working class. "It was my fault. Cathy never wanted the job, but I convinced her. The money was too good to turn down, and I'd always fancied playing a toff. We were a double act, you see? I played the piano, she danced, and we both sang and acted. We worked on the south coast in summer, then London in the winter. We were lucky to get anything at this time of year, so I jumped at the chance."

I marched forward then as I was almost as disgusted by his part in the plot as his fake brother's. "So you accepted money to help kill an old man?"

"No, matey. Nothing like that. All we knew was that we had to stay in character the whole time we were here. If anyone saw through the act, we wouldn't get paid." His tears came in short bursts, and he pointed across the audience to the savage. "That chap told us it was all a game to test how good a detective the famous Lord Edgington really was. He said no one would get hurt, and that he had some sort of potion to make it look like the old man was dead. You know, like in 'Romeo and Juliet'."

"That was a play, you foolish man." Grandfather failed to control his anger. Apparently, actors aren't the cleverest people. "What I don't understand is why you continued the scheme after Lettice was murdered, and it was clear that this was no game."

Tiffin still looked downcast, but I was more interested in Devyn, who remained exactly where he'd been standing throughout. He watched and listened intently but hadn't moved a muscle.

"Lettice, or rather, my Cathy, suspected things weren't right, but I thought she was worrying over nothing. She'd arranged to meet Devyn in the garden after she'd finished talking to Christopher. We argued about it, and so she went alone to tell him she was quitting. How I wish I'd gone with her now." The poor chap set about drowning himself in a puddle of his own tears. "I even saw him striding back into the house with a look of evil on his face, but I just kept playing the piano and having a jolly old time. As soon as I knew she was dead, I realised what an idiot I'd been. I wanted to tell you. I really did. But he said he'd kill me if I uttered a word."

"It's not too late, you cretin!" Devyn finally roared and, rather than one of the inspectors or the uniformed officers approaching that burly chap, Dorie stepped in to keep the peace. He suddenly didn't look so brave! "Don't you touch me, you massive–"

Before he could finish his insult, she had picked him up off the ground like a small child and slung him over her shoulder. "Mr Lord Edgington, sir? What shall I do with this?"

"Wait just a moment, Dorie." My grandfather circled his finger in the air, and she turned so that he could address the real villain. "If you hadn't killed the woman we knew as Lettice, I might never have realised who you really were." His gaze was made of pure steel at that moment and, without looking away, he issued an order to his subordinates. "Constables, arrest Ned and Betty Crower as accomplices to their son's murder of Hugo Templeton-Swift, his son Devyn and the actress who played his daughter."

There was a gasp of shock from various members of the audience. I noticed that Wilhelmina put her head in her hands and wouldn't look up again for some time. What I didn't understand was how her parents could be involved if she wasn't. Perhaps this was another of grandfather's teases.

"We never laid a hand on no one," Ned shouted, as the police put him in shackles. "We might have kept the old fellow dozy, but we never planned to kill 'im. That was our Nathan's doing. And none of this was our idea, it was all–"

"Oh, shut up, you stupid man." Betty managed to land one last slap around the back of her husband's head before the officers seized her. "Don't say another word."

"The Crowers were in their cottage when the actress was killed. There was water all over the flagstones and they would have surely heard the commotion but denied any knowledge of it. Under the pretence of an interview, I gained access to their house in order to look at a family photograph of the whole Crower clan. The man calling himself Devyn was in the picture, skulking away at the back of the group. Even beside the seaside, he looked thoroughly miserable."

This was another opportunity for me to curse my poor skills of observation, but a revelation of my own came to me at this moment. In the chaos of that busy scene, I stepped forward to speak. "Old Hugo said that he was human before *she* came. He wasn't referring to Christabel but Betty. She was *the one*! She was keeping him drugged to have an easy life. Which explains the expensive radio, the comfortable accommodation and the fancy clothes they're wearing. Hugo wasn't a generous employer. In fact, he barely employed enough staff. They were swindling the poor chap."

"Very good, Chrissy," my mother beamed, and Christabel, that truly wonderful, kind woman, came over to thank me with a hug. I always knew she was innocent.

"Inspectors Simpson and Simpson," I continued, feeling most imperious as yet another conclusion exploded in my brain. "Arrest Dr Merrick. Not only did he supply the morphine to incapacitate his patient, he intentionally misdiagnosed his ailment." I walked over to the fourth and final culprit. "I suppose you reduced the dose you gave him when it was time to find Hugo a wife to blame for his forthcoming death. It wouldn't surprise me if this whole thing was your idea from the start. I've no doubt you would have taken a healthy cut of the inheritance once the plan was complete."

Merrick was clever and wouldn't say a word. Not that it would do him much good. Hatching a plan with the likes of the Crowers was only ever going to land him in prison.

"Excellent work, Christopher." Grandfather winked at me, and a broad smile graced his lips. "You've outdone yourself again."

CHAPTER THIRTY-FOUR

When the criminals had been carted off to the police station, and Riverside Keep was calm once more, we had dinner on the terrace beside the house. It was one of those beautiful Spring days when the warmth in the air stays around long enough to enjoy every last minute of sunshine. It was an evening full of the promise of what summer would bring – though I predicted that, come July, it would rain non-stop and, if we ever made it to the seaside, I'd have to wear a mackintosh instead of a swimming costume.

As Halfpenny served the first course of oatmeal cannelons on a bed of rocket, and Todd filled our glasses, Christabel travelled through waves of sadness and joy. She had suffered more than any of the suspects – with the obvious exception of Cathy the actress, I suppose. The constant reminders of her third husband's demise would stay with her for a long time, but she managed to address the party with stoic determination.

"Lord Edgington, I will never be able to thank you for what you've done."

Grandfather – who was sitting very comfortably on not one but three cushions! – leaned around the circular cast-iron table to pat her hand. "There is no need to thank me. I was only doing my job."

"That's not true. You went far beyond what anyone could have expected. You trusted me when most men wouldn't have. And I was wondering…" Her soft words faded out completely then.

"You were wondering why?" The wily old fox had read her thoughts.

"That's right!" Like an easily gulled yokel at a carnival fortune-teller, she was cheered by his simple prediction.

"It was really not so very difficult, my dear. For one thing, my trusted friend Vivian Highley-Summers had once held you in high esteem, and I've never known that fine lady to be wrong in her judgement. But the purest sign of your innocence was that you willingly handed me the medicine you were administering to your husband. When I discovered it was really morphine, I realised that you couldn't have known what you were giving him and that someone had engineered our arrival here in order to obtain Hugo's estate."

"Oh, I see," I said, feeling ashamed of myself for not realising this sooner. "I'd assumed Betty had been putting the morphine in her master's food. Which might actually have made her slop taste better."

Far from dismissing the idea, he nodded encouragingly. "Yes, I considered the same possibility myself after you were so affected by Henrietta's Apple Charlotte. Perhaps that was how they dispensed it in the beginning, but it would have been difficult to ensure that only Hugo ate the poisoned food once Christabel came to live here. So they made her administer it instead."

"It's the treachery of Dr Merrick I struggle to comprehend." The widow put her hand to her mouth then, as if discovering the secret anew. "He was so convincing in all the advice he gave me. He visited so many times to check on poor Hugo that I could never have imagined it was an act. The Crowers' betrayal is easier to accept; I disliked them from the day I arrived. But he seemed so concerned for my husband's health."

"I've been thinking about the doctor," I explained. "And the only thing that makes sense is that he employed the Crowers on Hugo's behalf. The real Devyn wouldn't have come all the way from New York just to hire a few members of staff. I believe that he is just as responsible for what happened here as that thug Nathan Crower."

Grandfather didn't say anything at first, but smiled proudly, as though to imply, *I taught that boy everything he knows!* At least he didn't explain what a wonderful delegator he was… again.

"Very good, my boy. And I concur wholeheartedly. It was clear that, for the conspiracy to work, the Crowers would have needed information on the family's past. Merrick had been Hugo's friend and doctor for many years, and I believe he saw the opportunity to swindle a wealthy old man who was entirely alone in the world. He must have put the idea of marriage into Hugo's head and promoted our innocent Christabel here over any more suspicious-minded candidates. It's hard to know quite how much money he would have made from it, but the plan was his from the beginning; you can mark my words."

My mother had a rather comical – yet extremely wise – doubt of her own. "What I don't understand is how you put up with the food here for so long, Christabel. I've never eaten anything quite like Betty Crower's sandwiches before."

The widow was quick with an explanation. "To be perfectly

honest, I was terrified of her. I asked Hugo to hire new staff when I first arrived, but then his health deteriorated, and my priorities rather changed. If the truth be told, I tried to eat as little of the meals here as possible and made regular trips to the bakery in town." She truly was a woman after my own heart.

"'She's the one!'" I quoted. "Hugo said that once per course during dinner on Friday night. It was only after Grandfather revealed Betty's part in the plot that I realised the words coincided with her trips to deliver food."

With our work over, the victorious detective was in a dreadfully good mood. "This case really does prove the need to travel with a full staff of servants. Imagine what we'd be doing right now if I hadn't thought to bring Henrietta along with me."

My mother was still unconvinced. "You do realise that you have two hands, Father? Perhaps learning to cook could be the next item on your list of ambitions."

"Hmmm..." He considered the possibility. "It's an interesting suggestion. But I know exactly what I'm doing as soon as Chrissy finishes his exams. I have arranged for a–"

"Grandfather?" I interrupted him then, as I thought I'd probably rather not know what terrible challenge awaited me. "I still have one or two questions about the case, if you don't mind."

"Of course." He sipped his white wine and waited for me to begin.

"What will happen to Gary or Clive or whatever the fake Tiffin's name really is? Has he committed any crime?"

The great detective considered the point. "By not sharing the information he possessed after Lettice was murdered, he may well have. But I feel he has suffered enough for his mistake. The police have plenty on their plates tonight without worrying about that tragic character."

This was not the only gap I wished to plug. "I don't see who wrote to the real Devyn in New York. The Crowers wouldn't have done it, so was it just due to bad timing that he sailed home this week?"

To my surprise, Christabel had an answer. "I wondered if it was Wilhelmina who wrote to him. You see, she tried to talk to me once about Hugo's health but was clearly too nervous to say anything directly. I hadn't understood what she was afraid of at the time, but I

225

realise now that it was her own family who frightened her."

"I believe you're right." Grandfather slowly closed and reopened his eyes like an ever-so-ancient owl. "Ned and Betty always wanted us to talk to their daughter rather than to them. That was because Wilhelmina didn't know the full scale of their plans. They'd kept her in the dark, but she had her suspicions and, unable to express them to you, she wrote to his three children in the hope that their presence might solve the problem. It seems that only Devyn had forgiven his father enough for whatever had gone on between them to return. Unfortunately for everyone, he arrived here after Nathan Crower. If he'd come any earlier, perhaps no one would have died."

A shiver passed over me as I imagined this different reality that had so nearly come to pass. It was at this moment that the maid in question appeared at the side of the house. She had a carpet beater in one hand and looked determined to use it.

"Wilhelmina?" my grandfather called, then addressed us once more in a whisper. "Let us get the answers from the horse's mouth, as it were."

Dressed once more in her maid's smock, the tragic thing trundled over with her eyes low. She was clearly ashamed of her part in the proceedings and could barely look at my grandfather. "Yes, M'Lord."

"I wondered if you could tell us what you know about the events that occurred here this weekend." He quickly followed this statement with a qualification. "Not that I suspect you had anything to do with the crime itself, of course."

She glanced at me, of all people, and I tried to encourage her. "Only if you feel comfortable, Billie."

She breathed in for courage and began her tale. "I never thought my brother would kill no one. I knew he wasn't straight, like, so when he turned up here, it were obvious he was up to no good. He's swindled plenty of folk out of their money before, but I never thought he'd be violent."

"Your parents must have known," Grandfather put in a little sternly. "They maintained the deception that the three people claiming to be Hugo's children were really his offspring. Such a trick would only bear fruit if their father was dead."

Her face turned redder, and her eyes shone in the light of the setting sun. "Maybe they knew about Hugo, but he was an old man. They'd never have gone through with it if they'd thought that Nathan was going to kill whoever got in his way. That's why he and my ma argued in the kitchen this afternoon.

"Lettice knew it was no game they were playing, and she threatened to expose him if he didn't let her and Tiffin leave with the money he'd promised. By the time I knew anything about it, she was already dead. I know I should have told you then, but I couldn't shop my own family like that. Ma and Pa might not be angels, but they're not bad in themselves. Nathan's always been the scapegrace in the family. He was born rotten, and I'm glad to see the back of him."

Grandfather became a little more severe in his manner. "You're right. You should have told us what you knew the moment we arrived here. But I don't believe that your silence is reason enough to condemn you to prison." As the girl cried, he relented a little. "I know you tried to help Hugo. Tell us about the letters you sent."

She rushed to answer him. "The first one I took to the post office really was from Mr Templeton-Swift himself, M'Lord. And the second one was just as I said too. I found it in a pile of letters that wanted sending. I see now that it must have been my brother what wrote it. I suppose my parents found out about the one that Hugo sent you and had the idea."

"But before that, child. Did you write to the three siblings?" My mother could have charmed the truth out of a fire-breathing dragon and her tender tone gave the girl the confidence she required.

"Yes, miss. I saw the condition that the old master was in, and I knew it weren't natural. I couldn't be sure who was poisoning him, but I thought that one of his kids could find out. I got their addresses from his office but only heard back from the real Devyn the day before he arrived. I never knew he came to the house until you identified his body."

"You hapless creature," Christabel said, but her kindness did not have its intended effect.

Wilhelmina was crying huge raindrops of tears by now and could take the shame no longer. "I'm sorry, sir, madams. If that's all, I'll be back to my work." She didn't wait for an answer but scuttled off towards the kitchen.

"The poor, wretched thing." Christabel watched her leave. "I will keep her on if she'll stay. To come from a family like hers and remain so pure is a sign of great character."

Grandfather looked at her through the corners of his eyes. "She would not be the first person to achieve such an accomplishment, my dear."

Some contented grins passed around the table just then, but I had more questions to ask. "So what was all that nonsense about Big Jock Pocklington? And how do you know anything about the Highlands of Scotland?"

Grandfather's face transformed as he let out a laugh. "I honestly don't. Our family have a lodge somewhere up there, but I'm no hunter myself and neither is the actor who we knew as Tiffin. There is no Loch Gerald or Muir of Invergussie. I made them up to confirm that he really wasn't a Templeton-Swift. As for Big Jock Pocklington, the devilish bando player, well, that was just as an extra detail to add to the fun. Bando is a Welsh game, not Scottish. Though that is the extent of my knowledge on the topic."

Mother was overcome with laughter by this point and, try as she might, Christabel couldn't resist the infectious sound. "You're terrible, Lord Edgington. That poor man must have been petrified of you ever since you arrived."

"Just as long as you weren't, my dear. That's all that matters."

"Next question," I said, as they would have gone back to complimenting one another if I hadn't. "How did Tiffin and Lettice know to say the same thing when I challenged them on the conversation I'd overheard?"

Grandfather raised his chin to look down his nose at me and I knew he was going to say something superior. "I would have thought that was obvious." Yes, that'll do!

Luckily, my mother was on hand to set him straight. "Really, Father. In what way was it obvious? Everything that happened this weekend was steeped in complexity and confusion."

"Not at the beginning," he replied with more than a touch of irritation in his voice. If there was one thing my grandfather couldn't tolerate it was being criticised… or corrected… or wrong in any way. In fact, now that I think about it, there were lots of things he couldn't tolerate. "But with all we have since learnt, and the timing of the various incidents that have taken place, I thought you might be able to identify the reason."

I assumed this meant he wanted me to answer my own question, and so I did my best. "Ummm... well, perhaps they really had seen me leaning out of the window." He gave a slight shake of the head and so I followed up my first guess with a better one. "In which case they must have planned for the eventuality."

We all waited for Lord Edgington's verdict, and he made sure to torment us with a few seconds of pensive silence.

"Precisely!" His eyes shone with approval. "I've no way to say for certain, of course, but that's just the conclusion I formed. You see, they were actors. They'd prepared their parts and were ready for such scenarios. The fact that they were separated from one another when you interviewed them showed that they would need to be careful. Their tortured past with their father was an important element of the personas they'd created for themselves.

"Don't forget that Dr Merrick knew all about Hugo. I'm sure he would have provided the Crowers with the information that the actors needed. However, they were unaware of the cause of the family rift and had to improvise. It was a matter that Hugo would not discuss in any detail with Merrick, though he did admit to Christabel that it was linked to the death of his first wife. When you spoke to Lettice and Tiffin you learnt so little that it suggested there was something not quite natural about the story they presented."

I was no longer surprised by the guile and cunning of men, but the sheer scale of the plot we had uncovered was unlike any of our previous investigations. Laughing a little, I repeated my favourite refrain of the day. "I really did discover nothing of interest whatsoever."

Grandfather smiled and pointed out another element of the case that I had overlooked. "The only major misstep that Nathan Crower made, aside from choosing an inordinately complicated plan in the first place, was to rely on two substitutes to do the job for him. I don't know if you noticed, but he would stand back and let them talk whenever they were together. He clearly didn't trust his acting which, as a conman himself, was more than proficient. He certainly maintained his accent well enough."

The way he spoke of our culprit made me wonder something. "Grandfather, did you cheat?"

"I beg your pardon?"

"Did you call Scotland Yard to learn whether anyone in the Crower family had a criminal past? It would have made the rest of your discoveries far simpler to divine."

He looked affronted once more. "No, of course I didn't." He bristled for a few moments before finally conceding, "Well... I may have asked the question, but I am yet to receive the answer. The very fact that I thought to ask, though, is a real feather in my cap. Now, do you have any more questions, or should we ask Halfpenny to bring the main course?"

The truth was that there were fifty questions I could have put to him, but I limited myself to just one more. "Yes, my very last."

Grandfather dabbed his lips with his checked cotton napkin and drummed his fingers on the table in anticipation.

"What has Devyn's abattoir got to do with Hugo's death. It clearly proved he was a bloodthirsty chap, but it was hardly a guarantee that he was a killer."

"Think again, Christopher. The false Devyn claimed to have been in America for a decade and, from what he told us, had lived at the very lowest level of society. He wouldn't have called the place he worked an *abattoir*. Americans prefer the term *slaughterhouse*. His speech was peppered with such examples and, after so long abroad, I would have expected some hint of a transatlantic influence."

I'd never known any Americans – though I had once met a fake one – so I really couldn't blame myself for this failing. "How would you expect me to know that?"

"It is a detective's job to know everything."

"And it's just such comments which put me off investigating any crime with you ever again. I may improve my abilities of deduction, but I very much doubt I'll be able to learn about absolutely everything, even if I live to be your age."

I thought he would reply with one of his insouciant looks then, but he responded quite serenely. "Hmmm... perhaps I was being a little over-ambitious. No one can know absolutely everything."

"Oh, I wouldn't say that, Grandfather." I popped a crumb of

bread into my mouth. "In fact, I've always considered you quite the know-it-all."

"Such impudence, Christopher." A scowl seized his face, and I thought I was in trouble. He managed to maintain this displeased look for a few seconds before a laugh emerged from deep within him. "You little rascal."

"We should be careful," my mother said. "He's becoming just as brazen as I was at that age."

The great (and easily vexed) Lord Edgington folded his arms and looked away across the delightful garden. "Heaven forbid."

CHAPTER THIRTY-FIVE

We stayed one more night at Riverside Keep so that dear Christabel could adjust to the new life she was facing. And, by the time the cars had been packed for us to leave the next morning, two visitors had arrived to look after her.

"David!" the good widow screamed when a blue Triumph 10/20 pulled up in the drive and a boy of nine years old stepped out. The little chap sprinted across the gravel towards his mother, and I couldn't have felt happier to see them reunited.

"This was your doing, wasn't it?" I asked my grandfather, but he said nothing as he walked towards the car to greet the driver.

The truth is that, though he did not have any special powers and certainly possessed no psychic abilities, from time to time, Lord Edgington could do magic. Vivian Highley-Summers got out of the driver's seat and the three of us stood together, watching the happy scene.

"I appreciate your coming," he eventually muttered with a slight bow.

"You know I'd do anything for an old friend," the Junoesque beauty declared, and I was uncertain whether she was referring to the woman whose son she had just delivered or the man who had set the plan in motion. I was also not entirely sure I wished to find out, so, as the pair of them looked at one another in comfortable silence, I went to sit in the Aston Martin and tried to concentrate on my book. Delilah soon bounded over to claim the comfiest seat for the journey. I swear she'd got heavier since we'd arrived in Hanging Langford.

"Home, Todd," my mother said as she got into the Rolls. "And perhaps we could take a more direct route this time?"

"As you wish, Madam." The chauffeur climbed into the front seat and the vehicle rumbled away. The other servants followed in their endless parade of cars and, with a kiss of the hand for Vivian, Grandfather would not be far behind.

As we drove off the property, he looked back at the cheerful trio who remained in the doorway of the grand abode. "I told you that we came here for Christabel. You can see now that this was all for her."

I didn't have to ask any more questions. I knew just what he meant. I'd assumed that we'd driven to Riverside Keep in order to measure a woman's guilt, but I should have known better. Grandfather was an Arthurian knight at heart and, though it may seem old-fashioned by modern standards, he had taken up the quest to save a woman in peril, not condemn her.

"You know, Christopher," he said, looking down at the book in my lap. "More often than not, it's the monsters on earth of whom you have to be vigilant, not the creatures from Mars."

We reached the long straight road beside the meadow and, with a toot of his horn, he shot off past the rest of our convoy. I closed my eyes as tightly as possible until we got back to Surrey. No matter how bad a driver I was at the time, I was surely a lot safer than that maniac.

He drove me to school directly, but when we stopped in front of the sturdy brick building, I didn't feel like getting out of the car. We'd been through so much that weekend and I wasn't ready to go back to my normal life quite yet.

"Christopher, I have one last question for you," he said, turning off the motor. "Have you considered becoming a detective? I mean, have you given it any serious thought?"

I was mulling it over at that very moment. "Of course, I have. And I know it would make you happy, but there's a small problem."

"Oh, yes. What's that?"

"Well, we've just investigated our ninth, tenth and eleventh murders, and I still haven't solved a single case."

He became unexpectedly happy on hearing this. "Gosh! Is it eleven already? How time flies when–"

I decided to cut short his response. "I would love to be like you, Grandfather. I would love to make a name for myself in the police or go from case to case, bringing killers to justice as we do now. But I'm no genius."

"Neither am I, my dear boy." I had to raise my eyebrows at this, as I'd never heard him suggest such a thing. "I mean it. Though I may project an air of superiority, I can assure you that it is simply a mechanism I have perfected to keep those around me off guard. I'm no more a genius than you are an electrician. But I'm good at my job, and do you know why?"

I looked into his stormy grey eyes then, and I could see that there was something different about him. He was calmer, softer, more open, and so I shrugged my shoulders and waited with interest to hear his response.

"I became a good detective by working very hard for a very long time. I'm not saying I don't have some basic intelligence, but so do most people. The truth is, Christopher, that investigating a few cases and hoping that you are Sherlock Holmes is like picking up a cricket bat and expecting to hit a ball like W.G. Grace. Any man who has excelled in his field will have spent years mastering his craft, whether he be a worn-out old copper or a young prodigy. Without time, commitment and practice, even the most innate talent will go to waste."

I said nothing to this, but Delilah clearly agreed as she let out a loud bark and Grandfather ruffled her ears. I thought about his words and tried to work out what I wanted to do with my life. In fact, they stayed with me for days, even as I walked into my history exam the following week.

I suppose I must have felt more nervous when coming face to face with savage killers – the time one of them tried to murder me with a spear was certainly no thrill. But it was hard to imagine anything so vein-poppingly terrifying as taking my place in a school hall with fifty other boys at separate desks and turning over my exam paper to discover…What exactly? I could hardly look.

Describe in detail current or past theories for why Stonehenge was constructed on Salisbury Plain, and why its continued preservation is significant for British heritage.

I had to turn it back over again because I could hardly believe my luck. I half expected Grandfather to pop up at the window and confess that he'd bribed my teacher to change the exam. After five seconds, when he hadn't appeared, I took out my pencil and began to write.

The End (For Now…)

Get another

LORD EDGINGTON ADVENTURE

absolutely **free**…

Download your free novella at
www.benedictbrown.net

"LORD EDGINGTON INVESTIGATES..."

The seventh full-length mystery will be available in **Autumn 2022** at amazon.

Sign up to the readers' club on my website to know when it goes on sale.

ABOUT THIS BOOK

As **"The Tangled Treasure Trail"** was such an emotional story, I wanted to have some fun this time around. **"The Curious Case of the Templeton-Swifts"** is a classic detective romp in a country house but with a dose of weirdness bubbling under the surface.

The book also shows the end of Chrissy's school life and hints at what might be to come. Much like my narrator, I've thought a lot about where his path will take him and it's a difficult balance to keep his charm and innocence and also have him develop as a detective. If you read Golden Age crime fiction, and even right back to Sherlock Holmes, it is not the assistant's job to outdo the detective. Watson and Hastings never solve cases where Holmes and Poirot fail to, but I know that a lot of my readers would like to see Chrissy come into his own, and so it will be interesting to discover what I can do with that theme.

I love writing about families. My mother is one of five sisters and I'm one of three brothers. I'm constantly interested in the way relatives interact and the gulf in difference between one family and another. As the youngest sibling, I was always the hard done by, sensitive one but, now at the very end of my thirties, I can see how lucky I am to have two big brothers. I think the softening of my views on the matter has come out in my writing, and the relationship between Chrissy and Albert is also changing as the series continues.

In terms of the setting for the novel, that starts with the book cover. My wife and I search for images together and then she sets about making them look beautiful. This time, we came across a manor in Wiltshire. That's all I know about it from the photo website, but with a little bit of investigation (Lord Edgington taught me everything I know!) I've narrowed it down to either Lake House, in the village of Lake, or the nearby Wilsford Manor, which was built in a similar style.

Both houses have claims to fame. Lake House is currently owned by the singer Sting, and Wilsford Manor once belonged to Stephen Tennant – the Bright Young Thing who inspired the character of Fabian Wallace in my previous book. I hope that's the one as it would be yet another wonderful coincidence that my haphazard plotting and research has brought about. The village of Hanging Langford, and all the other names in the book (yes, even Nether Wallop) are real places in Wiltshire. Its landscape, winding rivers and wildlife have really inspired me, and I hope to visit when I go home to the UK this summer.

The book granted another opportunity to use my map from 1925 and chart a course across the English countryside using the A-Roads that had only recently been established. I knew that I wanted Chrissy to visit Stonehenge at some point, and it seemed the perfect place for a picnic. In my lifetime, the stones have always been roped off, but in Chrissy's day he would have been able to sit where he wanted and even climb on them – it's probably a good thing that's no longer the case.

Last, but most importantly for me, the book has another connection to my father. One thing I haven't mentioned about Dad before is that, later in life, he became a magistrate. He had worked for the court service in our area in the eighties and was put forward for the unpaid role by a colleague he knew from that time. Dad loved sitting with a panel of his peers and I'm sure he was a very fair magistrate. He heard any number of sad, moving and also funny cases and the anecdote that Lord Edgington tells at the dinner table about the boy who stole a suit for his own court appearance really happened. Dad also liked to tell the story of a man who had been arrested with a kilo of cocaine. He claimed it was for his own personal use and had only bought so much as it was cheaper to buy in bulk. I hope, for his sake, this was a lie!

My father was a brilliant storyteller and always loved making people laugh. It was a sad day for him when his Alzheimer's was so severe that he had to retire as a magistrate. Even as the disease progressed, he never gave up wanting to entertain people and put them at ease. I really hope he would have gone on at length about my brothers' and my recent achievements. In fact, I'm pretty sure he was proud of us even before we'd got much living done. Every book in this series is dedicated to my dad, Kevin Benedict Brown, so thank you so much for helping me pay tribute to him.

If you loved the story and have the time, please write a review on Amazon. Most books get one review per thousand readers so I would be infinitely appreciative if you could help me out.

THE MOST INTERESTING THINGS I DISCOVERED WHEN RESEARCHING THIS BOOK...

Unlike in the last book, I won't have to write an extra novella to explain all the research I've done. As it takes place in the country, and not the city, there wasn't nearly so much work required this time around, but I still discovered all sorts of incredible things.

Let's start with the most famous landmark in the book, the ancient standing circle of Stonehenge. All the facts in the novel are true. The land had recently been bought on a whim in 1915 by a man called Cecil Chubb, for the equivalent of half a million pounds in today's money. He bought it to stop the stones being taken from the local area, and it really is incredible that so much of the circle was still present at the time. In the 1920s, the neighbouring land was bought with donations from the public to stop overdevelopment, as houses and other buildings had started to appear nearby. Since then, the historic site has remained in public ownership, and you can still visit – if not picnic within the stones – today.

One of the first major archaeological digs at Stonehenge was carried out between 1919 and 1926 by a man called Lieutenant-Colonel William Hawley. Hawley conducted most of the work on his own but made any number of incredible discoveries – as Edgington reveals in this book. He was the first person to uncover evidence and formulate the theory that the site had held a sacred funerary role early on in its existence. He also proved that the site had been used by different people in different centuries, even before the stones were erected. Though the truth of his theory was not accepted in his lifetime, it is now the widely held view. I think it's incredible that a man working largely alone could achieve so much with limited technology at a time when archaeology was at a far more primitive standard than it is today.

Speaking of technology, no, the Electrolux Model V vacuum cleaner Chrissy spots isn't an anachronism. I love including mention of the domestic appliances that were available in those days and this invention came on the market in 1921. What's amazing about it is just how similar it looks to some models available today – unlike the Miele rotary washing machine from the period, which more resembles a butter churn. The Model V vacuum was advertised as a luxury item, suitable for everything from a light clean about the house to removing loose hairs from a horse.

Sometimes I'll discover a reference that I can't resist including, even if it doesn't strictly fit in with historical records. Devizes prison, which Edgington mentions, had actually just been demolished in 1926. However, it was such a phenomenally interesting prison (and I couldn't find any other in the region, anyway) that I had to mention it. Those with a good memory might remember Chrissy learning the word *panopticon* in the second novel, and this was a perfect example of one. Though built in 1867, it looked like something out of a sci-fi film, with a huge tower in the middle and cell blocks arranged in a circle around it. The idea was that the inmates would assume they were being watched at all times and not do anything naughty.

Regarding my characters, I borrowed the name Lettice from another Bright Young Thing. Lettice Mildred Ashley-Cooper was the daughter of the ninth Earl of Shaftesbury, and, in the Second World War, would go on to become a flight officer in the Women's Auxiliary Air Force before working her way up to corporal. The female aviators didn't fly combat missions but were involved in certain espionage and reconnaissance flights and they also transported wounded soldiers and supplies.

I took the name Tiffin from an early twentieth century cake, which lives on as a chocolate bar. Tiffin is also a posh old surname and the word for the Indian custom of having a light meal in the afternoon, which replaced afternoon tea at the time of the Raj. Devyn, meanwhile, is the name of the seventeen-year-old grandson of one of my readers who enjoys these books. Hello Devyn! I hope you don't mind lending your name to a brute. Oh, and in case anyone is wondering, yes, Inspectors Simpson and Simpson are inspired by the lookalike detectives, Thomson and Thompson, in Tintin.

A Lord Edgington novel would not be complete without fine(ish) foods and entertainment. There were two interesting dishes I came across when writing this book. Poor Knights of Windsor Pudding dates back to the seventeenth century, and the recipe is very similar to French toast – though early versions recommended serving it with rosewater. It seems the exact reason for this strange name is lost to us but, in 1346, knights captured by the French at the battle of Crecy were forced to sell their estates to raise ransoms and return home. Edward III subsequently granted them a salary and lodging at Windsor castle in exchange for their daily prayers for king and state. Perhaps the name came because they all had a sweet tooth! We may never know. A more modern dessert is Cherries Jubilee which, it is believed, was made in 1897 for Queen Victoria's Diamond Jubilee. It is a flambeed cherry and liqueur dish that was served to the monarch by August Escoffier, the pioneer of French Haute Cuisine, who had such a massive influence on early twentieth century cooking that he was known as the "king of chefs and chef of kings".

As for entertainment, we were treated to not one but two Harry Champion songs. I made a massive effort this time to look for British music from the early part of the century that was not of the music hall variety, but I failed so I stuck with what I know. Champion was a hugely successful comic singer and comedian who was largely popular with working-class audiences, so it's funny to hear Edgington singing his songs. Written by Charles Collins & E.A. Shepherd in 1915, "The Girl with the Golden Hair" is a *boy-chases-girl* song of a type that was common at the time and contains all the sauciness of a limerick. "You can't help laughing can yer?" written in 1913 by Lawrence and Carter, became a staple of Harry Champion's act and refers to his previous hit songs and his success as a performer in the first verse. As a result, experts on turn-of-the-century musical acts may be at an advantage in working out the twist in this book.

I've referred a couple of times in the series to some of the grand theatres in London in the twenties. By far the most spectacular was The Alhambra in Leicester Square. This vast, palatial building, built with a huge dome and Orientalist-style minarets, was opened in the mid-nineteenth century as The Royal Panopticon of Science and Arts but soon became a theatre. It dominated its surroundings and drew controversy for having a Parisian can-can act so seductive that the theatre's licence was temporarily revoked in the 1870s. It remained popular into the new century but was sadly bulldozed in 1936 to make way for the Odeon Cinema, which still stands today and holds the biggest screen anywhere in the UK.

Another, though far less savoury, ghost of London is the Old Nichol slum. It was located in the east of the city and was notorious for the tragic conditions in which people lived throughout the nineteenth century. On average 8.6 people lived in each tiny house, and in one three hundred and seventy square metre plot of land there were fourteen hundred houses, with most only having access to water ten to twelve minutes a day. The area became known for theft and prostitution and, from the 1860s onwards, people demanded change, but it wasn't until the twentieth century that a new estate opened in its place with better housing. Sadly for the people living there, like Vivian and Christabel, they were simply moved out of the city to similarly poor areas further east. The same thing happens in London today, but it's high-rises and executive housing blocks that tend to go up in place of family houses.

Sticking with miserable topics, I had to look into the laws for drugs and alcohol to write this book and I discovered that it was only in 1920 that drugs like opium, heroin and morphine were criminalised. Before then, addictions were treated as illnesses rather than criminal offences. I also discovered that, during Victorian times, the average Englishman drank half a gallon of spirits whereas, in Australia it was ten times that. What's more, before Europeans reached New Zealand in 1840, the Māori people had no form of alcohol. As you can see, I sometimes get distracted by incredible unrelated topics, and my research goes off at a tangent.

So, to finish with something more cheerful, let me tell you about Dick Whittington, former mayor of London and beloved folk hero. Richard Whittington was born in 1354 in the Forest of Dean (where the next Lord Edgington novel is set!) and was elected to be a councilman, sheriff and later Lord Mayor of London – serving four terms in total. He was also a brilliant mercantile businessman and amassed a fortune in his lifetime which he bestowed to the city. His legacy helped rebuild my beloved Guildhall (featured at the end of "The Tangled Treasure Trail"), build hospitals and libraries, set up a charity fund which continues to exist today and – perhaps most impressively – construct a public toilet for one hundred and twenty-eight people that was washed clean at high tide each day by the River Thames, in order to avoid unsanitary conditions in a poor neighbourhood. He is best remembered today though for being the focus of a British pantomime which tells the story of his rags to riches trip to London and his incredible cat. It's an example of truth being more compelling than fiction. What a legend!

Thank you so much for reading (or listening) to this book. By now, I'm sure you all know that I love murder mysteries, I love history and I love my readers. If you could spare a minute to leave a review at Amazon or Audible, I'd be phenomenally grateful.

ACKNOWLEDGEMENTS

Writing and putting this book together in the space of two months has been a massive challenge that was not helped by me going away to a four-day music festival just before publication. All of my releases are collaborative efforts, and I couldn't manage on my own, so thank you very much to everyone involved. I hope I haven't forgotten anyone.

My wife Marion creates my covers and does all of the web and graphic design work we need. My daughter Amelie inspires me to get out of bed every day and spend hours typing away and laughing at my own jokes. Thank you, too, to my crack team of experts – the Hoggs and the Martins, (**fiction**), Paul Bickley (**policing**), Karen Baugh Menuhin (**general brilliance**) and Mar Pérez (**forensic pathology**) for knowing lots of stuff when I don't. Thanks to my fellow writers who are always there for me, especially Pete, Rose, Suzanne and Lucy.

Thank you, many times over, to all the readers in my ARC team who have combed the book for errors. I wouldn't be able to produce this series so quickly or successfully without you, so please stick with me, Izzy and Lord Edgington to see what happens next…

Rebecca Brooks, Ferne Miller, Melinda Kimlinger, Deborah McNeill, Emma James, Mindy Denkin, Namoi Lamont, Katharine Reibig, Sarah Dalziel, Linsey Neale, Karen Davis, Taylor Rain, Terri Roller, Margaret Liddle, Esther Lamin, Lori Willis, Anja Peerdeman, Kate Newnham, Marion Davis, Sarah Turner, Sandra Hoff, Karen M, Mary Nickell, Vanessa Rivington, Helena George, Anne Kavcic, Nancy Roberts, Pat Hathaway, Peggy Craddock, Cathleen Brickhouse, Susan Reddington, Sonya Elizabeth Richards, John Presler, Mary Harmon, Beth Weldon, John Presler, Karen Quinn, Karen Alexander, Mindy Wygonik, Jacquie Erwin, Janet Rutherford and Anny Pritchard.

"THE TANGLED TREASURE TRAIL" COCKTAIL

A cocktail that has fallen out of fashion in the last fifty years but, in 1926, was the height of cool. Its origins are fairly murky, but there are a few indisputable facts about the Jack Rose. It's from the east coast of America, was invented sometime around the turn of the twentieth century and, though rumour suggests otherwise, it does not take its name from the gambler Jack "Baldy" Rose who was a witness in the 1912 murder of bookmaker Herman Rosenthal – a case so sensational it was mentioned thirteen years later in Fitzgerald's The Great Gatsby".

But I decided to include the drink in this book for its link to Ernest Hemmingway's 1926 novel "The Sun Also Rises", in which the narrator enjoys a Jack Rose in the Hotel de Crillon in Paris. It was also one of Steinbeck's favourite drinks and, as I spent my university years devouring such American literature, I couldn't resist this rash of connections.

As for the drink itself, the ingredients aren't so exotic that most people wouldn't be able to mix one, so long as you don't mind finding a substitute for the applejack – an American liquor which is made by freezing cider and removing the ice before fermenting and distilling the liquid. The most famous brand of applejack, Laird & Company, describe themselves as the oldest distillery in the USA, with production going back to the turn of the eighteenth century.

Ingredients...

> **50ml applejack (or any apple brandy such as calvados)**
> **25ml lemon juice**
> **25ml grenadine**
> **Ice**

You just shake all the ingredients with the ice for ten to fifteen seconds to cool and then serve in a martini glass. What could be more delicious for a summer party (or when outing a killer)?

The idea for the cocktail pages was inspired by my friend and the "Lord Edgington Investigates…" official cocktail expert, Francois Monti. You can get his brilliant book "101 Cocktails to Try Before you Die" at Amazon…

READ MORE LORD EDGINGTON MYSTERIES TODAY.

- **Murder at the Spring Ball**
- **Death From High Places** (free e-novella available exclusively at benedictbrown.net. Paperback and audiobook are available at Amazon)
- **A Body at a Boarding School**
- **Death on a Summer's Day**
- **The Mystery of Mistletoe Hall**
- **The Tangled Treasure Trail**
- **The Curious Case of the Templeton-Swifts**
- **The Crimes of Clearwell Castle** (Coming Autumn 2022)

Check out the complete Lord Edgington Collection at Amazon.

The first three Lord Edgington audiobooks, narrated by the actor George Blagden, are available now. The subsequent titles will follow through the year.

WORDS AND REFERENCES YOU MIGHT NOT KNOW

Gruntled – there is some evidence that this word existed by 1926, but it was popularised in the Jeeves and Wooster books from 1938 – not that Chrissy would know that.

Surveiling – I love using obscure words that people will have no trouble understanding and the verb form of surveillance is one of them.

Horological – to do with time i.e. his namesake in the corner is a grandfather clock.

Sop – an over sentimental, silly person – as in soppy. It originally came from sop, meaning to soak.

Pay box – a wooden cabin where you pay. Not an expression I was familiar with, but when Cecil Chubb gave Stonehenge to the public, he granted permission for such a box to be established where visitors would pay not more than one shilling – presumably it has been adjusted for inflation.

Blow me tight! – An antiquated expression of surprise, i.e. wow!

Londonian – a rare adjective for things or people from London.

Postie – a common enough word, in Britain at least, for a postal worker.

Ambulation – movement/walking.

Jounce – to shake something up. I particularly like it because it is presumed to be a portmanteau of jump and bounce

Abattoir – a place where animals are slaughtered.

Bill Sikes – the baddy in Oliver Twist. Booooo!!!!!

In a merry pin – another antiquated expression for someone who is in a good mood.

Hoyden – a wild young woman, or one who acts like a boy.

Inculpate – to blame, frame, entrap.

Balderdash – of uncertain origin, it originally referred to a mixed-up drink but came to mean a mess of words and now means nonsense.

Supernumerary – the theatrical term for a non-speaking actor in a play or opera.

Amphibolic – something which can have two opposing interpretations. In other words, it is something unclear or of uncertain meaning.

Vociferate – to say something strongly and with conviction.

Hectorer – someone who hectors or berates.

Yardarm to yardarm – laid end to end or very close. A yardarm itself is something to do with sailing, but even with a dictionary, I don't completely understand what it is.

Dunderhead – idiot, numbskull. I thought this might be too modern, but it is actually from the early seventeenth century.

Kip – to sleep

Cyma moulding – a common type of decorative moulding that has two curves to it.

Tomrig – a rude or wild girl, much like hoyden above.

Not the full shilling – "not all there" for someone who is a little batty.

Brouhaha – noise or fuss. I love the etymology of this word. It comes from French medieval theatre and was said by actors playing the devil in disguise as a religious figure. It is thought to be a distortion of the Hebrew words for "blessed is he who comes in the name of the Lord."

Parvenu – much like calling someone nouveau riche or an arriviste, this suggests that a person has moved up in the world without having the accompanying culture, manners or class. How very snobbish!

Carrollian – the adjective for anything that might resemble something from "Alice's Adventures in Wonderland". Taken from the penname of the book's author Lewis Carroll.

Namby-pamby – weak, insipid. Which was the nickname of an eighteenth-century poet who was often mocked for his sentimental verses.

Gordian Knot – something that is impossible to solve or, indeed, untangle.

Arcadian – another word for pastoral or bucolic, taken from the name for an ancient Greek region that European poets saw as a rural idyll.

Woesome – another uncommon word that is easy to understand. The opposite of awesome perhaps? Woeful is obviously more typical.

Inseverably – yet another uncommon word that is easy to understand. Impossible to sever.

Adagio dancer – a special kind of music hall or vaudeville dance act made up of a dainty female acrobat balancing on her strong partner.

Scapegrace – lazy, unprincipled, graceless.

Junoesque – stately, mature beauty

CHARACTER LIST

Hugo Templeton-Swift – wealthy investor in his eighties, who fears someone is trying to poison him.

Christabel Templeton-Swift – his much younger wife with a mysterious background

Tiffin Templeton-Swift – his oldest son who lives in Scotland

Lettice Templeton-Swift – his only daughter who lives on the east coast of England.

Devyn Templeton-Swift – the youngest sibling who has sailed in from New York

Doctor Merrick – the local doctor

Betty Crower – the cook at Riverside Keep

Ned Crower – her husband, the gardener

Wilhelmina "Billie" Crower – their daughter the maid

Regular Characters

Lord Edgington, The Marquess of Edgington – our seventy-six-year-old detective. A wealthy landowner who previously worked for Scotland Yard.

Christopher "Chrissy" Prentiss – Lord Edgington's seventeen-year-old grandson. Trainee detective, bird mis-identifier and cake connoisseur.

Violet Prentiss – Lord Edgington's daughter and Chrissy's mother. She's not a bad detective herself.

Todd – Lord Edgington's chauffeur and one of Chrissy's heroes.

Cook (Henrietta) – Cranley Hall's increasingly itinerant cook

Halfpenny – Cranley Hall's aging footman

Alice – One of the Cranley Hall maids

O'Driscoll – her husband, Cranley Hall's gardener.

Delilah – the smartest and most adorable golden retriever in the history of literature.

THE IZZY PALMER MYSTERIES

If you're looking for a modern murder mystery series with just as many off-the-wall characters but a little more edge, try **"The Izzy Palmer Mysteries"** for your next whodunit fix.

Check out the complete Izzy Palmer Collection in ebook, paperback and Kindle Unlimited at Amazon.

ABOUT ME

Writing has always been my passion. It was my favourite half-an-hour a week at primary school, and I started on my first, truly abysmal book as a teenager. So it wasn't a difficult decision to study literature at university which led to a masters in Creative Writing.

I'm a Welsh-Irish-Englishman originally from **South London** but now living with my French/Spanish wife and presumably quite confused infant daughter in **Burgos**, a beautiful mediaeval city in the north of Spain. I write overlooking the Castilian countryside, trying not to be distracted by the vultures, hawks and red kites that fly past my window each day.

When Covid 19 hit in 2020, the language school where I worked as an English teacher closed down and I became a full-time writer. I have two murder mystery series. There are already six books written in **"The Izzy Palmer Mysteries"** which is a more modern, zany take on the genre. I will continue to alternate releases between Izzy and Lord Edgington. I hope to release at least ten books in each series.

I previously spent years focussing on kids' books and wrote everything from fairy tales to environmental dystopian fantasies, right through to issue-based teen fiction. My book **"The Princess and The Peach"** was long-listed for the Chicken House prize in The Times and an American producer even talked about adapting it into a film. I'll be slowly publishing those books over the next year whenever we find the time.

"The Curious Case of the Templeton-Swifts" is the sixth novel in the "Lord Edgington Investigates…" series. The next book will be out in the autumn and there's a novella available free if you sign up to my readers' club. If you feel like telling me what you think about Chrissy and his grandfather, my writing or the world at large, I'd love to hear from you, so feel free to get in touch via…

www.benedictbrown.net

Printed in Great Britain
by Amazon